A Collection of Worlds
The First Adventure

Jo L Parker

Cover art by Teresa Cheung

"There is no way around - there is only the way through,
And things always take just as long as they do."

To my beautiful Auntie Kathy:
You always had faith that I would find my way.
Thank you for your unconditional love & support.
You will stay in my heart forever.
I miss you.
Love,
Jo

Chapter 1

Miracle Child

I remember the first time I learned that there were other worlds besides mine. My brother Richard taught me about other worlds when he had to live in a different one than me. I was seven years old and lived at home with my father John and my mother Alison, but Richard had to live in the hospital. Richard was very sick. His world was only one room whereas mine was a large house and a big city. Richard's world was pure hospital white while mine was a vibrant array of colours: trees, flowers, dirt, rainclouds, and buildings of yellow and red. Richard's world was safe and contained, mine was wild and open.

Then I turned eight, Richard was allowed to leave the hospital on my birthday. I was elated, Richard could finally leave behind his hospital world and join my exciting home world! I envisioned him becoming my best friend. Enthralled with my new role as a big sister, I planned out every event from holding him for the first time to teaching him to walk and ride a bike. I would instruct him in all the ways of dirt, colours, and the vibrant life that existed outside that hospital room.

It did not go like I thought it would. Instead of Richard leaving the hospital world behind and coming home, he brought the hospital world with him. I watched Richard's world descend into mine like a small white invasion. Suddenly the dirt was evicted and every surface was cleaned. Tubes from the hospital room were still attached to him and a large clunky machine stuck close behind to help him breathe. In one birthday, the hospital marched into my world and set up camp in my parent's room.

Everything changed after that. The colours faded from the flowers that sat neglected in my mother's garden, the light dimmed from my parents eyes as they grew increasingly tired, and some of the white from the hospital made its way to the corners of their ears in the wisps of their hair. This was rather more dull than I had thought.

At least I still had the foundations of my world: the tall brick house with the soft yellow kitchen, the green living room a step down, and the overstuffed rust coloured armchair that sat in the corner across from the fireplace. There I would curl up in my father's lap every night and listen as he read stories. No matter how much hospital white Richard brought into the house, the richness would never drain from the tales my father told. Tucked in the safety of home and the warmth of my family, I disappeared into the stories and allowed myself to be rocked to sleep by my father's soothing voice.

Then I was nine and Richard was one, he could breathe on his own and the tubes marched back to the hospital world. Richard still visited, going often to make sure he was strong enough to stay at home. Nurses in their spotless white uniforms would hug him and kiss his face when they saw how big he was. Wiping tears from their eyes they would look at my parents and tell them over and over that Richard was a perfect 'miracle child.'

One day when Mother had taken Richard to an appointment and Father and I were left home alone I asked him, "What's a miracle child?"

He smiled, put down his paper, and took off his glasses. "It means," he said patiently, "that we are extremely fortunate to have Richard at home and that it

3

surprises everyone when they see that he is not so sick anymore."

Not so sick anymore, I turned that information over in my head. My father looked at me thoughtfully, waiting for me to ask the question he could see brewing in my brain.

"Is he still sick?" I asked.

"He will always be a little bit sick and he will always get sick a little bit easier than you."

He tapped my head softly and smiled. When I asked why it was so, my father explained that Richard was born too early and so his lungs were weak and his body could not fight germs as well as other people.

"That is why he needed the tubes to breathe and why everything has to stay so clean," he said with finality.

That made sense. I didn't particularly enjoy helping clean the house everyday but it would be easier not to complain about chores now that I knew it was to keep Richard safe.

"Do you have any other questions?" Father's tired face looked at me with sympathy. "Your world has been pretty turned upside down hasn't it."

I shrugged my shoulders. "I like my world better than Richard's world."

"What do you mean?" Father asked, sounding rather amused.

"I mean that Richard's world doesn't have an outside. His world is only inside and it is very clean and very white. I like outside, there are lots of interesting things out there. If I was in Richard's world, I couldn't go outside. A world without outside seems like a very sad world." I did my best to explain myself.

Father chuckled, "Well, that is certainly one way to look at it."

He picked up his paper and began scanning the pages. The sound of the clock ticking was the only thing that interrupted the silence. I enjoyed the quiet sometimes, it let me think. I sat very still and tried to sort through what Father had just told me. Just when I was on the verge of a breakthrough that would allow Richard to start living outside, the front door opened. Mother carried Richard into the kitchen, she looked distraught. Without a glance in my direction she placed Richard in a jumper that hung in the doorframe leading to the living room. Gurgling happily Richard began bouncing up and down. He had a new purple elephant clutched in his hand and he waved it around happily.

"John," Mother said, her voice wavering slightly.

"Alison," Father replied in a lighthearted tone as he looked up over his paper. Seeing the concern in her face Father folded the paper, crossed the kitchen quickly, and guided her to the study at the end of the hall. I heard the door close softly behind them and I wondered what was the matter. I had never seen mother look so pale and they only closed the door when they were discussing very private matters. I tiptoed through the heavy carpeted hall and pressed my ear to the door to try and hear what they were talking about. Hushed whispers raced back and forth for a moment and then there was silence. Father sighed heavily and I heard a sob escape from my mother.

"Shh," my father comforted. "It's alright." His voice was soft and gentle. Heat rose to my face, Mother never sobbed like that. Something very serious must be going on.

Retreating from my post, I went to the kitchen where Richard was bouncing up and down in his jumper. He had been so small when they first brought him home, I remembered thinking that he had hardly looked human. In one short year he had transformed from the wrinkly white bundle that was constantly plugged into a breathing machine to an actual baby with fat wrinkly arms and legs and two small teeth poking through his gummy smile. He had chubby pink cheeks that sagged like a chipmunk and bright green eyes that locked on me as I sat down in front of the jumper. I held out my finger to him and he clutched it in his tiny fist, squealing with delight and thumping his feet on the floor as he jumped even wilder.

I thought about him being a 'miracle child' and concluded that we were lucky to have him in the house. Maybe we didn't have separate worlds after all, Richard and I, maybe we shared the same world. Perhaps he hadn't even turned my world upside down, he had just shown me what a miracle looks like.

Chapter 2

Mr. Sploot

A week went by where Mother and Father routinely disappeared to the study. I never knew what they were talking about and I soon stopped worrying. If there was something they wanted me to know they would tell me.

Richard got a cough and I wasn't allowed to play with him on the ground anymore. The only time I could play with him was when he was in his jumper in the doorframe. Red fuzz had started appearing on top of his head and it bobbed up and down frantically, clinging to his scalp for dear life as he jumped around. He liked me, when I would sit on the floor with him he would wrap his tiny hand around my fingers and squeal loudly.

Another week went by and groups of people started coming over. Sometimes there were only two people and sometimes there were more; one man was always there. He was tall and thin with a pointed nose that turned to the left at the end. He had a pocket watch on a gold chain and wore a blue pin striped suit. He had a bald spot on the back of his head and a neatly trimmed silver beard. He carried a briefcase but never opened it. Whenever he came calling, I was quickly turned out into the yard while he led people around the house. He made me very curious. I would watch the windows to catch glimpses of him. I very much wanted to know why he dressed so fancy and what was in his briefcase.

I got my answer one evening when we were all sitting down to dinner and a knock came on the door. Father answered and a moment later escorted the man in the blue suit into the kitchen. The man was carrying his mysterious black briefcase in his left hand.

"Mr. Sploot," the man in the suit said, snapping his heels together, and offering me his hand. I shook it, staring at him, and saying nothing. He smiled and turned his attention to Father. "So sorry John, I didn't intend to intrude. I wanted to discuss an offer with you that came in this afternoon just before we closed up." Mr. Sploot's voice was vibrant and rich.

"No intrusion at all," Father waved his hand to dismiss the apology. "Alison and I were wondering if the Smyth's would be putting in an offer, they had seemed so interested."

"Oh but that's business," Mother fussed. "Bill, won't you join us for dinner and we can discuss this properly over tea?"

"Alison, I don't want to trouble you."

"Don't be silly! You've been such a help to us and the least we can do is feed you." Mother always loved having company stay for dinner. "Besides, I've made an apple pie for dessert and goodness knows we don't need to eat all of it ourselves."

I thought I would have been quite happy to eat the pie all by myself but, unfortunate as it was for me, Mother loved to share her baking.

Mr. Sploot smiled and took the empty seat beside me. "Ah, when you put it that way," he patted his stomach, "how could I turn down your homemade pie?"

Father chuckled, "It's how she got me."

All the grown ups were laughing. I sat confused. I laughed a little so I wouldn't look too out of place. The briefcase was staring at me from beside Mr. Sploot's chair. It had silver clasps that were closed tight - intriguing.

Mr. Sploot was served dinner and the grownups chatted away, using big words that I didn't understand. I stared at Richard who was sitting in his highchair, lost in a private game with his stuffed elephant. Suddenly I felt very alone. There was the grown up world going along on one side of me and Richard's world on the other. It seemed I didn't fully belong in either and I felt lonely. The grown ups had each other and Richard had his elephant but I had nobody. For the first time, I wished I could jump into Richard's world. He didn't seem lonely, he was smiling and revealing a new tooth that had appeared. He locked eyes with me and gurgled, a string of drool travelling down from his mouth and sticking onto the top of his elephant's head. He laughed, delighted with himself.

When the meal was finished, Mother shooed the men into the living room and I helped her clear the table.

"Why is he here?" I asked, passing her a plate.

"He is helping us with some business," she said, scrubbing it clean.

"What business?"

"Grown up business."

She dried the plate and put it in the cupboard. She looked down at me and smiled. Something was different in her smile. Her voice seemed strained and tired and her face seemed more heavy. The light in her eyes was quieter.

"Once it is all settled we will be able to tell you about it," she glanced at me imploringly, "alright?"

"Alright," I agreed, growing more curious by the second.

I invited myself into the living room where the men were sitting. Soon after, Mother came and sat in the rocking chair and announced that the pie was cooling. Richard was cradled in her arms, looking 'milk drunk' as Father called it. His cheeks were red and droopy, his eyes looked wobbly as if they couldn't focus on anything, and in no time at all he was snoring. Richard was put to bed and Mother passed around pie and chamomile tea.

I devoured my dessert and waited quite impatiently for the grownups to finish theirs. Finally, mother took the dirty plates to the sink and Father lit his pipe. I squirmed up into his lap and rested my head against his shoulder. Mr. Sploot adjusted his coat and began explaining something about the Smyths making an offering. I didn't know what that meant but I was content to sit and listen. I eyed the mysterious black briefcase that sat at Mr. Sploot's feet.

"It is a sound offer, John," Mr. Sploot said. "More than you had been hoping for. It would make you enough money to afford the Blufferton property."

"It is definitely sooner than we were thinking," Father replied, his words were weary and dull.

"It is such a good offer though," Mother said as she entered the room. I noticed that her face looked hopeful for the first time since Richard had come home.

Mr. Sploot leaned forward, "I know it's sooner than you wanted, but I would look at this all the way through before turning it down."

His bony hand reached down and flicked the silver clasps of the briefcase case. I wriggled out of Father's lap and sat on the floor to peer inside. It was lined with red silky fabric. On one side there lay a crisp stack of papers, the rest was empty. Mr. Sploot took the papers out and passed them to Father.

"Why don't you and Alison take a look at these privately for a few minutes? I can keep Hazel occupied."

Father took the stack of papers in hand and he and Mother headed to the study. Mr. Sploot chuckled softly as he pulled the briefcase onto his lap and patted the couch seat next to him. Curious, I took the seat. Mr. Sploot smelled like after shave and pipe smoke, I liked

13

him. I leaned into his side and waited for the secrets of the case to be revealed.

"How old are you, Hazel?" he asked.

"Nine and one-eighth," I replied importantly. "I know fractions."

"Nine is a very good age indeed," a light kindled in his eyes as he spoke. "I was nine when I started collecting."

"Collecting what?" I asked.

"Worlds," he whispered. "I am an adventurer."

Briefcase Pockets

I was dumfounded and let my mouth hang open in awe. Mr. Sploot certainly did not look like the adventurer type.

He nodded very seriously and said, "Let me show you."

He reached into a pocket in his suit and pulled out a small pair of spectacles which he propped on the end of his long crooked nose. He opened his briefcase further and revealed countless pockets in the lining. How had I failed to notice these earlier? There seemed to be hundreds! It was as if they had appeared out of nowhere. Some pockets were closed with buttons, some with zippers, some with clasps, some with elastics, some with draw strings, some with magnets, and some with contraptions I didn't recognize at all.

Carefully, he unzipped one pocket and took out a small leather pouch. He shook the pouch and it grew to the size of a sheet of paper.

"Watch closely," Mr. Sploot instructed.

He shook it again and the leather jumped off and revealed a framed picture of a cloudy sky. He took a deep breath and blew across it. Clouds rushed off the edge of the picture and fell down to the floor. I watched the fluffy white mist tumble and dance across the room before fading to nothing. Behind the clouds there was a yellow house with a white porch. On the white porch sat a boy and a dog. The boy was dirty and wore tattered overalls that were ripped off at the knees. The boy's dog was white with splotches of black and extraordinarily bright blue eyes. The dog was bigger than the boy and had his paws stretched protectively across the boy's lap.

"Trickle," Mr. Sploot said, pointing to the dog. "He helped me learn how to be an adventurer."

Mr. Sploot snapped his fingers and Trickle stood up and licked the boy's face. He looked like he was whispering in the boy's ear. The boy in the frame laughed, pulled a small brown book out of his pocket, and scribbled something down. Mr. Sploot waved his hand over the frame and the clouds came back into the

16

picture. They turned grey and then black and rain started pouring down from them. The water gathered on the bottom of the frame. It collected into puddles, into ponds, and finally into a great river that picked up the house and carried it, the boy, and the dog, out of the frame. Mr. Sploot shook the frame one last time and the leather case leapt back over to cover the picture.

"Was that you?" I gasped.

"Yes," he nodded, "many years ago."

I tried to imagine Mr. Sploot as a young boy, the young adventurer with the great dog. Was this old man with the briefcase really the small adventurer in the magical picture?

"What happened next?" I pleaded.

Mr. Sploot tucked the frame safely away in his brief case.

"Adventures," he stated.

"What adventures?" I asked.

"Many."

"I want to hear the stories."

"Those are not stories I can tell you now."

I was very disappointed.

"Why not?" I protested.

"Because I might spoil it for you," he said with a smile. "Why do you think adventurers have adventures Hazel?" he asked.

I thought for a long time but could not come up with an answer. "I don't know," I replied, looking up at his face.

"Because nobody tells them how the story ends and so they stay curious. They want to experience the magic and they want to learn the truth," he said.

"Will I have an adventure?" I asked.

"Yes, if you accept the invitation. If you decide to be brave, resilient, and wise." He tapped his temple with his finger. "Do you know what it means to be brave?"

"I know what brave means," I said. "It means that you go to the basement even though it is scary or sleep in the dark even though you are afraid."

"That is exactly right," Mr. Sploot said, looking rather proud. "What about what it means to be resilient?"

I shook my head. I had never heard that word before.

"To be resilient," he began, "means to stay in the basement even if there was to be a loud noise. It means to go back to sleep in the middle of the night even if you had a bad dream and woke up in a fright and it was still dark. It means to not give up just because something got a little bit tougher."

I nodded with solemn understanding. "Like when I learned to ride a bike and I fell but I kept trying?"

"Mmhmm," he muttered and nodded his head. "Some people would never get back on the bike. True adventurers always get back on the bike."

A little glimmer flared up in my heart - I was a *true* adventurer.

"How about wise? Do you know what it means to be wise?" he questioned.

"I think it means to be old," I said; it was the best answer I could come up with.

Mr. Sploot looked at me quite seriously and said, "Do not let anyone tell you that you have to wait to be old to be wise."

I liked how he talked to me. He didn't talk to me like I was a child and knew much less than he did. He talked to me like I was just as smart and capable as he was. I wished more adults talked to children this way.

"Being wise means that you look at things all the way through and do not just accept them for what they seem to be on the outside," he said.

"Like your briefcase?" I replied. "I didn't know what was inside until you opened it."

"Exactly that," he exclaimed. "From the outside it looked like a boring briefcase but that could not be further from the truth."

I giggled, "It isn't boring at all."

"Yes, things can be quite boring on the outside and very exciting on the inside."

He opened another pocket in his case, one with a sort of dial you had to twist and turn. Inside was a black chunk of rock, it looked dirty and dull. He held it between his fingers and said, "This is a coal."

"Like from the fire?" I asked.

"Exactly like from the fire. Now watch." He guided my hand to hold the coal in my palm. He dug deeper into the pouch and sprinkled some fine glittery powder over the rock. The coal bubbled and white streaks shot through it, illuminating webbed lines across the surface. Blackness cracked and pieces of dull rock broke away, crumbling into nothing and disappearing before they even reached my lap. I watched transfixed as the lump of coal birthed a diamond, perfect and priceless.

"Fire dust," he explained, "reveals the true nature of something. It burns up the pretend and shows what is real."

I started making a mental list of everything I was going to sprinkle fire dust on.

"But there are two sides to this coin," he lowered his voice and looked at me like I must pay very close attention to what he was about to say next. "Sometimes things seem wonderful and are in fact terrible."

He reached back into the pouch and pulled out another diamond and placed it in my palm. Looking at the pair of sparkling jewels in front of me, I could not tell one from the other. Once again he sprinkled fire dust over my hand. I watched intently. The diamond that had already been tested with the fire glowed and shone brighter than before but the new diamond whizzed and groaned and streaks of blackness poured over it. The darkness spread from the top and wrapped itself around until it covered the rock completely. Now, the once shining diamond looked even more dull than the lump of coal he had handed me first.

"Would you have been able to guess that the second diamond was a fake?" Mr. Sploot pointed to the dull rock.

I shook my head.

"No one could have," he continued. "Sometimes it is quite impossible to tell what is true and what is false by the outside appearance. That is why we need to look at things all the way through. Sometimes, we need help to do that."

"So being wise is sprinkling the fire dust on everything?" I asked.

"No," he replied. "Unfortunately fire dust only works on certain things. It is also extremely rare. It can only be found in one volcano in one world and it is an incredibly difficult journey to get there."

I was distraught. "How am I supposed to be wise without fire dust?"

"Fire dust is simply a tool, that is all. There are many tools that help adventurers see all the way through things." He retrieved a small apple from another pocket. "Let's pretend this apple is given to you. You have a choice, you eat it or you can decide not to eat it. Look at it. Does it look like an apple that would be good to eat?"

I nodded. It looked delicious. It was shiny and smooth and smelled fantastic.

"Let's look at it all the way through," he said.

He took a knife from another pocket and cut the apple in half. Even though the outside was flawless, the inside was rotting and soggy. I gagged when a worm poked its head out of the core.

"Yuck!" I protested. "The outside lied!"

"The outside did lie didn't it? It made you believe that because the outside was beautiful, the inside was beautiful too. Sometimes a beautiful outside is merely covering up an ugly inside."

He returned the items to his briefcase and continued his speech, "Fire dust is merely a tool for the wise. You will learn many more tools as you grow up and have your own adventures. For now, just begin to look at things all the way through. Do not accept them or reject them based only on what they look like on the outside; and ask your conscience what is wise. Many times our conscience knows what is wise before our head does."

I soaked up this advice and vowed to myself that I would always look all the way through things.

Mr. Sploot reached into another pocket and pulled out a small book, brown and very plain looking.

"These are the lessons from my very first adventure," he said as he passed it to me.

I opened the book. Inside the cover was a picture of Trickle, he winked at me. Hand written notes were on every page. Notes such as:

Don't trust the parrots, they repeat whatever they hear.
Watch out for the silver tongue, it sounds nice but tells lies.
It is not wise to follow the Emu.
Listen to the owl, even when you don't like what he says.
The rocky trail smooths and the smooth trail cracks.

If you repeat whatever you hear, you are a parrot and
therefore untrustworthy.

I recognized the book as the one the boy had written in on the porch in the picture frame.

"You can keep that," Mr. Sploot said.

I gladly accepted it. "Thank you Mr. Sploot."

"You're welcome," he smiled. "I have a feeling you are going to need it more than I in the coming months."

"Why?" I asked.

"Because," he said. "You are about to begin you own adventure."

Chapter 4

Home is not a House

It turns out that Mr. Sploot had known something that I did not. Mr. Sploot, so it seemed, had retired from adventuring four years ago and become a realtor. The offering the Smyths had made was to pay Mother and Father a lot of money to live in *my* house.

"It's not fair!" I had pleaded with Mother and Father. "Why are the Smyths getting *my* house? This is my world not theirs."

I could feel my face turning red as hot angry tears filled my eyes. Mother looked like she was about to cry but she just sat quietly and looked at Father.

"Well," Father said patiently. "Remember how we talked about Richard's weak lungs?"

"Yes," I responded, sniffing hard to keep my nose from running.

"The factories have made the city air too dirty for him and it will hurt him very much if we stay here. We would not be able to keep him at home. He would have to go back to the hospital and stay there forever."

I dropped my head and thought of Richard's smiling little face and how he grabbed my finger and laughed. Richard was just a baby, too little to know all the trouble he was causing. I knew he couldn't help being sick but I felt a flare of fiery anger spark in the pit of my stomach anyway.

"Everything is always about Richard isn't it," I muttered, letting some of the anger slip out of my mouth.

"Hazel!" Mother looked hurt and disappointed. My anger weakened under her pained stare. I focused on jamming my toes into the carpet and staring at the patterns it created.

"It's what babies do," Father said quietly. "I have something to show you, come with me."

He offered me his hand and we left Mother in the living room. We walked to the back of the house and into the study where all the secret councils were held. Father and I sat across from each other in high back chairs with milky cushions and polished wooden frames. He pulled a black album off a bookshelf and

26

held it up for me to see. In the first pages there were pictures of a young man in a black suit and a young woman in a white dress. They were holding hands in front of a little white church.

"We look different don't we," Father chuckled.

"That's you?" I asked.

"And your mother," he said pointing to the smiling girl in the photo.

He turned a page and showed me a cozy apartment with big windows and paintings hanging on the wall. Standing by one of the paintings was my mother, she wore a beautiful dress and her hair was done up in way I had never seen.

He pointed to the picture, "That was her first painting that sold to a gallery."

"Wow," I whispered.

It is an odd thing to look at photographs of your parents when they were younger. I wished the pictures would move like the pictures in Mr. Sploot's briefcase.

Father turned the page and showed me the same woman with a swollen belly, her hair down, and her smile broad. He pointed a finger to her tummy; "That is you," he said. He flipped through pages of photos showing a growing belly, a 'SOLD' sign in front of the apartment, an art sale, a family moving into a tall brick house, and a baby girl being brought home.

"When you came into our lives, or into our world as you would say, you changed everything."

His words sat in my stomach and took away the last of the anger I had felt towards Richard. Instead of anger I felt a heavy sinking feeling, I felt guilt.

"We left the apartment world because you needed more room. Your Mother left her art world because you needed more attention and she loved you more than the brushes and paint."

He closed the book and ruffled my hair, bending down to look me straight in the eye

"You were your own sort of miracle, Hazel."

"I was?" I asked.

"Of course you were," he smiled, "your Mother was told she would never have a baby. Now she has two. There is nothing in any world that is worth more than you and Richard. That is why when one of you requires us to leave a world behind and move on to another one, we do."

I thought about this quietly before asking, "Is this an adventure?"

Father chuckled softly, "Yes Hazel, it is a big and wonderful adventure."

"I don't like the idea of going somewhere new," I said. "I thought that when you went on adventure you got to come home after. Why are we leaving home and letting the Smyths have it?"

"We aren't leaving home," he replied. "We are taking it with us."

"The house?" I asked, rather perplexed.

"No, not the house, the house is what is staying with the Smyths; but home is not a house, Hazel. Home is here," he pointed to his heart. "It is family, it is love, and laughing and all of the things that we brought with us when we moved into this house."

I knew my father was smart, but something about this particular argument seemed off. Home was the brick house, the fire place, the armchair where we read books, and the kitchen that Mother cooked in. Home didn't seem like something you could take out of a house and place in your heart.

"Are you sure?" I questioned.

"I'm sure. You will see. We will take home to the next house. Taking home to new places *is* the adventure."

I supposed I could go along with it - if it was an adventure. I helped Mother and Father work to get ready. I watched in a daze as boxes were packed, papers were signed, and finally we were dropping keys off at Mr. Sploot's office on our way out of town.

When we said goodbye to Mr. Sploot, he squatted down on the ground to look at me in the eyes.

"Do you have your book?" he asked. I knew he was talking about the one with the writing and the picture of Trickle.

I nodded and patted my backpack; "It's in here."

"Good, keep it safe for me. Remember to be brave, resilient, and wise. Do not be afraid and do not be discouraged." He winked when he finished speaking and shook my hand in a firm goodbye. I felt positively grown up.

The last thing I remember about the city world was looking back through the window of our rental car to give a final wave to Mr. Sploot. I watched as he grew smaller and smaller until he and the city dissolved into a rusty road and an open sky.

Chapter 5

A Gold Fish & A Turtle

Endless fields, rolling hills, and clouds drifted by as we drove and drove. Richard slept in his baby carrier beside me, Father's eyes were fixed ahead, and Mother sat beside him crocheting furiously as she always did when forced to sit still for long periods of time. The car rocked and swayed and the engine hummed softly. The humming turned into a bubbling and the bubbling into a river. I was sitting on a rocky bank throwing purple stones into green water. A large fish with shiny gold scales and a long orange silky moustache popped his head out.

"Won't you stop doing that," he reprimanded. "You've nearly squashed my spinach garden."

"Sorry," I replied, surprised that the gold fish could speak, and with such authority too.

The fish crossed his fins and leaned over to rest on the bank. "Is this your first adventure?" he asked.

I nodded; "How did you know?"

"You've got that new adventurer look in your eye," he replied.

"I do?" I was puzzled, how did the fish know about adventurers?

"I could see it a mile away," he waved a fin to emphasize his point. "I haven't seen such a young adventurers since…" he paused, tapping his scaly chin several times before finishing his thought, "Well it must have been old Bill Sploot!"

"I met him!" I cried, jumping up and accidentally knocking another purple pebble into the water with my foot.

"Hazel! Now you've bruised my Tiger Lilies," he pointed down in distress.

"I'm really terribly sorry," I apologized, folding my hands in front of me.

"Not to worry," he sounded sincere but his gold face looked sad and he sighed.

"How can you have flowers under water?" I questioned curiously. I had never seen flowers underwater.

"Tsk tsk tsk," he clicked. "You will see that world later. These young ones, always so enthusiastic. One world at a time don't you know, it's the only way to travel."

I didn't know what he meant.

"You must learn to go slow," another voice spoke from behind. I jumped and turned around, knocking even more stones into the water and causing the fish to moan in dismay. The voice had come from a small turtle with a red stripe that was sitting on a log.

"Learn to go slow," she repeated, "The fast race to nowhere but the steady arrive where they're meant to be."

I was still confused.

"That's one for the book," the gold fish said.

"I don't understand," I said looking back in his direction.

"Don't tell me you haven't got a book!" he exclaimed before disappearing under the shiny water with a splash.

"An adventure book," the turtle explained. "Every adventurer needs their own adventure book."

Just as quickly as he had disappeared, the gold fish returned to the surface. He had a small brown book tucked under his fin. It looked just like the one Mr. Sploot had given me.

"Here," he said, reaching to pass me the book.

I took the book in my hands and opened the cover. There was a message scrawled across the first page.

"Read it aloud," the turtle instructed.

I cleared my throat and read the words:

"Write down the lessons so you do not repeat the mistakes."

As I read the words, they faded away and left the page blank. I gasped in surprise but the turtle and the fish seemed unfazed, nodding slowly and saying 'mmhmm' in perfect synchronization.

"Always write," the turtle said.

"And always read," the fish added.

"Yes," agreed the turtle. "It important to read, to remember what you know."

"Yes," chimed the fish. "Important as well, don't forget to put the sunshine in. You will need it if it gets dark."

The turtle nodded emphatically as the fish passed me an orange pen.

"Write it down," the fish said.

"The sunshine?" I asked.

"No dear," the turtle said patiently. She repeated her lesson word by word as I copied her reminder down in my most careful handwriting: *Learn to go slow. The fast race to nowhere but the steady arrive where they're meant to be.*

"Don't forget," the fish said. "Always write!"

"And aways read," the turtle finished.

I put the little book in my dress pocket and thanked the gold fish.

"It is a gift," he said, "and the best thing to do with a gift is to honour the giver by using the gift for good. So use it, write down the lessons."

I nodded.

"It's time to wake up. We are here," he said.

"What?" I asked, very confused.

The fish disappeared under the water without answering. The turtle crawled off the log, into the river, and silently swam away. The ground started shaking gently and the world shone a bright flash before being swallowed up into night.

"Come on Hazel," it was Father's voice talking now. "It's time to wake up. We are here."

It had all been a dream.

It must have been.

Chapter 6

Number 7 Blufferton Way

Finally I woke up enough to get out of the car. We must have driven a long time, it was almost night now and the sun was low in the sky. The clouds shone orange and pink and cast a magical lighting over the new house. It was an old house that was painted blue and white and had a large front door with a crooked sign in the middle: *Number 7 Blufferton Way.*

The sidewalk that led to the house was weathered and cracked and little flowers grew through the gaps in the cement. Richard woke up bawling and Mother told me to go explore the house with Father. When I started walking, I noticed an unusual lump in my dress pocket.

Upon investigation I found the lump was a little brown book with an orange pen tucked inside - the gift from the fish.

"Where did you get that?" asked Father, having noticed my treasure.

"From a fish who knew Mr. Sploot," I replied.

Father looked at me with his head tilted and laughed. "Well isn't that interesting. What an imagination you have."

We walked up the crackly sidewalk and through the front door. The house was magnificent inside! There was a room just for coats and shoes where the floor had a funny pattern made of flowery squares with circles inside of them. The 'mud room,' as Father called it, opened up into a kitchen that had a shiny wood table and glossy cupboards. The oven was green and there was a small wood stove right beside it.

There was a living room a step down just like in the old house but this one had a large door that could slide open and closed. It had a fire place and a couch with a big window to look out over the lilac bushes that lined the front yard.

Further in there was a narrow staircase that led to a small room at the top of the house. There was a large window on each side of the room, a chimney running through the middle, and a wall painted with animals. "Your room," Father announced. "What do you think?"

"It's beautiful," I said as I ran to the wall and petted a zebra that was so realistic that I half expected it to move.

Mother and Father had a room at the bottom of the stairs, across a corridor, and behind a heavy door. Attached to their room was a separate bath, a nursery for Richard, and a large study for Father. It was a terrific new house and a wonderful place to start having adventures.

In no time at all our things were moved in and the house began to feel more like home. Father worked hard to fix it up. He repaired leaks, fixed squeaks, replaced lights, resealed windows, and repainted every wall and ceiling (all but my animal wall, which we all agreed was far too beautiful to cover up).

The country air smelled like flowers and sunshine and Richard's cough faded. Mother relaxed and laughed more. It seemed that life had found its rhythm once again and things would be alright after all.

Chapter 7

Mr. Art's World

Blufferton Way was on the last street of a very small village. There were no factories and only one motorcar which was owned by a man called Mr. Art. Mr. Art not only owned the only motor car in town but also the only shop. The shop was a square brick building with a flag flying from the top. Inside was a grocers, a meat cutters, a post office, a clothes shop, an ice cream parlour, a book store, and a toy store all in one. It was a funny little store and until Father started working there, Mr. Art ran it all by himself.

Mr. Art was a rolly-polly man with a very round tummy and a large fluffy moustache that curled up at the ends. He said it was his wife's cooking that did him in. "The best in the county," he'd always say. We learned that if he ate something and said it got 'second place,' it was the highest compliment. "Nothing can beat my Gladys' cooking," he'd brag. "The best you can even hope for is second place."

He was a jolly old man, he knew everyone by name and everyone knew him. When someone came into his store and bought too many items for them to carry, Mr. Art would simply close the store so he could give them a lift home in his motorcar.

We quickly befriended Mr. Art and Mrs. Gladys. When Richard had to be taken to the clinic for a checkup, which happened regularly enough, Mr. Art would loan Mother and Father his motorcar and take me to stay at his house. Mr. Art and Mrs. Gladys lived at the end of a winding red dirt road in a forest of tall trees. Their house was closed in by a large black gate and fence. It was the biggest house I had ever seen. It was white and had two stories. There was a water fountain in the entrance and seventeen bedrooms that all had their own bath and closet. There was a piano in the living room and bookshelves reaching so high that I could barely see the top. It was impressive to say the least.

"You must have a lot of money," I said one day when we were having cucumber sandwiches at the long kitchen table.

He laughed out loud and remarked, "A lot of money? I gave all of that nonsense away a long time ago."

"Then how do you live in such a big house?" I asked. "It takes a lot of money to live in a big house."

"Not so," he corrected. "I did not choose this house and I did not pay for it either. I inherited this house."

"What's inherited?" I asked.

"It means I got it as a gift from my father."

"Tell me the story?" I asked. Mr. Art was a gifted storyteller and every time he graced me with a tale I would sit completely enraptured.

"A long time ago, before there was a village, there was my great great great grandaddy and his sweetie," he began. "They had come from a long journey on a boat and were looking for a place to set up a new life, a 'new world' as he would have called it. He and some friends cleared trees from this property and built a lodge for everyone to live in. My grandaddy was very wise and so the people made him the mayor of their village. They worked together for years to build up the settlement and people eventually built their homes and moved out of the lodge. When they found themselves living in the lodge all alone, my granddaddy and his sweetie decided to fill it with children. Gradually they built a family and when grandaddy left the lodge, his son took over, and the same with his son, and his son, until eventually it was handed to me. It's a family legacy. I didn't earn it and for a long time I didn't even want it."

"Why didn't you want it?" I interrupted.

"I wanted to runaway, to have grand adventures, and be far from everything I knew. I wanted excitement and to see what else this world had to offer," he said solemnly. "It was a fool's errand. I didn't know enough to listen to the wise words of my family and I didn't find what I thought I would. One day I woke up alone, hungry, cold, and with no money at all. I realized I had to go back to the village, back to my family, and beg for forgiveness. So I walked and walked until I reached the gate of this house. When I arrived there, my father was waiting for me. He greeted me with tears of gladness and outstretched arms saying:

'Welcome home my son.'

'I don't deserve to be called your son,' I had answered him. 'I left you and I made a mess of my life. I am sorry. Let me tend to the maintenance of the yard and house and live on the grounds. I will work for free and I won't be a bother. I am ready to live right.'

'You will live in *your* house. We are your family and we love you. You are my son and you have come home - this is a day of rejoicing.'

And my father decided to throw a party for the whole village. Everyone came and we celebrated into the night. I did work to help around the house and I did it with gladness in my heart because I knew what a blessing it was to have a home again. When he was old and hunched over, my father decided to leave the lodge and retire in the village with his friends. He entrusted the house to me. It was a gift. I did not earn it and I do not deserve it."

"I think you deserve it," I said. "You are nice and you worked hard."

He chuckled, "I didn't always work hard and I wasn't always nice."

"No he wasn't," Gladys joked as she entered the dining room and filled our cups with iced tea. "He has learned a lot from his adventures, haven't you dear?"

"That I have," he smiled at her.

"And you have honoured your father with this house," she stated, taking a sip of her tea. "You have done good things with it."

Mr. Art nodded, "When a great gift gets passed to you, the only thing to do is to humbly accept it and honour the giver by using it for good."

I gasped, wasn't that what the fish had said?

"That would be one worth writing down," Mrs. Gladys winked at me.

I heard the gold fish echo in my ear, "Write down the lessons."

Later that day, after Mother and Father had picked me up and taken me home, I found my brown book and wrote down the lesson: *When you are given a gift, humbly accept it and honour the giver by using it for good.*

Chapter 8

Lori-Anne, Cowie, Uncle Art & Auntie Gladys

Richard got a cough when the weather turned crisp and Mother got worried.

"I think we need to go back to the clinic," she said to Father.

"Well there's no telling how long we will have to stay there," he replied. "If they have to intubate him we could be there for a week or more. I just don't know how I would manage that with work. Perhaps you could go alone?"

Mother teared up, "What if something happens?"

Father sighed, "You're right. Let me talk to Art."

Mr. Art said it would be his pleasure to loan them the motor car for as long as they needed and that I could stay in the house with them.

"I do hope she isn't afraid of dogs," he had told Father. "My daughter Lori-Anne has just come home.

Life has been hard on her lately so she is back for good and she brought her Great Dane, Cowie, back with her."

Father assured him I would be fine and the very next day I found myself at the end of the red dirt road, sitting in the piano room, sharing the couch with a dog that was much bigger than I. He looked familiar, like I had seen him before. He was tall and mostly white except for his left ear, his right foot, his knees, and a splotch on his back. He had blue eyes and ears that stood straight up as if he was listening to everything. Once you looked at him you instantly felt that he knew far more than you ever would.

Lori-Anne was a vibrant lady. She wore long sleeves and colourful pants. Her hair was ginger and curly and hung in a long ponytail down her back. She had bangs she was constantly blowing out of her face and she liked to laugh a lot. She had moved back in with her parents with nothing but her dog and a suitcase full of books.

"Terrible shame," I heard Mrs. Gladys say to Mr. Art one night while they were sitting on the back deck and didn't know I could hear.

"Why?" Mr. Art asked.

There was quiver in Mrs. Gladys' voice when she spoke, "I just don't know why life had to be so hard for her. I am so grateful she is back but I worry she will never be the same."

"Oh Gladys," Mr. Art said tenderly. "She will never be the same and it is better that way. Her adventures have shown her truth and brought her back home. She had to go through the pain to learn about love, just like I had to. She is better now than she ever has been and she is going to be just fine."

"You're right," she replied softly.

Cowie licked my face and almost knocked me over. His tail was wagging and banging on the wall, announcing our presence. I patted his head and followed him out onto the deck. Mr. Art and Mrs. Gladys were sitting together on a chesterfield drinking hot tea that smelled like apples and cinnamon.

"Are you ready for a story Hazel?" Mr. Art asked.

"Yes sir!" I replied enthusiastically.

He laughed loudly, "I am not that old, young lady. Call me Uncle Art, please."

"Okay Uncle Art," I said.

"And call me Auntie Gladys," beamed Mrs. Gladys.

I hugged her, "Okay Auntie Gladys."

The three of us walked into the living room one after the other. Uncle Art lit a fire and selected a book from the shelf, Auntie Gladys knit in her rocking chair, and Lori-Anne sat in an arm chair with her legs crossed and a daydreamy look in her eyes. I lay on the floor next to Cowie and listened to the story. As Uncle Art's strong voice filled the living room, I felt the same comfort that I did when I was reading with my father in our old house in the city. What an adventure I was having. In the city I had one home but now in the village, I had two (*and* a dog). My heart was full to the brim. I drifted to sleep with my head on Cowie's side and a smile on my face.

Chapter 9

Seven Brown Books

It was a rainy day; the kind where the rain falls down gently and sweetens the whole world. The grey clouds dimmed the sunlight, the water drops cooled the air, a fresh smell filled the lodge, and fires crackled in all the hearths. Auntie Gladys was busy cooking, baking, and singing in the kitchen. Uncle Art was sitting in the living room flipping through a thick volume that had very big words and no pictures. I was wandering around the house looking for Cowie and Lori-Anne.

I found them in a little round room in the top left corner of the house. The room had a slanted roof and a big window seat. Lori-Anne was lounged on the seat, cushions propped up behind her back, Cowie laying across her legs, and a small brown book open in her hand. It looked like an adventure book.

"I have one of those," I said, pointing to the brown leather cover.

She smiled and folded the book over her thumb.

"Do you?"she asked. "Where did you get it?"

I told her about Mr. Sploot and his positively fantastic briefcase and how he had given me his first book.

"Fascinating," she sounded genuinely intrigued.

"Where did you get yours?" I asked.

"Well this one," she held it up for me to see, "I got from a special place very far away from here, you wouldn't know it. A lady named Sylvie gave it to me."

"That's a pretty name," I said.

"She is a pretty lady," Lori-Anne replied. "Do you have a book for you to write in?"

I nodded, "I already wrote something in it."

"Splendid," she replied, placing her book down beside her. "What did you write?"

"I wrote two things. I wrote that the fast race to nowhere but the slow get somewhere they're meant to be. And I wrote that when you get a special gift you should honour the giver by using it for good," I said.

50

"At least I think that's what it was. It was something that Uncle Art told me the other day."

"Very good lessons indeed," she commended.

Cowie gave a sleepy yawn and moved his head slightly. He barely opened his eyes to acknowledge my presence. Lori-Anne stroked his sleepy face.

"Where did you get the book you write in?" she asked.

I tried to pause and think of what Mr. Sploot had told me, I had to be wise and look at this all the way through. Something in me didn't want to tell Lori-Anne about the gold fish and the turtle. After all, Father thought I had imagined it. What if I told Lori-Anne the true story and she thought I had imagined it too? It did seem made up. I had thought it was a dream myself, after all. Besides, how could a fish or a turtle talk? Yet, it seemed so real... and I had the book... how could I explain that? The book was a gift from the fish and it had the lesson from the turtle written in it. It had to be true. I sighed loudly, it seemed I couldn't tell the story of the book without telling the story of the fish and the turtle. I swallowed hard and prepared myself for Lori-Anne to think I was making up stories, or worse, to laugh at me.

"I got it from a gold fish with a spinach garden," I said sheepishly.

"Oh?" she asked, raising her eyebrows. "I got one of mine from a gold fish once. One of my first ones."

"Really?" I asked, relieved she had not pointed and laughed. Lori-Anne was suddenly becoming much more interesting.

"Yes, really," she said with a smile. "I was twenty two years old and I met a fish that lived in a green river. I thought I had dreamt it all actually, but when I woke up I had the book that he had given me. How could I explain that?"

"That is what happened to me!" I nearly shouted with excitement. "I told my father but he thought I was imagining things. I think he thought I was making up a story for fun."

"He probably thought you imagined it simply because he has never met a fish who gave him a brown book," she said matter of factly. "People often choose to believe that if they have not experienced something then it doesn't exist. That is a sad mistake."

"What do you mean?" I asked.

She paused for a moment to think before answering, "Sometimes, when the truth is particularly difficult to accept, people would rather believe their own stories

52

than believe the true story. When you tell your father something that he has never heard of and never seen, it sounds more like fantasy than reality and is therefore difficult for him to believe. So he tells himself something that makes sense to him, he tells himself that you are just playing pretend. But just because he does not believe the true story does not mean that it isn't the true story. Do you understand?"

I nodded, "I think so."

These were advanced ideas and I was doing my best to wrap my head around them.

"It's just," I stammered, "it's hard hard to know that the fish was real when you tell someone what you saw and they think you made it up. It makes me feel a little bit crazy. How do I *know* that it wasn't all a dream?"

I felt that Lori-Anne would be able to handle my doubt and help answer my questions. She talked to me like Mr. Sploot had, like an intellectual equal and not a child.

"Do you believe it was a dream?" she asked.

I considered what Mr. Sploot said about asking my conscience. My conscience believed the fish was real, beyond a shadow of a doubt. How else would I have gotten the book? I had never taken anything from a dream before and brought it home with me. No, my conscience told me that the fish was not a dream and it was not made up.

"No," I answered with finality. "No I do not believe that it was a dream."

"Then you believe it was real," she stated.

"But a fish with a book just doesn't make sense," I replied. I wasn't trying to argue, I was merely trying to sort out the nonsensical nature of my experience.

"The more days I am alive, the more I learn that the world is far too magical a place for everything to make sense," Lori-Anne replied with a smirk. "Have some faith young Hazel."

"Faith?"

"Trusting that what we cannot explain is still real," she said. "Faith is one of the biggest tools of the wise."

Lori-Anne certainly seemed very wise.

"How do you get faith?" I asked.

"It is a choice. You choose to have faith over and over again and it grows with time," she said. "You can start by having faith that the fish was real and having faith that your book is real. You will see in time, the world is a very magical place."

"How big is your faith now?" I asked.

She giggled, "Faith is not something you can measure that way. It's something you feel."

"Oh," I muttered. I couldn't feel my faith yet.

"How many books do you have?" I asked.

"Seven," she held up her hands to show me the number.

"Wow," I whispered. I wondered how many Mr. Sploot had.

She nodded, "Always remember to write and to read. You are always on an adventure and you need to remember what you know."

I drank up that advice and hastily excused myself to my room. I pulled out my own little brown book and thought about what she had said. I took a fancy black pen from the desk drawer and sat down to scribe the lesson: *Faith is the choice to trust that what we cannot explain is still real.*

"I will choose faith over and over," I whispered to myself quietly as I closed the book.

Chapter 10

Cowie Crosses the Stars

Almost a week had passed and Mother and Father still had not been able to come home with Richard.

"He is going to be fine," Father assured me on the telephone. "He just has to finish some medicine before we can come home."

I missed them. I loved my home with Uncle Art and Auntie Gladys but there was something about my parents, Richard, and our new house that I so desperately wanted back. The rain had stopped and I was sitting on the back deck brooding. I heard the click of Cowie's feet across the deck and turned to see his massive frame strutting toward me. He sat down beside me and I leaned into his strong side.

"I wish I could aways have you around, Cowie," I said. I then began pouring my heart out to the dog. I

56

told him all about Mr. Sploot and his magical briefcase, moving, the gold fish, my brown books, and how much I missed my parents and my brother. "I wish Mother and Father could come home with Richard soon. I miss them. I am sad because Richard gets to see them everyday and I don't even get to hear their voices everyday. They have been gone so long and sometimes I worry they will never come back. Do they love Richard more than me?"

I felt silly for asking a dog a question.

"Of course not," a deep voice came from Cowie. Startled, I snapped my head around to look at him. He winked a sparkly blue eye at me.

"What?" I asked.

"Woof," he replied.

"I'm nuts!" I said out aloud.

He winked a sparkly blue eye at me again. I heard Lori-Anne's voice in my head telling me to have a little faith. I remembered my promise to choose faith over and over. I had to trust that what I couldn't explain was real.

"I know you talked," I said.

"I did," he replied. "I just wanted to tease you."

He stretched out his front paws and let out a yawn. I could hardly believe it, a dog that talks! This was the best moment of my life.

"They love you just as much as Richard by the way," he interrupted my thoughts.

"How do you know?" I asked.

"Because I know what true love is and what it looks like."

"You do?"

"Yes. I had an adventure that taught me," he said.

We sat silently for a moment, watching the sun sink low. Something strange was happening in the sky. Instead of the normal orange and pink sunsets, the sun was turning blue and the sky was turning green.

"It's time to go Hazel," Cowie said as rose to his feet. I could smell cinnamon buns baking in the oven and hear Auntie Gladys singing in the kitchen.

"But there's cinnamon buns baking and Auntie Gladys said I could have one right out of the oven," I replied.

"We will be back in plenty of time for cinnamon buns," Cowie said, picking me up by my dress collar and standing me on my feet. "Don't you want to have an adventure?"

I nodded, it seemed like cinnamon buns would simply have to wait.

"Do you have your books?" he asked.

Again I nodded.

"Then there's not a moment to lose. Adventure doesn't always give you a second invitation. The sky is right and I hear the call, it's now or never." He stooped his shoulders down so I could climb onto his back.

"Hold on tight," he said.

I wrapped my arms around his neck and squeezed his side with my legs. His powerful body ran across the yard and jumped the fence. We ran through the forest and into the last trails of sunlight, leaving the lodge behind us. Grass under his paws turned to snow, which turned to puddles, which turned to a body of clear water.

We were running on water! A calm glass sea stretched out endlessly before us and behind. The blue sun had set and the stars spread out in front of us. Every step Cowie took caused a sparkle of shimmering light. Soft pink, purple, and orange mixed together in the ripples made by his paws. Eventually the water faded into nothing and we were running across the sky with only the stars holding us up.

A very long way off, between two stars, a black circle seemed to be growing. The closer we got the bigger the black circle got. A minute went by and it started to look less like a circle and more like a triangle. Another minute went by and I saw a mountain peak with a moon rising up behind it. Another minute and we were close enough that I could see a tall black mountain with a blanket of trees, cliffs, and waterfalls that led to a pebbly beach. We seemed to be approaching it at a great speed and I was beginning to worry that we would crash right into the rock face. Suddenly, just before I could finish imagining fatal disaster, Cowie took the last strides across the stars and landed gracefully on a dark shale beach. The mountain towered above us, the peak far above eye view. I turned my head around to look at the sky we had crossed. Stars sparkled above and ocean stretched endlessly behind. We had run across the stars, not a bad start to an adventure.

Chapter 11

Newton

"You can walk on your own feet now," Cowie instructed. I slipped off his back and walked beside him. The beach was covered in smooth black shale that was cool to the touch. We walked for about a minute when Cowie started whistling a low tune a few measures long. I heard a rustling in the bush to our left. Again Cowie whistled. Again a rustle sounded. I could hear my heart beat in my ears and I was starting to feel nervous about what might be lurking in the shadows. Cowie whistled the tune a third time and a final rustle shook the bushes before a shadowy figure darted into view. The shadow was about two feet long. It scampered low to the ground as it quickly made its way across the beach to stop right in front of us.

"Well I was wondering when you would arrive," the shadow spoke in low tones. He had a fancy accent and a dramatic flare to his voice that gave his words great finesse.

"Only landed about a minute ago Newton," Cowie replied. "Good to see you old friend."

"And you," Newton said. A cloud moved and a crystal ray of moonlight shone down like a spotlight on the beach. The shadow melted away to reveal Newton. He was bright orange, had a long tail, a scaly body, spikes on the sides of his stomach and head, and short squashy limbs.

"What are you?" I asked.

Newton looked up at me in disgusted confusion.

"Are you a lizard?" I guessed. He did look similar to a lizard I had seen at the zoo once.

Newton sat up on his hind legs and crossed his chubby arms, "I beg your pardon ma'am, but I most certainly am *not* a lizard." His chin puffed and he hissed momentarily. "I am a *dragon*."

Cowie chuckled, "That may be taking it a bit far."

"It is not!" Newton replied defensively. "I am, by definition, a bearded *dragon*. If I was a lizard and not a dragon I would be called a bearded lizard and that would be simply horrible."

"Are you really a dragon?" I questioned.

Newton rolled his eyes before he flared his beard and hissed again. This time, a stream of fire shot out of his mouth and ignited a pile of sticks.

"Could a lizard do that ma'am?" he asked. I conceded that he must indeed be a dragon.

"You just aren't like the dragons in the stories," I tried to explain; it didn't help.

"Oh don't get me started on the stories!" the tiny dragon was now waving his hands frantically. "How are any of us regular dragons supposed to live up to those ridiculous expectations? Flying through the sky, with scales the size of cedars and a wingspan bigger than a castle. Ridiculous I say, ridiculous. It sets everyone up for disaster. Dragons feel so inadequate they are ashamed to show their faces in public. Ignorant animals don't believe we *bearded* dragons are real dragons because we can't fly or knock down a forest with a single claw. Quite frankly, I don't know why everyone fancies *those* dragons so much anyway. Why are they always getting all the attention? We bearded dragons are much more sophisticated and agreeable." He finished his rant with an emphatic stomp of his foot. Once he calmed down he leaned against a branch by the fire, crossed one leg over the other, and folded his arms indignantly.

I sat down on the shale. The breeze blew across the water and I shivered, wrapping my arms around myself to warm up. Cowie came and sat on the ground behind me, blocking the wind. I was grateful for his warmth. Newton kept throwing bits of shale on the fire to keep it going. The shale would glisten, crack, and release a powerful heat before simmering down into a soft green glow. I wondered if Father knew you could burn shale like firewood.

Between the fire and Cowie, I was quite warm and began to relax. This day had been quite exciting. Gentle waves were lapping up on the shore and a chorus of crickets chirruped in the distance. Everything blended into a soothing symphony that cradled me into a sleepy state of delirium. When my eyes were closed and I lay very still, the animals began to talk.

"Isn't she a bit young to be an adventurer?" Newton asked.

"She was invited," Cowie replied. "Do you remember Bill Sploot?"

"How could I forget the ol' chap," the bearded dragon said. "Good lad, good lad. Always kind to us dragons. What's he to do with her?"

"He gave her his first book."

At Cowie's words the bearded dragon breathed a heavy sigh.

"He must have seen a bit of himself in her then I reckon," he said slowly.

"He must have," Cowie agreed.

There was silence for a minute and I nearly drifted off but Cowie spoke up again, "He was her age when he climbed the peaks."

"Was he now?" the dragon replied. "Seems like so long ago you know. The story is so old it isn't even true anymore."

"True is true," Cowie said.

"Indeed," the dragon murmured. "They know she's here you know - the weasels."

"Oh dear, already? How?"

"The magpies," Newton said. "Blasted grease feathers got wind of your approach from a great white shark they say. The news that Cowie was arriving with an adventurer spread as fast as that," he snapped his fingers together.

"I suppose there will be no rest for us. We will have to start first thing in the morning."

"Aye," said the dragon. "Does she know anything yet?"

I struggled to follow the conversation in my half asleep state.

"No," replied Cowie gently. "She's keen on adventure but it seems best not to tell her too much too soon. One step at a time."

"Not how I would do it," sighed the dragon. "But she is in your charge."

"For now," Cowie said.

The dragon launched into another longwinded speech but I could no longer hear his words. Sleepy warmth overtook me and I drifted into dreams.

Chapter 12

Wordy

"Up you get," I heard an unfamiliar voice. "Enough lazing around."

Scaly hands rocked my face back and forth. I was startled when I opened my eyes and saw an orange face staring at me. I jumped back and yelled, "LIZARD!" The lizard jumped back and hissed.

"Newton," Cowie scolded. "Is this really how you want to start the morning?"

"She called me a Lizard!" Newton waved his arms dramatically. "Honestly, haven't we been through all of this last night?"

I shook the sleepy cobwebs from my mind and tried to focus. "I'm sorry, it was an accident… I forgot" I said meekly.

"Of course you did," Newton sounded sarcastic. He rose up on his hind legs and muttered, "She yelled at me first you know."

I was just about to start arguing my case when Cowie stood up and interjected, "No time for such nonsense. It doesn't matter who yelled at who first and who is to blame. We have a much bigger task at hand."

"What is that?" I asked.

"Climbing the mountain," he answered.

I looked up at the towering black mountain. It reached above the clouds so high that I couldn't see the top. How were going to get to the top if we couldn't even see it? I hoped desperately that Cowie knew the way.

"Why do we have to climb the mountain?" I gulped down the stress that settled into my throat.

A massive owl flew down from the trees and lighted gracefully on the beach. He stood roughly three feet tall. He was covered in brown feathers and had yellow eyes that peered out from underneath bushy white eyebrows. A monocle was balanced on his beak and gave the appearance that his right eye was disproportionately larger than his left. His ears stood up from his head like horns and twitched back and forth. He cleared his throat and spoke in a deep billowy voice, *"Because yooooou have accepted the invitation of adventure!"*

"Who are you?" I asked in awe.

"My name is Wordy, and I am the keeper of time.

Speaking of which, we are running behind!"

He reached under his left wing and pulled out a large pocket watch that glowed a dim yellow. When he pressed a button on the side, the face lifted and released a circle of swirling clouds that glowed different colours. The clouds drifted out of the watch and formed a mystical globe that hung in front of his face. It was certainly the most interesting watch that I had ever seen. He shook his head and muttered something to himself. He snapped the watch shut and the clouds disappeared in a puff. He turned around majestically and Cowie nudged me to follow as Wordy walked along the beach. I fell in step behind the owl. I had never seen an owl walk before and found it rather interesting. He waddled along, his feathers crisscrossed neatly on his back, his chest up, and his head held high. While he walked he spoke:

"Atop Murky Mountain in the realm of the weasels,

A traveler is imprisoned in the castle of Feazel.

A terrible mistake how she came to be here,

She has to get home for disaster is near.

Seventeen days is the time that you have,
To right what is wrong and give the lost back."

I had so many questions. "What am I supposed to do to help?" I asked, sounding rather more afraid than I intended. I cleared my throat and tried again, "I mean that I have only just arrived and I don't know the first thing about Murky Mountain, or weasels, or castles of any kind."

Without pausing to look at me, Wordy continued:
"A while ago you did not believe,
That owls could talk but now you're talking with me.
Do not be discouraged and do not be afraid,
The sky opened for you and it makes no mistakes.
The adventure invited and you accepted the call,
And what is life without adventure? It is no life at all."

I thought about Mr. Sploot telling me that I would have adventures if I accepted the invitation. Like it or not, I seemed to have accepted this as my first adventure. I swallowed the lump that was threatening to close my throat with anxiety. Cowie walked beside me and tucked his head under my hand. I stroked his fur and breathed easy again.

"You are okay," Cowie reassured me.

I heard Newton grumbling about how fragile adventurers had become. "Of course she's okay, nothing has happened yet," he whispered under his breath.

Mr. Sploot had told me to be brave, resilient, and wise. I mustered all my bravery and, in the most confident voice I could find, asked Wordy, "Where do I start?"

Wordy answered,

"Go straight up the mountain and cross the purple cliffs,
Where the crows give their treasures to the platypus Fritz.
Avoid paths with blue stones for they lead only to trouble,
Heading for trouble will make the time you spend double.
Stay on the trail, or you will get lost,
And no matter what, do not listen to the fox.
Write in your book and read it every night,
So that you can learn, the steps that are right.
Remember your goal, to get to the top,
And if your conscience says no, you best better not.
Look for the truth and the truth you will find,
But pity the adventurer who leaves it behind.
Learn from the lessons of those who went before you,
Wisdom is found in the book of Bill Sploot."

By the time he had finished his speech, we arrived at the start of a very narrow and rocky trail. Wordy turned to face me and placed a wing on each of my shoulders.

"I regret I must leave - there is so much to do.
Stick close to Cowie, he will help you!"

I had many questions for Wordy but before I could ask even one, he flew up into the trees and out of site.

"Show off," muttered Newton.

"You're just jealous he can fly," chortled Cowie.

"I am *not* jealous," Newton twisted his face in disgust. "And why did he say Cowie would help you, as if I am not even here? He could have said Cowie AND Newton will help you, or Newton AND Cowie-"

"You aren't a senior guide yet," Cowie cut Newton off. "Wordy didn't mean any offence by it."

"Sure he didn't," Newton began lamenting that Wordy would have said his name if he had in fact been a regular storybook dragon.

"What's a keeper of time?" I asked when Newton was finished complaining.

"It means he's incredibly bossy," Newton replied. "Shouldn't you be writing?"

I paused for a moment. Unsure of what he meant.

"The instructions," Cowie reminded me.

"Of course!" I pulled out my adventure book. Cowie patiently listed the directions one after another until all of the notes were recorded in my book.

Chapter 13

Francis

Directions in hand, the three of us began to trek up the mountain. The trail was narrow and grew very steep. Newton quickly got tired and rode on Cowie's back. It was hard work and I found myself feeling quite tired and hungry. My mouth watered thinking of Auntie Gladys' cinnamon buns at home. My stomach growled and I wished we had thought to bring snacks. We came around a corner into a large garden full of very oddly shaped trees. On each tree grew a different kind of fruit: oranges, apples, mangos, lemons, pears, peaches, and many that I had never seen before.

"Blueberries!" Newton started jumping up and down excitedly on Cowie's back.

"And bananas!" Cowie barked happily.

The fruit tasted even sweeter than it did at home and we gorged ourselves on the endless supply. After eating as much as we could, Cowie, Newton, and I all stretched out in the sun and closed our eyes. Newton's face was smeared purple by the berries and his lips fluttered against one another as large snores escaped his mouth. Cowie's breathing lengthened and let me know that he too had fallen asleep. Though I closed my eyes I could not find rest. I was too distracted trying to keep up with my racing thoughts about the adventure before us.

When my brain paused for a brief moment, I noticed a humming coming from further in the garden. Curious, I got up and followed the sound. Through the banana trees, past the mangoes, and through a maze of raspberry bushes with sharp thorns, there stood a short white fence. The white fence had a sign on it that read: LOOK ALL THE WAY THROUGH. The fence was encircling a sparkling tree with silver leaves and gold fruit hanging from its branches.

"Wow," I whispered, awestruck by the radiant beauty. I leaned on the fence to take a closer look. When I did so, the humming stopped and a dark orange fox gracefully jumped off one of the low hanging branches and laughed, "Oh dear - you caught me singing."

"That was you? I thought it was the tree."

"How silly!" the fox shook his head and smiled, a dashing smile full of stunning white teeth. He came up to the fence and peered at me with very dark eyes. He had tall ears with black tufts of fur on the points and a long bushy tail. His fur was well groomed and glistened in the light of the tree. "I daresay I haven't seen you here before. Are you new to these parts?" he asked. His voice was rich and beautiful. I felt I could listen to him talk all day.

"Yes I am," I replied.

"Well allow me to welcome you," the fox bowed low.

"Thank you," I blushed.

"What brings you to these parts?"

He sat back and curled his tail around his feet. Something about him looked positively regal, like he ought to be sitting on a throne and not on the ground.

"I'm on an adventure," I replied.

"Oh how exciting," he said. "Not often an adventurer comes through these parts anymore. It's been so long since I've met one."

I offered no reply. Wordy's voice echoed distantly in the corner of my mind, almost too far back for my ears to hear: 'Do not listen to the fox,' it called. After a moment of silence I started to say that I had better be going back to my friends but the fox interrupted before I could finish.

"What kind of friend would I be if I let you pass by without offering you a gift?" he asked.

I paused. I didn't think that the fox and I were friends but the idea of a gift intrigued me.

"You see," he said as he hopped the fence gracefully, "This is a very special tree. The fruit has a supernatural power that will make you *always* wise." He pointed to the sign with a sleek black paw and he read out the words: "look all the way through"

"I read it," I said. "I met a man named Mr. Sploot who told me to look at things all the way through. He said that is how I could become wise."

"Oh you met Bill Sploot did you?" the fox said coyly. "Well, did Mr. Sploot tell you that there was a 'Look All the Way Through' tree? You can have all the wisdom in the world just by eating one of these fruits." He gestured to the shimmering gold tree behind him.

I stared at the fox quietly and let his words play over again in my mind. I considered what Mr. Sploot had said about how the wise used tools to help them. Was this fruit a tool? The fox grinned at me as if he could see my thoughts work through my head.

"This fruit is the only tool you will ever need," he said in a low voice that was rather haunting. The words sounded sweet but something about them didn't feel right. I reached into my pocket for my brown book, I wanted to see if Mr. Sploot had written anything on the subject of gold trees. Before I pulled it out, the fox stretched out his paw and stopped my hand. "No need to bother with that nonsense," he said. "Just try the fruit, you won't regret it. It is the easiest way to wisdom."

I could feel my conscience bubbling up in protest. This fox was making me feel more uncomfortable by the second.

"Why would you trust Wordy anyway? Or Cowie? How do you know they are safe?" he asked coyly. I didn't like him asking these questions, they were too hard for me to answer. "Come over the fence, just try a bite of the fruit," he coaxed again.

I didn't think wisdom could be as simple as eating a piece of fruit and I didn't believe that the fox had the right idea. Still, would it hurt to take a closer look?

The fox continued to persuade me to come over the fence and try the fruit. His voice pulled me in like a magnet and eventually drowned out my conscience. All of a sudden I felt one foot leave the ground as I prepared to take a step over the fence. Before my foot touched the grass on the other side, a bone shaking howl split through the trees and I turned to see Cowie bounding towards me. Newton was holding onto Cowie's ears for dear life and bouncing wildly on the back of the dog's neck.

"Francis you snake!" Cowie growled. "Get behind me Hazel."

The spell of the fox's voice broke and I was flooded with panic. I fled behind Cowie and watched the fox back slowly towards the gold tree. His back was arched up like a cat and his teeth were bared.

"She came to me," he hissed. "Seems someone left her alone. Who am I to let an adventurer pass by without offering the wisdom of the tree?"

Newton puffed up his beard and yelled at Francis, "As if there is any wisdom in your tree. I ought to set fire to your tail!"

Francis laughed and Cowie growled, "It isn't worth it Newton. Francis knows what's coming to him. Come along Hazel."

Francis leapt back into the tree and began humming again. As we turned and walked away from the garden and back to the road I heard his singsongy voice call, "Remember I offered you the easy road, Hazel."

Newton crossed Cowie's back and stood up on his hind legs while screaming, "Don't make me come back there and set fire to your whiskers you slithering LIZARD!" He lost his balance and tumbled off Cowie's back in a heap. Cowie ignored Newton's outburst and spoke as he walked beside me.

"Francis tells lies. That is why Wordy told you not to listen to him."

"I couldn't remember," I responded sheepishly.

"Francis does have a way with words. His voice makes it hard to think clearly," Cowie explained. "That is why you must read your book and make sure you know what you know so that when he tries to talk to you, you *know* not to listen to him - no matter how nice he sounds. And you must not wander off on your own again. You must always have Newton or I with you."

I nodded and apologized.

We walked silently for a moment and I thought about what Francis had said about the wisdom in the tree.

"What would have happened if I ate the fruit?" I asked.

"You would have become a silver tongue," Newton chimed in.

"A silver tongue?" I asked.

"Honestly Newton," Cowie protested, "Don't you think it's a bit soon to be bringing this up?"

"No I do not. I think she ought to have been told this right at the beach," Newton argued before proceeding to explain. "Silver tongues are creatures who's tongue has turned silver and who therefore can only speak lies. They work for Feazel. Their job is to convince adventurers to abandon their journey and join the Feazel's side."

"Why didn't Wordy tell me that?" I asked.

Newton rolled his eyes, "What is this attitude? As if someone has to tell you every little thing. You have got a conscience haven't you? I bet your conscience was telling you that you best better not listen to Francis."

A weight sat on my chest when I realized he was right.

"But why did the tree look so beautiful if it was all lies and why did it have Mr. Sploot's lesson in front of it? Looking all the way through is a good thing, isn't it?" I was confused.

Cowie smiled, "If you were to have thrown fire dust on that tree it would not have looked so beautiful. It

80

would have been a withered black bush with thorns and burrs and fruit that tasted rotten and soggy."

"Where can I get fire dust?" I asked in a hurry.

Newton looked aghast, "Honestly Hazel - what *is* this attitude about? This entitlement? Fire dust is a completely different adventure."

"Patience," was all Cowie said on the matter. I wasn't sure if he was speaking to me or to Newton but I resigned myself to not ask any further questions.

We came to rest at a crystal blue river and I flipped through Mr. Sploot's book. One of the pages read: *Stay with your group. If you go out alone you go looking for trouble.* The next page said: *Watch out for the silver tongue because it sounds nice but tells lies.*

"Isn't that true," I whispered to myself closing Mr. Sploot's book. I opened my own adventure book and read Wordy's instructions over and over again until I could recite them. I would not be fooled again.

Chapter 14

A Fork in the Road

After my run-in with Francis I was very purposeful to stick close to Newton and Cowie and read my adventure book at night. Sometimes while we walked I would flip through Mr. Sploot's adventure book and read the lessons he had learned on his first adventure. Although many of the pages didn't make sense, I was trying to memorize as many as possible. I had learned two today: *do not stop at the watering hole because the price is very high* and *throw the ball for the hyena.*

When we stopped for the night I lay on the ground against Cowie's back and let the instructions tumble over one another in my mind. I wondered who was trapped at the top of the mountain and what the journey would be like to get there. Seventeen days certainly did not seem like very much time to climb a mountain and rescue a prisoner.

The wind rustled the tree leaves as it blew around us.

"Sixteen days," Newton announced when we woke up and started climbing higher up the mountain.

"Why is called Murky Mountain?" I asked.

"Because of the water in the lake at the top," Cowie replied. "It is murky and that is why the weasels like it. They hide their secrets in Murky Lake and then they think no one will know about their deeds."

"Oh," I responded, just as confused as before.

"The badgers like it too," Newton added. "Feazel is the reigning monarch in the castle and he is a badger. Terrible brute, the leader of the silver tongues."

Feazel certainly sounded terrible.

Newton continued, "And there's the legends of the lake monster-"

"Not now," Cowie gave Newton a stern look.

I did not want to think about a lake monster, Feazel was enough horror to imagine for now. I pictured a badger with a royal robe and a crown on his head with hundreds of weasels at his feet. I shuddered and shook that image from my brain. I didn't want to dream up how it would feel to go into that castle.

We climbed higher and higher up the mountain. The rocks turned pale and we came to a place where the road split in two. There was a large greyish pink bolder in the middle of the fork and on it there sat a red squirrel. The squirrel had tall pointy ears and a plump body. She was sitting and working on a needle point and didn't see us coming.

"Hello Edith," Newton greeted.

Edith jumped with a loud squeak, her needle point flew one way and she flew the other.

"Goodness gracious me, why do you insist on sneaking up on a squirrel like that?" she stood up and pressed a hand to her chest. She retrieved her needlepoint and returned to her post on the rock. "Wordy told me I should sit here today, said an adventurer would be coming by."

I stood there awkwardly.

"Edith, meet Hazel," Cowie introduced.

Once again Edith threw her needlepoint. "Oh dear me, I am so sorry love I didn't even see you there." She rushed over and scampered up my leg and perched on my shoulder. She squeezed my cheeks, inspected in my ears, and made a quick run around my hair. "Good," she said. "No mites,"

I was confused.

"Mites?" Newton shouted. "What on earth would she be doing with mites?"

"You should always check to be sure, got to keep things clean," she clicked her tongue, ran to fetch her needle point, and scampered back to her rock. She moved in an intense blurry frenzy.

"Simmer down Edith, if you move any faster you might outrun your tail," Newton joked.

"When did they put the split in the road?" Cowie asked, ignoring the banter.

"Last week," Edith replied. "It was the moose. They said they didn't like the other way and so they made their own."

I looked down both sides of the fork, they looked identical. I wondered if fire dust worked on roads.

"Hmm," Cowie muttered to himself, looking at the fork.

"Those moose, so alternative," Newton shook his head.

"How do we know which one leads up the mountain?" I asked. Wordy had said nothing about a split in the road and I had no map.

"Oh oh oh I know!" Edith shouted. She disappeared in a flash, leaving her needle point spinning on the rock. A moment later she zoomed back with a gold pocket watch that looked very much like the one Wordy had carried.

"A thing-a-ma-jig," Edith said when she placed it in my hand. I pressed the button on the side. There was no cloudy globe and no shining colours. On the inside there was a single black arrow that read: *Up the Mountain.* The arrow swung back and forth for a moment before pointing down the left fork.

"Well," Newton said, "There you have it. Left is up and up we go."

"What's down the right road?" I asked Edith.

"Only the moose know," she replied.

"The Sweet Grass Forest, man," A lazy voice spoke behind us. It was a moose with very tall skinny legs, a shaggy head, and massive floppy ears. I could feel the heat of his breath on my neck. Everyone turned and gave their attention to the towering creature. He looked as if he had just woken up. "This road," he lifted a hoof to the left, "is too narrow. It gets real scary in some places. I tried to go that way once but I turned around and came down the right trail." He pointed his hoof down the right fork, "I know *this* is the better way."

"Why is it better?" I asked.

Newton covered his eyes with his scaly hands and shook his head in frustration, "why bother even asking."

"It's a short cut," the moose said. "I've been a guide on this trail for…" he paused and thought, "almost forever now I suppose."

"Jack," Edith rolled her eyes, "you just went down that trail for the first time last week and you're not a guide."

Jack shook his head, knocking trees with his antlers as he did. "Not so Edith, I've been in the Sweet Grass Forest for years. And I *am* a guide. I led a possum all the way up to the circle just a few days ago. "

"That possum was going to the same meeting that you were," Edith sounded exasperated.

"What's the Sweet Grass Forest?" I asked.

"The best place in the world," Jack looked down the trail longingly. He wore a silly smile on his face. "You should come see it sometime. The grass there is delicious, much better than the stiff grass on the higher mountain trail. It's the perfect place to relax. Plus it's a shortcut to the Council Circle."

I started to ask what the Council Circle was but Newton finally burst, "Honestly we don't have time to waste, Hazel. We know which way to go so let's go."

"Simmer down, Newton," Edith said, cutting the thread of her needlepoint and tying it off at the end. "If you move any faster you might outrun your tail."

Cowie laughed. Newton crossed his arms and glared at Edith.

"Thank you for the thing-a-ma-jig," I said.

"You're welcome," Edith smiled. "Mind that you keep it away from the crows."

I pulled our my book and wrote: *Keep the thing-a-ma-jig away from the crows.*

"Will do," I assured Edith.

Cowie nudged my arm and we bid Edith goodbye. When we walked down the trail I could hear Jack trying to persuade her to come to the Sweet Grass Forest for a while, "Seems like you could use to relax, man. You're so uptight."

"Honestly, Jack-" I didn't hear the rest of Edith's reply for her voice faded into the distance behind us. I flipped the thing-a-ma-jig over in my hands and wondered why I would have to keep it away from the crows.

Chapter 15

Priscilla

We hadn't walked long when I started to see what Jack the moose had been talking about, somehow the path grew even more narrow and it was getting scary. It rose aggressively up and then dropped sharply down. The ground was covered in slippery loose rocks and I fell and cut my knee. Blood dried on my leg and the wound stung. The stinging got worse and I asked Cowie to look at it and make sure I was alright. Just as Cowie had stooped down to inspect my knee, a loud shriek pierced the air. The sound was followed by a tumble of rocks. A goose wearing a large pink hat with a funny bow on one side was sliding uncontrollably down a steep decline behind us. The goose crashed into Cowie who crashed into me. In the blink of an eye I found myself sprawled out on the ground in a pile of feathers, scales, and fur. Newton had still been on Cowie's shoulders and was so surprised by the crash that he had shot a stream of fire out of his mouth. The goose's hat had ignited and turned into a smouldering heap on the ground.

"Get *OFF* my tail!!" Newton screamed at me.

"Sorry," I apologized as I leapt off the pile. Newton raced away clutching his tail in his hands and stroking it protectively.

Cowie stood up and shook the rock dust off his coat before stomping out the remains of the fire from the hat. The goose sat up in a daze and brushed off her feathers.

"How clumsy of me. Quite embarrassing," her voice was sweet and soft. She went to adjust her hat and gasped when she realized it as gone. "MY HAT!" she cried when she saw the heap of ash on the ground.

"It was an accident," Newton defended.

"Well you owe me a new hat now," she growled.

"Accidents happen to the best of us," Cowie said calmly.

"Not as often as they happen to me," the goose clucked and wiped a tear from the corner of her eye.

"Where are you going?" I asked her.

"I was trying to find the market," she clucked. "I need a new outfit for my sister's wedding, but I fear I got lost."

"I don't know where the market is," I said. "But you could walk with us! We are bound to find someone who knows."

The goose happily agreed, expressing over and over how thankful she was not be travelling alone anymore. I learned that her name was Priscilla. She was from lower down the mountain by a place called Tipsy River. She seemed much better at talking than listening but I didn't mind, her stories were full of drama and intrigue. Cowie stayed quiet and led the way down the path. Newton remained lost in his private miseries; complaining about the clouds, the birds, the flowers, the breeze, and about a bee he said that was following him and whispering very unkind things in his ear.

I liked Priscilla. By the end of the day I knew everything there was to know about her. She was apparently very lonely for friends and we made a pact that we would be the best friends on the whole island. When I did manage to talk, I told her about the adventure we were on.

"How exciting!" she beamed. "I have always wanted to go on an adventure."

"Well you could join our adventure," I offered.

Newton sputtered in protest, "Cowie do something before this all gets out of hand."

Cowie stopped walking and addressed Priscillla, "Accepting an adventure invitation is quite serious business. Once you accept the invitation you must commit to seeing it through."

"I can commit - I can do that!" Priscilla cheered.

"There is a price," insisted Cowie. "If you dishonour the invitation to adventure, it may never invite you again."

"How would I dishonour the invitation?" asked Priscilla, astounded that Cowie would suggest that she could be capable of doing such a thing.

"Well you could trade your adventure book-"

"And *why* would I do *anything* like that?!" she interrupted defiantly. Glaring at Cowie she crossed her wings over her chest. "Hazel has invited me on the adventure and now I have accepted. That is that."

Cowie persisted in trying to explain the serious nature of adventures but Priscilla waved him off and insisted she was more prepared than he thought she was. Eventually he relented. "If she's going to join the adventure she needs he own adventure book," he said.

"Quite right," Newton let out a defeated sigh, "Wordy will have his eye on it. He will get her one. Imagine it, a goose on an adventure."

"I. Am. A. S*wan!*" she spoke in a staccato voice that expressed both horror and rage. Everyone stared at her unblinking for a moment.

"Whatever you say," Newton said quite unconvincingly.

I was too excited about Priscilla joining the adventure to care about whether or not she realized she was a goose. It was nice to have someone else to share the excitement with. Someone who, like me, had never been on adventure before. What did it matter if she had a small delusion of grandeur?

We poured through Mr. Sploot's book together and I told her all about his magical briefcase, the gold fish, the trip across the stars, meeting Cowie and Newton and Wordy, and our journey thus far. I trusted her with every secret detail and hidden hope. She was thrilled to be joining the journey. Talking must have exhausted her because as soon as we stopped to set up camp for the night, she fell fast asleep.

Cowie built a fire and Newton lit it. I leaned against Cowie's side and flipped through Bill Sploot's book. It wasn't long before Cowie fell asleep, his body rising and falling in the gentle rhythm of peaceful dreams. The sun sank low and disappeared. The stars shone above us and a full moon flooded the forest with milky white light.

Newton was sitting on the ground with his arms crossed and tail wrapped around his feet.

"What traveler is imprisoned?" I asked him.

"I don't know," he responded.

"Where in the castle is the traveler imprisoned?" I asked again.

"I don't know." Newton replied.

I paused.

"Have you ever been to the castle?"

Newton looked exasperated.

"Does your mind ever stop coming up with questions?" he asked.

I shook my head and smiled.

"No," he answered. "I have not been to the castle. I have been to the Murky Lake but I was very young and foolish then. Spending a great deal too much time with the raccoons."

"Do you think it is scary?" I asked. The image of a castle ruled by a badger and crowded with weasels made me feel queasy.

"I think," Newton spoke very slowly, "that worrying about whether or not the castle will be scary is a waste of time. We will only know what it is like when we get there. There are enough scary things to face in the mean time. Each moment has just as many scary things as it does and we will greet each one as it comes."

"I suppose you're right," I conceded.

"Of course I'm right," he huffed, "And write this down: If it walks like a goose, talks like a goose, and honks like a goose - it is *not* a swan." His voice contained just enough humour mixed with annoyance to let me know that he was done answering questions for the night

"Now," he said with finality, "there is a time and place for everything under the sun, but under the moon it is time to sleep. Goodnight Hazel."

I giggled quietly and wrote the lesson down in my book. "Goodnight Newton," I replied and watched him curl up on his stomach and tuck his nose under his tail. Not yet feeling tired, I thumbed through my adventure book. I remembered the fish telling me to put the sunshine in for when times get dark. I scribbled a picture of a sun on a blank page. I smiled at my art, closed the book with my pen serving as a bookmark, lay back against Cowie's side, and closed my eyes.

Chapter 16

Grynns

Soon everyone was snoring away and I was the only one awake. I tried to sleep. I closed my eyes, counted sheep, and made myself hold very, very still. Even so, my mind would not give in to rest. After what felt like hours, I sat up and looked around. The fire was now a pile of hot glowing coals. Clouds rolled across the sky above us and blocked the light of the moon. Deep in the forest I saw a little light glowing. It was an icy blue light that swayed back and forth softly as if it were a lantern hanging in the air.

I watched the light tilt back and forth as it moved slowly, very slowly, across the tree line. Curious. Silently I rose and took tentative steps towards the edge of the path, stopping where my toes just reached the boundary line between the path and the forest.

Newton rolled over in his sleep and mumbled something about entitled adventurers inviting deranged geese on a serious adventure; I froze and waited until his breathing evened out and the camp lay still again. Staring at my sleeping comrades made me want to stay by the fire. They looked so peaceful.

But then the light caught my eye once more. I didn't feel tired. I felt curious. Something about that light was positively enchanting. I had to know what it was. Surely it wouldn't hurt to just slip away for a moment. I had my adventure book, I would be alright.

"Stay on the trail or you will get lost," Wordy's voice played in my head. I dismissed it. I wasn't really going off the trail, it would still be in my site. Besides, even if I lost track of the path, I would still be able to see the light of the coals so there was no way to get *truly* lost. Confident in my cleverness, I decide to pursue the strange light.

One foot left the path, the other followed. I crept through the trees, being careful to make no sound. The whole forest was still, all except the swaying blue light. This was very exciting, for the first time I felt like a real adventurer, capable and independent.

The light was growing larger as I ventured deeper into the woods. One step at a time I took myself closer and closer to the blue, further and further into the forest and away from my camp. Time disappeared completely, the earth and sky faded from my mind, I could only see the little light. It sucked me into a vortex that blinded me to the rest of the world and made me see only itself.

Finally I could see the outline; a large dome lantern suspended on the end of a curved walking stick. The light was encased in a black iron cage that was twisted into an elaborate pattern.

I still could not see what exactly emitted the light. Was it fire that was in the cage? I couldn't tell, I had to get closer. Another step towards the lantern and I still couldn't see the flame - it couldn't be fire though, I had never seen blue fire. I walked several steps closer, so transfixed by the light that I gave no mind to what or who might be carrying it. Suddenly I found myself crouched in a bush right beside the lantern. Just as I had suspected, there was no blue flame. Suspended in mid air, glowing steadily, and rocking gently back and forth, a round stone glowed a very icy blue.

Forgetting myself for a moment, I whispered beneath my breath, "wow."

The lantern stopped moving. My attention snapped to the figure that was carrying it. It was taller than I by at least a foot, it was wearing a heavy dark cloak with the hood up and so I couldn't make out what sort of creature it was.

"Hazel, so you've come back," a soft voice called out from under the hood.

Who was that? It sounded familiar.

"No sense in hiding." The figure turned towards my secret place. "I know you're there," Francis's voice taunted.

My heart picked up speed and beat loudly in my ear. I reached into my pocket and pulled out my adventure book, doing my best to shrink away from Francis and escape back to the trail. He slipped the hood of his cloak off his head. I didn't remember him being so tall and menacing in the garden. His ears perked up and twitched in my direction. For a brief instant our eyes met, his looked like they were two glowing red coals. I screamed and whatever resolve I had to sneak away quietly instantly vanished. I turned and ran back through the woods as fast I could. I looked for the campfire and realized I couldn't see it. There was no sign of where I had come from and where my friends were sleeping. I was completely lost. I ran blindly. There was no light from the moon or stars which were

99

completely blanketed by thick clouds that began spitting rain down onto the ground.

Francis followed close behind me, laughing and telling me not to run. "Stop, Hazel! I only want to talk to you."

I didn't dare look back. I didn't want to talk. I didn't ever want to face Francis again. I ran as fast as my legs could carry me. Rain pelted into my eyes and I tried to shield my face so I could see. I tripped over a tree root and landed with a thud on the ground. My adventure book was flung down beside me and fell open with a splat. I covered my head with my hands and clenched my eyes, prepared for Francis to overtake me, but he didn't. There was a great blinding light of bright yellow before a piercing yelp. I glanced up just in time to see Francis disappearing into the forest.

My adventure book still lay open on the ground, but it was now glowing. The sun I had drawn was shining as bright as flames and had created a pool of light all around me. I picked myself up off the ground. The cut in my knee had reopened and stung badly. My adventure book started flashing it's light in a steady rhythm. It paused. A moment later a small and very soft yellow light answered it, blinking the same pattern.

I watched the little light get larger as it travelled through the woods towards me. It drifted through the trees gently and came to land gracefully on my knee. Had I not been in so much pain, I would have thought I was dreaming. This strange light was a lantern with butterfly wings. The wings drifted up and down very subtly as the lantern perched on my good knee. There was a little door on the face of the lantern that swung open. A tiny creature that resembled a honeybee stepped out of the lantern. He carried a small yellow case in his hands. He flew over to my injured knee and inspected the wound, poking it gently and humming to himself. After a thorough analysis, he reached into his yellow carrier and retrieved a small bottle of shimmering gold liquid. He uncorked the top and poured several bright drops on the cut.

As the drops splashed into the wound, I felt instant relief. The solution was cool and comforting, easing the pain and giving me a calmness. I took a deep breath and felt my heart start to return to a regular speed.

Nodding his approval, the creature corked the bottle and put it back in his case. He climbed into the lantern and waved at me gallantly before closing the door. The butterfly wings carried the lantern back into the forest and into the dark night.

Suddenly my knee felt fine, I felt calm, and had a clarity of mind that I had not had all night. My adventure book continued to glow as it hovered over the ground and beckoned me to follow it.

I rose to my feet and followed my book all the way through the forest, back onto the trail, and to my friends by the fire. I collapsed beside Cowie with a heavy sigh. My adventure book folded itself shut delicately and came to rest on the ground beside me.

"What's that on your knee?" Cowie asked. Evidently I had sat on his foot and woken him up.

"Uhhh...," I stammered for a moment, not wanting to explain my betraying Wordy's instructions and landing myself in an encounter with Francis.

Cowie smirked knowingly and rested a paw across my shoulder.

"It's alright Hazel. I'd recognize liquid sunshine anywhere. I am glad the Grynns could help you but you really shouldn't wander off the path again."

I nodded and didn't say anything more. I lay down on the ground and tried not to think too much about the events of the night. Cowie quickly fell back asleep and eventually, I did too.

Chapter 17

Underground Postal Service

"Fifteen days!" Newton hollered when we woke up.

Priscilla complained that she looked hideous from sleeping on the ground and said over and over that no one should see her in such an ungroomed state. Cowie said she looked just fine and we pressed on along the trail.

My knee was better this morning. The skin had grown over and there was no more wound, just a small white scar with a shape that resembled a sun. I wanted to ask Cowie about the Grynns but I felt that I better not ask now. It was best not to bring it up around Newton and Priscilla. I knew Newton would not approve and would have strong words for me if he found out what I had done. Yes, I had better wait to ask about the Grynns. For now I just decided to be grateful that Cowie had kept my nighttime escapade secret from the rest of the group.

The trees grew thinner and shorter until they were no taller than me. Large poky nests sat in the tops of the branches and great black and blue magpies flew in and out of them.

"Tattle tails," Newton muttered.

The magpies flew from tree to tree, tracking us along the path. We passed a group of three that were perched on the edge of a nest not far from where we were. I heard crackly bird voices whispering, or trying to whisper, to one another.

"That's her," one said.

"Can't be," another replied, "What kind of adventurer looks like that?"

"Right?" agreed a third. "She's too small and wiry."

"Well she has the dog," the first voice spoke. "Bill Sploot went to the castle with a dog, didn't he?"

The third spoke again, "but who ever heard of an adventurer travelling with a lizard!"

A crackle rose in Newton's throat and he puffed up his beard ready to blast the feathers of the magpie.

"You know Mr. Sploot?!" I turned to the birds.

They squawked in surprise and screamed in unison as they flew off into the trees, "Its seen us!"

"Blast you grease feathers!" Newton yelled.

"Grease feathers?" Priscilla asked.

"Ignore him," Cowie interjected.

"Have you been to the castle?" I asked Cowie.

Cowie nodded but said nothing. I wanted to ask what it was like but I held my tongue.

"Blimey are we going to a castle?" Priscilla piped up, flapping her feathers.

I thought I had mentioned the castle when I invited her on the journey, but perhaps she was too busy talking to hear that part.

"I don't think it's that kind of castle," I replied solemnly.

"A castle is a castle! I can't wait to see it," she clapped her wings excitedly.

Suddenly a gopher leapt out of a hole in the ground on the side of the trail. He was quite short and trim. Two large shiny white teeth protruded from his mouth and large brown eyes darted around wildly. He was carrying a big bag and wearing a green vest with silver buttons down the front.

"Hazel?" he asked, looking from face to face.

I raised my hand.

"Underground Postal Service!" He pointed to the badge on his vest. "I have a letter for you, from Wordy."

He passed me a paper scroll that was tied with a gold ribbon.

"Thank you," I said as I accepted it.

"We are at your service," the gopher saluted. "Keeping you connected wherever you go!"

"Anything for me?" Newton asked.

The gopher checked his bag and shook his head, "Not today."

"Who are you expecting a letter from?" Cowie asked.

"My mother writes to me," Newton defended. "She worries about me when I go on adventures."

"Priscilla?" The gopher called.

"Here I am!" Priscilla shoved Newton out of her way and stepped forward.

The gopher passed her a brown adventure book and she giggled with excitement as she flipped the cover open. Her eyes scanned the page and I knew she was reading a note Wordy had written. The gopher bid us good day and disappeared down the hole.

Priscilla snapped her adventure book closed with a determined scowl on her face. I asked her what the note had said but she refused to tell me. "I don't like what it said! I am not sharing it with anyone."

I showed her the page in Mr. Sploot's adventure book that read: *Listen to the owl, even when you don't like what he says.* She brushed it off with a flick of her feathers and said that that particular statement did not apply to her in this case. My conscience disagreed but I didn't feel like starting an argument. I untied the scroll and read my own note from Wordy:

"Hazel:

It has come to my attention,

that the weasels know you are here.

I need to make sure that does not inspire fear.

You are safe on the path if you do not wander off,

And when you get to the swings take the one that's on top.

Enclosed is a map of the castle for you,

Cowie AND Newton will help you decide what to do.

Take heart and have courage, keep your mind on the quest,

The times up ahead are the times that are best.

Wordy."

"Where is the map?" Newton asked.

"I don't know." I checked to make sure there wasn't a map attached to the letter.

"Perhaps he's forgotten it," offered Priscilla. "He seems like he doesn't quite know what he's doing."

107

"He knows what he's doing. He hasn't forgotten it," Cowie said. "Check the back, Hazel."

I turned the letter over and saw a drawing of an envelope on the other side.

"It's just a drawing." I held the paper up for Cowie to see.

"Is that so?" Cowie winked, "Interesting."

We kept walking and I kept staring at the envelope drawing. I had faith that the letter was real and I had faith that the envelope was real... but how was I supposed to open the envelope?

I remembered Mr. Sploot's briefcase and the picture frame he had shown me. He had shaken it to reveal the secrets. Perhaps...yes... that could be it! I shook the letter, nothing happened. Newton chuckled in amusement and Priscilla asked Cowie if I had gone mad. Cowie gave no one any attention and just walked steadily forward.

I blew across the envelope drawing. The paper quivered and the envelope opened. Shimmering dust fell out from inside and hung in the air. I shook the letter and watched as a silvery paper, which was folded many times over, fell out of the drawing and onto the ground. I picked it up and opened it carefully. It was blank.

"Notice that he said Cowie *AND* Newton this time," Newton said, puffing his chest and grinning.

Wordy said he had included a map of the castle, but where was the map? This was just a blank piece of pretty paper. I could not have been more confused.

"Newton?" The gopher reappeared. "I do have something for you."

He passed Newton a paper parcel that was tied with brown string. Inside, was a box full of baked squares and a note:

Newton,

These are for you and your adventure friends.

Stay safe.

Love,

Mom.

Cowie took a bite off the top.

"Hey those are mine!" Newton tried to block Cowie from sticking his nose in the box again.

"They say for your friends," Cowie retorted.

"And aren't I glad we're friends," Pricilla teased, helping herself to a square.

"We're *not*!" Newton glared at Priscilla as he moved to guard the box.

"I haven't got one yet," I said.

Newton groaned and rolled his eyes before offering me a square.

"I guess this means we're friends," I chuckled.

"*Adventure* friends," he corrected with a smirk.

The squares were deliciously soft and chewy like caramel. As I ate, I took out my adventure book and tucked Wordy's letter in the front cover. I knew I would need those instructions later. Squares, letters, and adventure books in hand, we pressed on down the trail.

Chapter 18

The Page Erases

Although Priscilla had started her journey as an adventurer with great enthusiasm, she was obviously getting tired of it. By mid afternoon she was complaining loudly about how her feet hurt, how dirty her feathers were, how little fun this was turning out to be, and how she was thinking of abandoning the whole adventure all together.

"You committed," Cowie reminded her.

"I thought you said you were ready for it," Newton added.

"I am *ready* for anything!" Priscilla snapped her beak at Newton.

I didn't blame Pricilla completely for complaining. The journey was very rough today. We slipped and stumbled and climbed perpetually uphill, it was exhausting. However, her complaining was grating on my nerves and making the whole ordeal much less bearable.

The sun beat down and slowed us all a great deal. We had to jump over a short but very deep crack in the earth, which I almost slipped into but Cowie pulled me forward. Priscilla refused help and nearly fell, knocking some stones with her foot. The rocks echoed infinitely as they fell down the seemingly bottomless pit.

Across the crack there was a sign hammered into the path:

"PROCEED WITH CAUTION

Many bumps. Chasm ahead."

A separate path split to the right, it also bore a sign:

"SMOOTH ROAD HERE."

"Well it's obvious which way we ought to go," Priscilla announced. Without asking anyone else or checking any instructions, she started marching down the smooth road.

"Wait!" I called.

"What?" she asked. Annoyed that I was challenging her.

"Blue stones," I pointed to the rocks that were scattered along the path. She looked at me confused. I opened my adventure book and read: *Avoid all blue stones.*

"Those aren't blue," she argued feebly. "They're more of a ... teal... or turquoise."

I raised an eyebrow and looked at Cowie for guidance.

"Look all the way through," he said.

Mr. Sploot's adventure book had something about a smooth road in it, didn't it? I flipped through the pages to see.

"This is silliness," Priscilla crossed her wings and stamped her foot. "We're wasting time. Why would you go to the chasm instead of down the smooth road? You almost fell into the chasm back there. Surely you don't want to challenge another one and risk falling to your doom."

I did not appreciate Priscilla's attitude today.

"Here!" I said, " *'The rocky trail smooths and the smooth trail cracks'* ," I read. It didn't make sense to me but it seemed to be all that applied here.

"You don't even know what that means," Priscilla retorted.

"Maybe not," I said. "But I do know that those stones are blue."

I pulled out my thing-a-ma-jig and flipped the lid opened. The arrow wavered to and fro and finally pointed towards the sign that said to proceed with caution.

"The thing-a-ma-jig says to go this way," I said.

"We don't have any more time to spare," Newton said as he prodded my back with his scaly finger.

"Come along Hazel, you've made up your mind."

Cowie nudged my hand and started walking. I followed him closely. Priscilla stomped her feet and let out a honk of frustration before she too followed Cowie down the path.

This path was very difficult. We struggled over large rocks with sharp edges and skated across loose stones. More than once I nearly lost my footing completely and started to fall off the edge of an embankment. After a few close calls I grew quite scared. Cowie walked right beside me and assured me that if I just stayed at his side I would be fine. I kept my hand on his neck and tried to focus only on getting to the smooth part of the road that was promised in Mr. Sploot's book. I repeated the words over and over in my mind: *The rocky trail smooths.*

Newton was riding on Cowie's back, his face very near my hand. He peered down over the edge of the path and suddenly I felt a heat flash across my hand.

"Ouch!" I yelled.

I turned to see little streams of fire coming from Newton's mouth as he struggled with the hiccups. His face had turned a greenish colour but his cheeks flushed crimson when I looked at him. He covered his mouth with his hand but small webs of fire still escaped through the cracks between his fingers.

"Don't mind him," Cowie said. "He's afraid of heights, gets the hiccups when he's nervous. Just close your eyes Newton."

Newton closed his eyes and eventually fell unconscious from trying to hold his breath in order to suppress the hiccups. Once asleep, his breathing returned to normal and the flames stopped shooting out of his mouth every two seconds. Some fur on Cowie's back was singed and my hand suffered a small burn but we finally crossed to smooth solid ground otherwise unscathed.

Just when I reached stable ground, I heard a screech from behind. Priscilla was tumbling down the cliffside. She plummeted down to the bottom of an embankment and started screaming that we should have taken the smooth road.

"*HOW* am I supposed to get back up to the trail?" she yelled furiously.

"You're a goose!" Newton shouted. "Fly!"

"I! AM! A! SWAAAN!!!!" Priscilla screamed. It took her a minute of yelling pure rage and fury before she had the self control to fly back to the trail.

When she rejoined our party, her face was flushed with anger and embarrassment. She stuck her beak in the air and walked off into the forest to pout.

"Stay on the trail or you will get lost," I reminded her.

"Honestly Hazel I have just about had it with you and your foolish rules!" she hissed.

I was just about to explain to her that the rules were wise and not foolish but Cowie stopped me.

"Give her a moment," he said.

We all took a moment to rest before heading along the trail. Mr. Sploot's book was right, the rough road got much smoother. A cool breeze brushed gently by and I found it very refreshing. I felt much more relaxed and began to enjoy the journey once again.

Eventually Priscilla started to get over her anger and began walking with the group. When we stopped for the night in a small clearing by a shiny river, Cowie sat and started talking seriously with Priscilla. Giving them some privacy, I walked to the edge of the river and started looking for some purple stones. I couldn't find any. I tossed a grey rock into the water anyway. Earnestly I waited for the gold fish to come scold me. I tried several rocks and nothing happened. I wondered where he was and how his spinach garden was fairing.

Priscilla and Cowie were talking in low hushed tones. There was a solemn air hanging around everyone when I sat back down at the fire. I leaned against a tree and Cowie came and stretched his paws over my lap. I stroked his head.

"I am sorry for my attitude," Priscilla said calmly.

"It is alright," I replied. I offered her a smile but she refused to make eye contact.

"Did you write anything?" I asked.

"What?"

"In your book," I pointed to her adventure book and quoted: "Write down your lessons so you don't repeat your mistakes."

Priscilla picked up her book, turned to a blank page, and wrote something down furiously.

"It's not working!" she cried. "The ink keeps disappearing."

"Well what're you trying to write?" Newton asked.

"It's a secret," Priscilla snapped.

"Well it must not be a true secret. You can't write anything in the adventure book that isn't true," Newton

117

said. "Adventure books will erase anything that isn't true"

"It *is* true!" Priscilla insisted.

"Unfortunately he is right Priscilla," said Cowie. "It is the responsibility of adventure books to erase any falsehoods."

Priscilla slammed her book shut and said that she was tired of being treated so unfairly.

"It's actually the fairest thing in the world," Newton said. "No one can write down anything that isn't true no matter who they are."

"Well I suppose then that it wouldn't let you write down that *you're* a dragon," Priscilla hissed.

Newton began to puff up his beard but Cowie placed a paw gently on his back.

"Please, not tonight," he said. "I've got a dreadful headache and we all need to get some rest."

"Fine," Newton huffed. "Only because you asked."

Priscilla and Newton lay in disgruntled silence. I stroked Cowie's head and tried to will his headache to go away. Priscilla soon fell asleep. Newton began snoring not long after her.

"I'm a dragon I'm a dragon I'm a dragon," he mumbled over and over again in his dreams.

"Cowie?" I asked. "What did Mr. Sploot's book mean when it said that the smooth trail cracks?"

"I don't know, I wasn't with Mr. Sploot when he learned that lesson."

"Oh," I replied, "I am just curious."

"Why? You chose this path for good reasons. Do not look back on the past and start wondering what would be at the end of another path. You picked this one."

"I know," I said. "I just sort of wanted to know."

"Would knowing help?"

I shrugged.

"Let me tell you something that you ought to write down," he said. "Where you set your focus, there you will go."

I wrote it down in my book.

"What does it mean?" I asked.

"It means that you are headed forward. Keep your mind and eyes both looking forward."

Where you set your focus, there you will go.

I thought about these words. I didn't want to go down the smooth road and I would stop looking there with my mind. I looked to the beginning of my adventure book and reread Wordy's instruction: *Remember your goal, to get to the top.* The top, that is where we were going and that is where I had to set my focus.

119

"Cowie?"

"What is it Hazel?" He sounded tired.

"What's a Grynn?"

He smiled. "I wondered when you would ask that. Grynns are the firefly fairies."

"They didn't look like fairies to me." I thought fairies were supposed to be delicate ladies with long dresses and musical voices that gave you magical dust that could make you fly. I also thought they were pretend.

"It would be wise if you stopped assuming that every picture in your mind is true and accurate,"he said.

I had never considered this. After all, in all the stories fairies were depicted the same as the pictures in my head. But this wasn't a story, this was reality.

"What's liquid sunshine?" I asked.

"It's the gift of the Grynns. Their jobs is to help adventurers who get lost in the dark. The liquid sunshine can cure any ailment: discouragement, loneliness, cut, bruises, being lost... anything really."

Amazing. I had many questions about how the Grynns got their liquid sunshine, where they lived, if they could give me some sunshine to take home, and how to locate them in daylight. Alas my body was tired and pulled my brain into dreams before I could get the answers.

Chapter 19

The Ferry

"Fourteen days!" Newton announced at the crack of dawn. "Hurry hurry hurry we can't miss the ferry! If we miss it that babbling idiot will delay us by hours. Up! Up! Up!"

For someone so small Newton could do a great deal of nudging and motivating. There is nothing quite like a small dragon voice screaming directly in your ear. It rang through my brain and rattled my nerves awake. Gradually his nagging rose everyone to their feet. We all wiped the sleep from our eyes, washed up in the river, mustered our best attitudes, and headed along the trail. I was quite impressed with the effort everyone seemed to be making to get along. Cowie called out pleasant things like a brightly coloured bird, a new flower, and how lovely it looked when the fog rolled through the valley. Newton agreed that it wasn't completely dreary and that was a nice change. I offered my observations on the interesting shapes of the clouds, how the road was much easier to walk, and how refreshed I felt after a restful night. Even Priscilla was far more cheerful this morning than she had been the night before and refrained from making any snide remarks at Newton. We chatted easily and walked side by side. It seemed we were all friends once again.

Just as the sun was coming up across the horizon we came down a ravine and to the side of a wide river. There was a raft with a long vine fastened to it. The vine pulled the raft from one side to the other, taking travellers back and forth. I wasn't certain how such a contraption worked, but I was too tired to ask too many questions this early in the morning. We had to wait in line while a small black bear in a yellow hard hat and orange vest lumbered from one side of the raft to the other doing the morning inspection. He began by checking the flags, the latches, turning the sign to open, adjusting his vest, and scrubbing a coffee stain off the reflective yellow stripe.

A group of otters splashed up onto the ferry deck and began chatting with the bear loudly. They were bouncing up and down and all yelling over top of one another. They seemed to be very excited about a warthog they saw fishing just up the river. They were pushing each other into the water, splashing wildly, and laughing a great deal. Newton was not having any of it.

"Why do otters always insist on wasting everyone's time? I know that they think life is all fun and games but don't they know that some creatures have actual work to do?"

Cowie hushed his complaining. A great polar bear came marching up behind us and stopped beside Cowie.

"Hello Mitch," Cowie greeted.

"Cowie," the bear acknowledged.

Cowie introduced me to Mitch who nodded gruffly in my direction. His face was very serious and I knew I must be on my best behaviour around him. He looked like someone who very much cared for rules and did not care for those who broke them. A dog was standing beside him and carrying a great pack full of grappling hooks, ropes, nets, and other contraptions. The dog sat silently beside Mitch while he and Cowie talked. He kept very close to Mitch and watched the bear on the ferry suspiciously.

"How are things looking today?" Cowie asked Mitch.

"You wouldn't believe it, Cowie. Another donkey caught on an edge in the ravine, trying to show off for

123

his friends. I can't stand it. Something needs to be done. They go into the woods to go camping and they absolutely disrespect the space. Fires aren't put out, garbage is strewn everywhere, and then they are calling for help because another one of them decided not to obey the signs I put out and they go wandering where they shouldn't. And after all that, they're mad at me because they got stuck."

"It is a thankless job you do," Cowie said solemnly, "but a noble one."

Mitch let out a sigh and turned his attention to me. "You pay attention to the signs and don't go looking for trouble. I don't want to go pulling you up off a cliffside because you wandered away."

I nodded very enthusiastically to let him know I would stick to the path and obey the signs. I didn't particularly want to know what would happen if Mitch had to rescue me out of a ravine.

Cowie and Mitch went on about Mitch's work. Newton chimed in often to let Mitch know that he was sympathetic to the struggle with foolish creatures. Priscilla was snoozing, standing up with one leg picked up off the ground, her eyes closed, and feathers folded. I watched the river raft.

By the time the otters had finished entertaining the bear, he had forgotten what parts of his inspection he had done and had to begin all over. He dragged his heels when he walked and laughed a lot at jokes that he made loudly and directed to no one in particular. Finally he decided his raft was river worthy, waved a little flag, and directed us one at a time onto the deck. Priscilla shook her feathers indignantly when we woke her. She glared at the black bear when he told he she was a very nice looking goose and refused to talk to anyone until we got to the other side.

Many other animals had gathered behind us. Impalas wearing running shorts stretched their legs and talked about how fast they could run the trail today, an alligator plucked a banjo and wailed about how he would never find love, and a long trail of armadillos traded theories about why this was probably the day that the raft vines would snap and we would all be drowned in the river. The bear seemed to find all the chatter quite amusing and he kept wandering around asking people whether or not they could swim.

"I can hold my breath and do the doggy paddle at the same time," he announced proudly; no one seemed very impressed.

The raft finally started moving along the river, it moved dreadfully slow. Newton apparently got seasick and started turning a strange shade of orange.

Cowie and Mitch carried on their conversations and reminded Newton just to keep his eyes on the horizon. I was writing down how to cope with sea sickness when the black bear came up behind me and told me that there was no writing allowed on his raft. I stopped writing and stared at him, unable to tell if he was serious or not. His crooked teeth split into a wide grin and he slapped the ground laughing.

"I have to write," I said. "I'm an adventurer, it's what I do."

He stopped laughing and stood up on his hind legs and pointed down the river.

"Well you ought to be writing about those characters down there. They're having quite a fun time. They don't waste their time writing. Know how to live in the moment those lot do." He pointed a hairy paw to the otters splashing in the river.

I didn't particularly like the black bear. It didn't seem like he knew very much about adventures. I told him I didn't have any interest in talking to otters and was just fine writing about sea sickness, if it was all the same to him. He shrugged and walked back to the armadillos who were laughing uncomfortably at his joke that he hadn't properly inspected the raft's vine in years.

Eventually the raft reached the other side and we went through another painful inspection process in which we had to help the bear tie up the raft since he had forgotten how. Finally we were stepping off the ferry and wishing Mitch good luck as he headed into the mountain terrain to rescue more donkeys.

The scenery on this side of the river was much greener than that on the other side of the river. The trail was smooth, the sky clear, and wildflowers perfumed the air with a delightful scent. The impalas darted ahead at a maddeningly fast speed, the alligator strolled mournfully far behind everyone else (eventually sitting in the shade and giving up on walking all together), and the armadillos chatted on in a furious but very slow moving mob behind us. It didn't take much time before we were surrounded by towering trees and blissful silence.

Chapter 20

An Alligator, a Parrot, & a Betrayal

Many twist and turns later, the trees cleared and we arrived at a town. There were lots of little houses made of branches and bricks. The town was built around a large blue watering hole. A sign was posted on the side of the path: "VACANCIES: Adventurers not welcome!! Surrender adventure books at the waterhole office. All violators will be reported to the WSS."

"What is the WSS?" I asked.

"Weasel Sneaky Service," Cowie replied.

"Terrible lot," Newton muttered, "Ruthless."

"Why aren't adventurers welcome?" Priscilla asked.

"Because it's a watering hole," Cowie stated. "The watering holes are all controlled by Feazel. They're managed by silver tongues and most who live in them are silver tongues themselves. We must not get distracted by lies or give the WSS any reason to interrupt our journey."

"Oh."

Priscilla still sounded confused.

We passed several homes with small gardens, flower pots, and different creatures lounging on their decks. Outside one home there was a family of rabbits having an argument about who left a mess in the den. I couldn't be certain but every time I looked, there seemed to be more bunnies running around. Little carts were parked at the sides of the road and different animals called out to us, tempting us to buy their crafts.

"The market!" Priscilla jumped up and flapped her wings. One cart was covered in hats and had a long silver framed mirror standing beside it. Priscilla squealed with glee and waddled over to the display. An alligator with a top hat, a black cane, and a bow tie assisted her in trying on hats of every shape, size, and colour.

Cowie, Newton, and I followed Priscilla. I didn't like the feeling I got when I arrived at the stand. The alligator looked at me funny and I felt very uncomfortable around him. We weren't supposed to stop at the watering hole - we were supposed to be focused on moving forward. Newton was looking furious, obviously horrified anyone would ever waste time looking at hats. I stayed close to Cowie, feeling safer with him beside me.

"We're not supposed to stop at the watering hole, it says the price is too high," I reminded Priscilla.

She snorted, "This isn't the watering hole, it's a hat stand."

"I am pretty sure this still counts as stopping at the watering hole." I shifted on my feet uncomfortably.

"Newton owes me a new hat," Priscilla replied sharply. She tried on a lavender piece with a peacock feather and a pearl on the side.

"Tawee Tawoo look at the pretty pretty bird!" A parrot whistled at Priscilla, making her blush.

"You should be a model," the parrot called.

Priscilla gasped and placed a wing over her heart, "I have always wanted to be a model."

"Don't listen to the parrot!" I blurted, full of concern. Everyone looked at me. I quoted Mr. Sploot's adventure book: *Don't trust the parrots because they repeat whatever they hear.*

Priscilla shot an angry look at me and snapped her beak, "You are just jealous because he thinks *I* could be a model."

She adjusted her hat and posed in the mirror, shaking her tail feathers and puffing up her chest. The alligator walked to stand beside her. "Such a jealous young creature," he said, pointing his skinny cane at me. Cowie let out a low rumbly growl and Newton ducked his head, trying to hide behind Cowie's ears.

"So jealous," Priscilla clucked in agreement.

The alligator stood next to her in the mirror and stretched an arm around her neck. "Why don't you stay here with me? You could model my hats. We can become business partners. You and I can make this the richest stand in the watering hole. You could have a great big house with a whole closet *just* for hats," his deep echoey voice crooned in her ear.

"That sounds wonderful," Priscilla swooned.

"Yes," he replied grinning. I saw a gold tooth in the side of his mouth glimmer in the sun. "All it will cost you is that little brown book that you keep tucked under your wing."

Priscilla paused. A flutter of panic flew up into my chest. I remembered how Cowie had warned her that if one abandons adventure, it may never invite again.

"We need to go," Cowie said firmly.

Priscilla looked longingly at her reflection. I looked in the mirror and gasped when I saw that Priscilla *was* a swan in the reflection.

"Stay here pretty bird," the alligator said.

131

The parrot chimed in again, "Stay here pretty bird!"

"We're friends and friends stick together," I snapped at the parrot.

"Are you really friends with these filthy adventurers?" The alligator glared at me and whispered into Priscilla's ear, "Seems to me that if they were *really* your friend they would support you pursuing your dream of becoming a model. You weren't made for adventure. You are such a beautiful *swan* - you should be modelling."

"Such a beautiful *swan*!" called the parrot. "Should be modelling! Tawee tawoooo!"

"Don't you see?" I said to Priscilla. "The parrot is just repeating everything he hears."

Priscilla glanced at the parrot doubtfully but the Alligator used his cane to guide her gaze back to her beautiful swan reflection.

"Abandon adventure," the alligator whispered, "live in luxury." He placed his cane back on the ground. I saw a silver tongue peer from the back of his throat as he spoke. Horror overtook me and I grabbed Priscilla's wing with my hand.

"Don't listen to him," I said. "He is a silver tongue!"

"A silver what?" she asked.

"Silver tongue," I replied. "He can only tell lies!"

132

Priscilla looked at Cowie who nodded solemnly. "We must be going," he said again. "No time to lose."

"Then take your nonsense ideas and go!" The alligator waved his cane at Cowie. "Priscilla my dear *swan*," the alligator whispered to her, "stay. You belong here, in the market, being adored, and celebrated for your beautiful looks."

"You belong here!" the parrot repeated. "Tawee Tawwooooo!" He called over and over.

"Just give me your book," the alligator whispered again.

Priscilla stared in the mirror a moment more and something changed in her eyes. She passed the Alligator her adventure book.

"No!" I cried as the alligator threw the book callously into the watering hole and it sank under the surface.

"I'm staying," Priscilla hissed, "I belong here."

"But Priscilla-" I pleaded.

"Go away Hazel! I don't want to be friends with any filthy adventurers!" She snapped her beak in my face.

Cowie nudged my hand with his nose. "Come along Hazel," he said. "Priscilla has made her choice."

I couldn't believe it. I kept a hand on Cowie's back and let myself be led out of the town. Newton placed a hand on mine when he saw a tear roll down my face. For once he sounded sympathetic: "Don't let it get you down. Friends come and friends go. Sometimes creatures can be kind in the beginning and turn cruel in the end; not always, but sometimes. It is just the way that it goes."

"It is her loss, truly," Cowie said heavily.

"Look for the truth and the truth you will find, but pity the adventurer who leaves it behind," Newton quoted Wordy's lesson. "You looked for truth and you found it. You recognized the lies of the alligator and the echoes of the parrot. You saw the truth. Pity Priscilla, she traded truth for her hat. All we can do is hope that it won't be to her complete undoing." I had never seen Newton so sincere and solemn.

"It will be alright," Cowie reassured me. "You chose right and now we must look forward."

"Where you look you will go," I repeated the lesson he had taught me last night. I brushed a fresh tear from my eye. Newton offered me the last square and I took it gratefully. I didn't look back as we left the watering hole, the noise fading away in the distance. I looked only down the road ahead and did my best to push Priscilla out of my mind.

Chapter 21

Mr. Marty

After we had left the watering hole we journeyed the rest of the day in silence. We travelled back up into thick forest where there were large boulders and high cliffs. Rain started to fall before the sun sank below the horizon and so our travels were cut short. We took shelter in the mouth of a large rocky tunnel. It took a long time to get a fire going and we were all shivering with cold from the rain. Newton complained incessantly that the whole tunnel smelled of wet dog. We huddled together in shivery damp discomfort.

"Is that Cowie I hear," a strange voice echoed through the tunnel. Cowie leapt up and spun around, rumbling a threatening growl. Newton screamed, a flame escaping his throat and sizzling as it hit the corner of my wet dress. Scratching noises from deep inside the cave made their way closer to us. Cowie's growl intensified. "Who goes there?" he called.

"It is I, Marty."

A rock chuck scrambled up to the cave entrance. He was fat and furry with a large nose and a yellow scarf. He had a puffy tail that curled around his feet as he stood on his hind legs. He was holding a brass lantern that glowed a flickery orange. I quickly inspected the lantern from a distance and determined that it was not a flying rock lighting the inside nor a Grynn. It was just an ordinary candle lantern, a small flicker of disappointment.

"Of course!" Cowie relaxed. "I should have known this was your tunnel. I didn't even recognize it in the rain."

"Not to worry not to worry," Marty replied. "I heard you were going to be in these parts soon. Wordy came by about a week ago, said you would be passing through here with an adventurer."

Marty scampered behind Cowie and offered me his hand. "Greetings young Hazel."

"How do you know my name?" I asked.

"Word travels fast in these parts I'm afraid," Marty chortled. He scampered to the mouth of the cave and looked at the clouds thoughtfully. "The rain isn't

136

supposed to let up until later tomorrow morning based on what I can see. Why don't you come back to my den. You can warm up and dry off. Why don't you have dinner, and stay the night? Get started in the morning after this downpour lets up."

"We'd be delighted," Cowie replied.

Newton emerged from his hiding place in the rock and clambered onto Cowie's back.

"Newton!" Marty exclaimed. "How you have grown since the last time I saw you. How is your mother?"

"She is well," Newton said. They chatted about his mother as we followed Marty further into the cave. Evidently everyone knew each other. I felt slightly out of place in the group and stuck close to Cowie's side. He smiled at me affectionately when I scratched behind his ear. He assured me that I was just fine and that I would like Marty's den very much. Along the walls there were pictures scratched into the stone.

"The children's work," Marty said with a proud smile.

Very deep into the tunnel, far from the entrance and the rain, we came to a spiral staircase carved into the mountainside. Around and around the spiral steps we climbed. I thought we were never going to reach the top. My feet ached and my legs were sore.

Just when I thought I was about to fall over with exhaustion, we arrived at a blue door with a very small window in the middle and six key slots running down the side. Marty rapped on the door sharply.

"What's the password?" A high pitched squeaky voice asked on the other side of the door.

"Pumpernickel," Marty answered. "Can't be too careful," he said to us over his shoulder.

One after another, the six locks clicked and the door swung open. A second rock chuck greeted us. She was slightly shorter than Marty and wore a pink apron and large glasses which hung on a colourful beaded chain round her neck.

"Cowie my dear!" she greeted, hugging him around his neck. Wordy did say you would be coming." She moved past him and embraced me in her furry arms. "And you must be Hazel. What an honour to have you here! Go and warm yourself by the fire while Newton and I get supper fixed." Much to my surprise, Newton did not seem at all perturbed about being drafted for kitchen prep and scampered happily into the kitchen, chatting easily about how his mother was doing, how insolent magpies were, and how backed up the postal service was becoming.

Mr. Marty hung up his scarf and reset all six locks on the door behind us. They were not like ordinary locks, they had spirals and gears and springs and clasps and levers and bands on them. I wondered how they worked.

After he finished locking the door, I followed Mr. Marty over to the living room where there was a roaring fire in a stone pit and a thick green carpet on the floor. Mr. Marty sat in a purple hammock that hung in the corner, put on a pair of knitted slippers, and began to smoke his pipe. Cowie stretched out by the fire and let out a heavy sigh. I knew how tired I felt; he must be exhausted too. I sat on the rocky hearth and stroked Cowie's side.

"So," Mr. Marty said, puffing on his pipe, "You're headed to the castle?"

"Yes," I replied.

"An honourable venture. That poor girl. I heard they had her held in The Stinky at first, but just today a dragonfly told me that she has been moved to The Stinky of Stinkies." His voice went very soft and quiet as if he was afraid someone might overhear. I was unmoved as I didn't understand the places he was talking about.

"You've heard the story haven't you?" he asked. Apparently taken aback by my lack of reaction. I didn't know what a Stinky or Stinky of Stinkies was and no one had told me about the traveller we were rescuing. I shook my head from side to side in reply.

"Oh dear me! You started the adventure without a story? That's no way to begin an adventure at all. Best get comfortable Miss Hazel, I've got a yarn to spin."

"He means he's going to tell you the story," Cowie clarified with a yawn.

"Barring any *further* interruptions," he shot Cowie a stern look, "I shall begin." Marty cleared his throat and his voice took on a daydreamy tone:

"A faraway world hidden under a crystal sea,
Is home to many creatures that you never thought would be.
People with blessings and powers of mind,
Two nations at war in a deadly divide.
A girl that's a healer sought help from the East,
On the back of a powerful and intelligent beast.
Torrential winds and events no one knows,
Landed her here in the nets of the crows.
Before any could help she was taken to the weasels,
And thus she was locked in the castle of Feazel.
In fourteen short days she must be back to her land,

A rescue that will take the most careful of plans.
The lost traveller must be returned before the new moon,
For to Dragon Healers, its rising is their doom."

"Lemon scone dear?" Mrs. Marty bounded into the living room, completely oblivious to the seriousness of the conversation. A small rock chuck hung off her apron and squealed, "Mama! Mama! Mama!"

"Tut tut tut," she clicked her tongue and wagged a disapproving finger at the child. "Guests first."

She passed me a plate full of pastries that were larger than my hand. I accepted one, though my appetite had greatly diminished due to the new pressures I felt after the story. This 'Dragon Healer' relied completely on me to be kept safe and I didn't have a clue what I was going to do.

"Thank you lovely," Marty said to his wife when she passed him the tray. Cowie politely declined, said lemon didn't agree with his stomach.

"Dinner will be shortly," Mrs. Marty called on her way back to the kitchen. "It will be splendid! Newton is making his famous potato salad."

"Delicious!" chimed Marty. "I haven't had that in years."

I chewed on my scone and the speech that Marty had just given me. Where had he said she was imprisoned? Oh yes, The Stinky. I sought consolation in that. "The Stinky doesn't sound like a very scary place at all," I said. I had been in many stinky places, like the root cellar back home or the basement in the city after it had flooded in the spring, and I was never *that* scared of them.

"Tsk tsk tsk don't be such a fool Hazel," Marty clucked his tongue.

I remembered Cowie's lesson about the pictures in my head not always being accurate. Putting aside my predisposition to the name, I asked Marty, "What is The Stinky?"

"Only the most desolate dungeon in the whole world," he replied. "It is a vile place it is, buried far under the dungeons in the castle. It is cold and the water from the murky lake trickles through the roof and runs down the walls. There is no light, no sound, no food, and no safe water to drink. That's where they put their prisoners that they want to break."

"What is The Stinky of Stinkies?" I asked feeling more afraid by the second.

Marty puffed on his pipe for a moment before answering. His hammock was strung up on chains that creaked knowingly as he swayed back and forth. He blew a circle in the air and waved it aside with his hand.

"In the bottom of The Stinky," he said quietly enough so that no one else could hear, "there is a trap door. Below that door lies The Stinky of Stinkies. No one has ever gone into it and come out. No one knows for certain what is down there. There have been no survivors."

I shuddered and felt my skin crawl.

"And that's where they put the girl?" I asked.

"That is what the dragonfly told me. And dragonflies never lie. Honest to a fault those creatures are. Wouldn't lie to save their own tails, any of them."

"What's a dragon healer?" I thought that sounded like a very intriguing thing to be.

"You will have to ask her when you meet her," Marty replied. "I have never met one myself."

"And how am I supposed to rescue her?" I swallowed hard and felt a weight sitting on my chest.

Marty puffed on his pipe calmly and leaned back. He genuinely looked unconcerned. He crossed his arms and sighed contently.

"Worry not Hazel, if the sky opened for you then you are the perfect one for the job. I am sure you will have a brilliant plan in no time."

I was glad Marty had faith. He seemed sure I would be fine. I gulped - I was not so sure of myself.

Chapter 22

Gold Gully Goblet

Dinner was wonderful. There were dishes piled high with wild rice, potato salad, homemade dinner rolls, and a a simmering vegetable curry. Mr. and Mrs. Marty had eight children, all boys. They sat at a separate table and talked louder by the minute. It wasn't long before they began getting rowdy and started to throw their dinner rolls at one another. Mrs. Marty got so tired of asking them to, "please pipe down," that she ended up sending them all to bed without any dessert (which was a delicious apple rhubarb bake). Cowie was too big to sit at the table so he stayed on the floor and I dished up his plate. Newton's potato salad was a massive hit. "A recipe from my mother," he said modestly.

"So what's the big plan?" Marty asked me when Mrs. Marty cleared the plates.

"I don't know yet," I replied, feeling rather foolish, for not knowing.

"Well have you got an idea?" he prodded.

I retrieved my adventure book and pulled out the silver paper, passing it across the table to him. "Wordy gave me this. He said it is a map but I haven't been able to sort it out."

Marty took the paper in his hands and walked over to a small end table that stood in the corner of the room. He reached into a narrow drawer and retrieved a sort of looking glass, round with a handle on each side and gauge on the lower right corner that had letters drifting around in circles. He came back to the table and placed the paper down, peering into the glass as he held it at various heights.

"Interesting," he said many times. Eventually he placed the looking glass down and lifted the paper to the light of the candle chandelier. He folded it and unfolded it, sniffed it, and dropped it on the floor several times, studying it carefully as it fell and letting out a triumphant 'ah-hah!' every so often. After several rounds of seemingly nonsensical experiments, he placed the silver paper back on the table and toddled happily into the kitchen.

"What's he doing?" I asked Cowie.

146

"Testing it," he responded.

"Really? He's got some odd methods," Newton stated. "Between you and me I think that-"

Newton never finished telling us what he thought for at that moment, Marty appeared above his head clanging two pot lids together and sending Newton flying into the air in a flurry of sparks, fire, and screams. The fire scorched the silver paper that lay on the table as Newton darted off the table and into the living room where he dove into Marty's hammock.

"Of all the nerve!" he screamed.

Marty acknowledged Newton's outburst with a hearty giggle and a 'gotcha.' Cowie chuckled but Newton did not seem amused. Marty placed the silver paper back down on the table and I watched as black writing danced across the page: "Sorry. Try again!"

"Just as I suspected," clucked Marty. "He's double fire proofed it. Amazing. Very secret indeed."

"What do you mean double fire proofed?" I asked.

"Watch and see," Cowie said.

It seemed Marty was quite enjoying solving the problem of the map. "Dear," he called into the kitchen, "Where's the Gold Gully Goblet?"

"It's in the canning room," Mrs. Marty answered.

"Oh no," Marty laughed nervously. "I can never find anything in there."

Mrs. Marty came into the kitchen, wiping her hands on her apron. "I'll go find it," she said.

"She's the only one who could." He chuckled.

She shot him a look and propped her hands on her hips.

"I've been meaning to tidy it up, I really have. I was going to do it today but things just got a little out of hand you know, it is busy with all you boys running around. Honestly, I will do it tomorrow."

"She's been saying that for years," he whispered to me with a giggle.

Mrs. Marty disappeared further into their home and returned a few moments later with something that looked more like a bronze jar than a gold goblet.

"Ahhhh yes!" Marty beamed excitedly. "Thank you my love! This will do the trick. This will cut through the double proofing."

He reached into the jar and took out something that looked like a handful of glittery yellow sand. It jumped and jittered in his hand as if it was alive. He sprinkled the sand onto the silver paper and levelled his eyes with the table to stare at it. For a moment nothing happened.

The sand wiggled and vibrated lightly but that was it. Marty looked at it intently, not even blinking.

Minutes went by and we all watched expectantly. Still nothing revolutionary happened. I was starting to become suspicious that Marty did not know what he was doing. Just when I was going to say that we should consider trying something else, a very peculiar thing began to happen. The sand stopped jittering and froze. Then it started slowly swirling across the page, subtly at first but picking up speed with every second. In a moment I could feel the wind of the sandstorm on my face. Golden sand sparkled and flashed as it whipped in tight circles, creating a fierce tornado. The flashing tornado danced across the paper in choreographed lines, burning up the fire proofing and revealing small traces of ink wherever it travelled.

I watched entranced as the tornado maneuvered across the page and unveiled the map before us. In the blink of an eye, almost too fast to see, the sand took its final pass along the page, leapt from the paper and into the Gold Gully Goblet, closing the lid securely behind itself.

The goblet spun around for a moment before coming to rest stationary on the table. Marty let out a childlike giggle, "Ahhh watching that never gets old."

The lines revealed by the tornado were fine brown calligraphy swirls that outlined a castle; the lines were so inconspicuously narrow and the labels written so small that I could barely make out the general shapes let alone decipher the details.

"How are we going to read it?" I asked desperately.

"Of course it wouldn't be so simple as fire proofing," Marty clucked in amusement. "We've just got to enlarge it somehow, enough so that we can read it."

"What if you shake it?" I offered, remembering how Mr. Sploot's leather pouch had grown.

"Worth a shot," Marty picked up the map and gave it a shake. Nothing happened.

"Here," he said as he passed the map to me, "You try." I gave it a flick and willed it to grow but again nothing happened.

"I wonder," Newton muttered. He had returned from his hiding and scampered up onto the table to analyze the map. "Do you think it's a Shrinks map?"

Cowie leaned his head on my shoulder. "Check the envelope again."

I pulled out the letter from Wordy and looked at the envelope drawing. I opened the lid by blowing across it and gave it a firm shake. A small emerald fell out.

"Brilliant suggestion Newton!" Marty exclaimed.

Newton beamed at the praise.

I was not sure what the significance of the emerald was. I watched Marty as he placed the emerald on the top right corner of the page, slid it along the edge to the bottom right corner, then along the bottom edge to the lefthand corner, and up the other side. In the middle of the top edge he stopped and said, "Ah-hah! It is Hazel!"

"What is Hazel?" I asked rather worried. "What is me?"

"Only one person can use a Shrinks map," Marty explained. I still wasn't sure what a Shrinks map was. "Their name must be written on the paper. Look." He gestured to the emerald that was sitting on the map. I went around the table to stand beside him and peered into the emerald.

Hazel

I gulped. There it was, clear as day. My name was written on the map.

"What's a Shrinks map?" I asked.

"It is a special map, one that can only be read from the inside," Marty explained.

"The inside?"

"Yes. A map is manufactured to be an exact replica of a place and then is shrunk every which way so that it can lay on a piece of paper. Every Shrinks map is different, of course, but there is always only one way in and one way out and only those whose names are written on the map can enter. It is up to them to make a legible map for anyone else."

I tried very hard to understand but the idea was foggy in my mind. My confusion must have been evident on my face. "Never mind the details. The point is that you must go into the map and chart it," Marty said, trying a simpler explanation.

"Alone?" I panicked, "Can't Cowie come with me?"

"I'm afraid not. His name isn't written on the map. Wordy sent this you said?"

I nodded.

"Well then, Wordy must have wanted you to go alone."

I knew Mr. Sploot had written that I must listen to the owl even when I didn't like what he said, but I wondered if Mr. Sploot had ever been told to go into an unknown map alone. I looked at Cowie in a fright.

"You will be fine." He assured me.

I didn't feel like I would be fine. Actually I felt like I was going to be sick. My stomach flip flopped into a small knot and I felt rather faint.

"You can take your adventure book with you," Newton added, "You will need it."

"I will?" I asked.

"Yes!!" Everyone chimed in unison, making me feel quite silly for having asked the question.

Marty cleared his throat and continued giving directions. "The map will only work once. You must make careful notes on everything you see. You will chart the castle and make your own map in your book. When you bring it back to the rest of us, we will be able to make a plan."

My mouth dried up and I nodded my head silently. Pictures of weasels and badgers and dungeons drifted through my mind. I started to tip back off my seat before Cowie steadied me. I stroked his head and tried to relax. In this moment I truly felt that I did not want to be brave and I did not want to finish this adventure.

I heard Mr. Sploot's voice drift through my mind, it was as clear as if he was standing beside me: 'It means to not give up just because something got a little bit tougher.' Well, things were a little bit, a *lotta bit*, tougher now that I was being asked to do this intimidating task;

but I needed not to give up. I had to do this. I was, after all, a true adventurer.

"The castle will be empty," Cowie interrupted my private battle.

"It will?" I let out a heavy sigh as relief flooded me. It would be much easier to face a castle if there were no badgers and no weasels.

"Of course," Newton chuckled. "Why would anything else be there? It is just a map after all." I let out a stressed laugh.

"Right," I said. "It's just a map." Even though I heard myself say the words, I didn't fully believe them.

"Ready then?" Marty asked. Straightening himself and clearing his throat.

"Now?" I protested.

"There's really no time to waste."

I knew he was right. I swallowed hard and nodded, agreement.

"You will be alright," Cowie reassured me.

"Of course she will be alright!" Newton rolled his eyes. "It is just a map. What has happened to make adventurers so fragile? Honestly."

Marty pressed the emerald into my palm and told me to cup my hands around it, shake it, and roll it across the map like dice.

"That will get you into the castle," he said. "When you are ready to come back to the den, take the emerald just the same, shake it, and throw it into the sky. Only do that when you are absolutely sure you are ready to come back to the den, for the map will only let you explore it once. And be sure you do not lose the emerald. If you do..." He sighed. "Well, let's just not think about that."

I could feel my eyes popping out of my head as my mind raced fearfully to the conclusion that I was about to be trapped in a map forever. Cowie nudged my arm and told me once again that I would be just fine. I steadied my breath, despite the fact that my heart was pounding in my ears, shook the emerald several times, and released it to roll across the map. No one could have prepared me for what happened next.

Chapter 23

Down is Up

All I could see was the emerald. The room disappeared around me in a zooming whirlwind. I felt myself falling though the air after the gem. It pulled me out of the den and into the map. It bounced through the castle gate, down a series of stone steps and landed with a deafening clatter in the centre of a large stone hall. I fell through the air and onto the cold floor. I did not spare a single moment before I leapt on the emerald, determined not to lose it. I tucked it safely into my pocket before standing to take inventory of my new surroundings.

I was no longer in Mr. and Mrs. Marty's den but in a vacant corridor. Grey stones rested crudely on top of one another to form shaky walls that leaned this way and that. The floor slanted to the left and a steady drip came from the ceiling. The air rushed out of my lungs and I froze in a moment of fear as I realized just how quiet the castle was. There was not a sound to be heard aside from the drip of the water. There was no wind, no voices, no music, no nothing. I steadied myself and took out my adventure book to chart the castle; that is what Marty said I was supposed to do. Though, where was I supposed to start? I had never made a map before. My heart sank in despair. How I wished Cowie's name had been written on the map and he had been allowed to come with me. I bet he would have known how to make a map.

"Oh I don't know what to do!" I cried to no one. My voice bounced off the far wall and echoed back to me eerily. I shivered. I didn't like this place one bit. I took out the thing-a-ma-jig from my pocket, full of faith that it would help me sort out which way to go. I opened the lid and watched the arrow spin around aimlessly, never coming to rest on a direction. With a heavy sigh, I gave up and closed the lid back over the face. It seemed I would have to figure this out all by myself.

Tentatively I walked along the echoey corridor. I had to jump across giant holes in the floor where stones had fallen through and no one had bothered to replace them. I wondered how the whole castle had not fallen to complete ruin yet. "Guess they're not much for maintenance," I muttered to myself.

Across many gaps, through a glistening spiderweb, and at the end of the corridor, there rose a staircase. A small green backpack rested against the first step. A note was taped to it. I read it aloud:

"*Hazel -*

Welcome to the map! I am glad you got in,
And now that you are here, you must quickly begin.
This backpack is for you to carry your tools,
Always keep the clasps closed, it wards off the fools.
At the top of these stairs you will come to a slide,
It will lead you to the gate, the way in from outside.
The castle is large, do not get lost in the detail,
Work smarter not harder and trust that wisdom will prevail.
Draw what you see and write down what you read,
And take careful note of where the rat keeps his keys.
In the office of Schultz you will find a great help,
Twenty-third from the left, on the thirty-second shelf.
Eleven is Feazel's most favourite number,
And to cross the final bridge, you must look over not under.
Take heart and show courage you are going to be fine,
Now hurry, be quick! And waste no more time.
Wordy."

The backpack was fastened shut with black buckles. They opened easily when I applied pressure to the sides. I was mildly disappointed to see there were no pockets inside as there had been in Mr. Sploot's briefcase. There was simply a single compartment that was closed by a zipper.

"*I forgot to mention,*" read a note tied to the zipper.

"*The zipper must be zipped to prevent any leaks or drips.*

~ *Wordy*"

I took a moment to jot the instruction down in my adventure book, just in case I forgot later: *Keep the backpack clasps closed and the zipper zipped.*

Carefully I placed my adventure book, letters, emerald, and thing-a-ma-jig inside the compartment and zipped it shut. I fastened the buckles together, swung the straps over my shoulders, and headed up the stairs. My footsteps rung through the stairwell as I clambered up the seemingly endless line of steps. Around and around I climbed until I could barely convince my legs to take one more step forward. Finally, I took the last step into a very small round room, I was breathless and sweaty. I was greatly confused as there was no slide to be found. In the middle of the room there was a red cord hanging from the ceiling. I wondered if that was the entrance to the slide. It was worth a try. I wrapped my hand around the rope and was just about to give it a gentle tug when something caught my eye. There was a stone in the wall opposite with a letter scratched on the surface. At first I couldn't make out what the letter was but the more I stared at it the clearer it became. An "S" followed by an "L" and an "I" and a "D" and… I squinted hard and wiped some dirt off the stone. Yes, that was definitely the remnants of an "E." I took a step toward the wall and placed my hand against the stone. It gave way under slight pressure. I pushed a bit harder and felt the stone budge forward. The stone slid back into the wall and fell in place with a soft click. I heard a grinding of gears below my feet and looked down just in time to watch the floor drop out from under me.

I screamed!

I was dropped straight down and caught roughly by the floor of a stone slide. The trap door swung closed above me with a heavy thud. A snap sounded and the slide chamber was lit an icy pale blue; illuminated by glowing stones that lined the walls and roof. My terrified cry transformed into squeals of delight as I was taken sharply to the left and to the right, in a loop upside down, and through a spiral so tight that it made everything dizzy.

The ride lasted for over a minute and my stomach flipped and crashed around inside of me. Just when I thought I was going to be sick from spinning, I felt the slide rise up beneath me and I began to slow down. There was another series of gears cranking and I watched a door swing open in front of me. I was shot out of the slide and into a large net. I bounced up and down several times before coming to rest on the black mesh. My head was still spinning and I had to lay still for a moment before I found the stability to scramble off the net and onto the ground. I stumbled haphazardly toward the castle, unsteady on my slide legs.

Reaching the gate, I stopped to take in the architecture. The outside of the black castle was menacing, towering hundreds of feet above my head; I couldn't see the top of it. I gulped and reminded myself to blink. How was I going to draw a map of this?

I whispered Wordy's instruction to myself, "Do not get lost in the details. Work smarter not harder."

I could do this.

I collected myself and focused on my mission, to map the castle. I wouldn't allow myself the luxury of feeling overwhelmed, there was simply no time for that. Besides, what was there to be overwhelmed by? Wordy trusted me to go into the map alone and chart it. He knew I was capable. Besides, Cowie had said I would be alone in the map, so there wasn't anything to be truly afraid of.

I ran around the perimeter of the castle as quickly as I could (being very careful not to step off the edge of the map) and realized the castle was a perfect square. There were three hundred steps each way around. I ran around a second time, just to be sure.

When I arrived back at the gate I pulled out my adventure book and drew a careful square. I labelled the slide, the net, the gate, and the bridge. It seemed Feazel's castle was completely cut off from the rest of the world by a chasm that stretched all the way around. "Is that what the sign meant when it said 'chasm ahead'," I wondered to myself. "The chasm of Feazel?" It sounded quite terrifying when I said it out loud.

There was only one way to cross the chasm and enter the castle, a very rickety old draw bridge that stretched from the castle gate to the mainland. It was a rotting wooden structure that looked unreliable at best. My stomach twisted itself into a knot as I pondered how we would have to cross it to reach the castle. If there was only one way in, then there would surely be creatures to guard it. Even if the crumbling bridge would agree to hold our weight, how were we going to sneak across without being spotted? This was looking more dire by the second.

I shivered at the thought of being apprehended on the bridge and thrown into the dungeons. The picture of that happening spurned the eery feeling that I was being watched. The hair on the back of my neck stood up and I thought that I could feel a pair of eyes boring into the back of my skull. I peered over my shoulder, just to be sure. I couldn't see any eyes. I reminded myself that Cowie had said that there would be no one else in the map, but I couldn't shake the feeling that someone, or something, was there with me.

Inside the castle gate there stretched a large vacant hall. The whole chamber seemed to scream and warn me that some uninvited peril lie ahead. Again, I pushed the thought from my mind. "

"No one else is here," I said quite loudly. "No one. My cheeks flushed in annoyance. Why was I suddenly feeling so afraid? I had to be brave. I had to be resilient. I had to be wise. Putting on my bravest face, I steeled my determination and tiptoed inside the door.

A large sign hung on the wall just inside. A purple sign with black letters: "STAMP TIME HERE."

A narrow table stood beneath it. A large book rested on the top, strewn with rows of names and numbers:

#8014	Skeeto	08:30
#0255	Stone	09:40
#3381	Nelson	10:30
#4420	Schmidt	11:15
#1002	Linus	11:58

The list of names went on for pages. On the very bottom of the page it was open to, there was a note:

"Anyone caught with their circular entertainment device on their post will have it confiscated and will clean The Stinky.
Schultz."

I copied the note into my adventure book, made sure the book of names and numbers was returned to exactly the position I had found it in and ventured further into the castle.

The floor of this corridor was covered in soft purple carpet. This carpet was the only thing about the castle so far that appeared new. Everything else was as decrepit as the corridor that the emerald had led me into first. I was grateful for the carpet. It cushioned my feet and silenced my presence.

About a hundred and fifty steps inside, halfway down the length of the castle, there was a wall. Five arched doorways opened up to their own routes. A drawing hung on the wall above the arches. A black star was painted on the bottom. It had crudely painted letters on it that read, "YOU ARE HERE." I analyzed the map and saw that the passages lead to: the throne room, the office of the nobility, the centre of recruitment of new weasels, royal chambers, and the dungeons. Quickly, I made a rough copy of the map to the dungeon. The map above the arches had many more details but I didn't bother to write any of them down. I knew that The Stinky was underneath the dungeons and so I only needed to be interested in that route.

The map directed me to: follow the arch furthest to the right, go straight to the end of the corridor, down a series of stairwells, through a door labeled 'number g,' and cross under a swaying bridge. I double checked my rendition of the map to ensure accuracy before I confidently walked through the correct arch.

Along the corridor were rows of paintings of grim badgers in royal attire. They had fat bellies, stuck up noses, glistening robes, and gold plated teeth. I tried not to look at them but it felt like their eyes followed me as I walked. I was grateful for the soft purple carpet that continued to cushion my steps, it made me feel more inconspicuous and reassured me that there was nothing to be afraid of.

As I walked, I noticed that this corridor felt much longer than a hundred and fifty steps. I looked back, I could no longer see the arched doorway I had entered through. I looked forward and realized I couldn't see the end of the corridor. Curious. I wondered how such a long hall could fit inside the square castle.

The corridor floor came to a place where it was no longer carpeted. It was crude uneven stone that had cracks and gaps. There were no more paintings of badgers and no more windows. The walls looked like they were caving in, ready to fall on me at any moment. I swallowed the nervousness in my throat and focused only on reaching the end of the passage, that I still couldn't see. Windows became fewer and fewer until there were none at all. Dim light was provided by occasional torches that burned a sad pale orange, cold and grim. Oh how I wished Cowie had been able to come with me!

Finally I could see the end of the hall and the entrance to the stone stairwell. I ran to the edge of the corridor, my heart pounding in my ears. I stopped stiff in my tracks when I reached the entrance to the stairs. Something was much different here than it had appeared on the map by the arches. That picture had only shown stairs leading down to the dungeons. Here,

166

there were steps that lead both down and up. A sign hung on the wall in between the two staircases:

DOWN IS UP AND UP IS DOWN

That didn't make sense. I checked the map again, there was no reference to stairs going up or to a sign that said such nonsense. I tucked my adventure book securely in my backpack and tapped my foot impatiently on the ground as I considered my options.

I looked up the staircase and those steps definitely went up. I looked down the staircase and those steps definitely went down. Perhaps the sign was a joke or a mistake. I knew I had to go down to reach the dungeons and judging the evidence that I had, I concluded that the down steps must go down.

I scrambled down the steps. Anxiously trying to find my way to the dungeon as fast as possible so I could get back to the security of Cowie and Newton and the warm den of the Martys. Down and down the steps took me, deeper into the rock every moment. The air grew stale and damp and the walls started to weep. I remembered how Mr. Marty had said that the water from Murky Lake seeped through the walls into The Stinky. "Yes!" I shouted. "I must be on the right track!"

The roof stooped gradually lower until I had to crouch in order not to hit my head. Roots and vines clung to the walls and moss coated the steps, causing me to slip and nearly fall. I came around a corner and faced a dead end. I stood there, hunched over and confused. There was no dead end on the map.

Why was everything so different here than on the map? Perhaps it was an outdated map. Or the vines were blocking the rest of the corridor. Yes, that could be it! Vines as thick as my arm were growing on the wall in front of me. Perhaps they had grown together and were simply obstructing my way forward. I pushed the thicket aside to see, hoping desperately that it would reveal a spacious hall with a tall roof as I was beginning to feel rather claustrophobic.

Something clanked against the rock when I brushed my hands through the damp greenery. A set of iron keys swung out from the vines. I picked them up to examine them. Crude letters were scratched into the side of the keyring: "RATS."

I reached for my backpack to note where they were. When I let go of the keys, they swung and knocked some moss off the wall, revealing an "I" carved into one of the rocks. There appeared to be another letter, partially covered by moss, carved next to it. Distracted from my adventure book, I brushed aside the rest of the moss to uncover the remaining letters.

168

As I uncovered the words, they read themselves aloud in a deep cackling voice that boomed overheard, "I told you so," it said, "Down is up and up we go!"

The roof shook and rocks started falling all around me. I covered my ears and my eyes as I felt myself fall to the ground before being shot upwards.

Chapter 24

Shultz's Office

The passage launched me up through the entire height of the castle. I landed on the roof with a thud and heard the passage close up behind me. My brain was ringing in my ears. I stood up and shook the rubble off my dress. My backpack was still on my shoulders and the buckles were still tightly closed. I opened it and quickly searched the contents to make sure I hadn't lost anything. Frustrated by my folly at not believing the sign, I took my adventure book out and scribbled: *Up IS down and down IS up. And the rat keeps his keys at the bottom of the wrong stairwell.*

As I flipped through the pages of my book I criticized myself out loud, "I should have paid attention to the sign!" I scanned the pages. Unfortunately, my drawing of the castle had not included any sketches of the roof nor noted any ways to get down from it. I snapped the book shut in frustration. How was I going to get to the dungeon now?

My thoughts were interrupted when I heard a crow caw in the distance. I froze and waited to hear it again. I heard nothing. "Great, now I'm hearing things," I chastised myself. How could I have thought I heard a crow. There were no crows in the map, I was alone.

I returned my book to the zippered pocket in my backpack and took a walk around the castle roof to see what I could see. I inspected the floor for any clues of trap doors. There were no obvious signs: no cracks in the roof, hinges, latches, handles, or anything to raise any suspicion. I walked along the edge of the roof, peering over the side of the wall as I went. The great height of the castle made me feel slightly dizzy. What a time to learn that I, like Newton, was afraid of heights.

At first I didn't see any way down. But there had to be a way. Surely I wasn't the first person to be stuck on the roof. Certainly someone had ended up here by accident before and found a way down. I walked around a second time, slower and more thorough than the first. Along the side of the wall nearest to the mainland, a grey ladder was camouflaged perfectly into the side of the castle. It was the same colour as the stones and was therefore perfectly inconspicuous. I wondered if using the term 'ladder' was too optimistic as it was merely a series of rickety rungs that were attached with soggy rope that looked rotten and weak. The whole contraption looked as if it would fall to shreds the instant any weight was put on it. I took another slow lap of the castle roof, hoping to find an alternative method. Much to my dismay, my final lap confirmed that this 'ladder' was my only option.

Trying to make myself as light as possible, I held onto the edge of the castle roof as I swung one foot over onto the first rung. It creaked loudly as it protested my presence. I swung my second foot over and listened to the wood groan in dismay. I felt the rope stretch and flex, barely holding on. I held my breath and took a step to the lower rung, moving my hands off the castle edge and onto the first rung. Shockingly the ladder held together.

The ladder seemed to go on endlessly. I climbed down and down, my legs and arms cramping. Though the ladder continued to protest, it cooperated and did not snap. I did not dare to look down and see how much further I had to climb. "It can't be too much further," I tried to encourage myself.

I passed through a cloud that was black and cold. I was too nervous to wipe my eyes when the water drenched my hair and made it cling to my eyelids. "No worries," I said to myself. "It will be fine when I get through the cloud. I must be at the bottom soon."

It did not get better, but instead it got worse. The cloud thundered and rain poured down, soaking my dress and blocking my vision. Water mixed with sweat ran into my eyes and made them sting. I couldn't see anything. I clenched my eyes shut and tried not to loose grip of the slippery ladder rungs. I focused my mind completely on holding on and reaching the end of the ladder. It seemed like hours, though it was probably only a few minutes, and I still didn't reach the bottom. The rain beat relentlessly and a fierce wind rose, pushing the ladder violently from side to side and making my teeth chatter in a frozen rhythm. My hands started shaking and I was loosing my grip on the rungs. I was about to give up all hope when all of a sudden my foot met solid ground.

I splashed down onto a stone balcony that was covered in puddles. I was soaked to the bone and felt as frozen as a snowman. Despite the chills and discomfort of the wind and rain, I smiled wholeheartedly; I was relieved to be off that ladder.

I wiped the hair out of my eyes and checked to see where I had arrived. The stone balcony had a black railing behind me and a tall window in front of me. The window was open a crack. I grabbed the frame and pulled as hard as I could. It was an extremely heavy old window but I was able to pry it open enough so that I could squeeze through. I tumbled out of the rain and closed the window quickly behind me.

A fire crackled in the hearth and a flood of warmth overtook me. I ran over to the fireplace and rubbed my arms frantically to encourage the feeling to come back to them. My body trembled and my teeth still rattled together but the exuberant success of surviving the ladder filled me with a satisfied warmth.

It took me several minutes before I could hold still enough to come back to my senses and remember my mission at hand. I looked around and took inventory of this new space. I was in a tall study with an elaborate chandelier hanging from the ceiling and intricately carved support beams stretching across the roof and down to the floor. In the centre of the room there was a large desk with a green swivel chair tucked against it. Bookshelves covered every inch of the remaining free space. Hundreds if not thousands of books occupied every available space in the shelf; it was like heaven.

I skipped over to one of the bottom shelves. Beautiful polished wooden slabs were labeled: shelf 1, shelf 2, shelf 3, shelf 4, and so on. I gasped and retrieved Wordy's note. Even though my backpack was soaked, the note somehow hadn't been ruined. In fact, everything inside the zippered pocket remained perfectly dry.

I scanned the letter: *In the office of Schultz you will find a great help.* This certainly seemed like an office. I consulted the name plate that rested on the desk. It was black with gold stamped letters.

SCHULTZ: Federal Boobytrap Inspector Agent 1."

This was it! *Twenty-third from the left, on the thirty-second shelf.* I scanned the shelves and located shelf thirty-two, by the window, about halfway between the floor and the ceiling and very far out of reach. I spotted a rolling ladder close to the window. Unlike the one outside, this ladder was sturdy and beautiful. It was red wood that was polished so intently that I could see my reflection in it. It bore decorative gold ivy along the handles and rolled along on gold plated wheels. I wish the outside ladder had been more like this one. I positioned the ladder under my target, climbed up to shelf thirty-two, and began counting from the left until my fingers landed on the twenty-third book. It was a very uninteresting looking book, thick with a plain black cover and no title or inscription. Taking it in both hands, I flipped to the first page.

"Protected F," I read. "For the trusted members of the Federal Boobytrap Inspection Headquarters Only!"

My reading was interrupted when I heard a rush of wind. I spun around just in time to see a gopher in a green vest, soaked from head to toe, jump through the window. He shook the water from his fur and collapsed panting on the ground. He looked distinctly ruffled, exhausted, and miserable.

"How did you get into the map?" I asked, shocked. I clambered down the ladder to meet him.

"Keeping you connected," he replied through gasps as he passed me a small piece of paper folded in half, "wherever you go." He sputtered some water out of his lungs and then disappeared out the window, closing it behind him once again.

I unfolded the paper and read the note:

"Danger is afoot, you have tripped a trap!
Quick throw the emerald, it's time to leave the map."

I recognized Wordy's handwriting at once. Terror filled me. I was no longer in the map alone. I heard a voice coming towards the door. "I am confident there

176

has been a breech!" the voice screamed. "The doorway to the dungeons spat someone out and set off the alarm. How else would that happen. Sweep the perimeter!"

Frantically I threw the black book into my bag and searched for my emerald. Footsteps landed nearer as the voice continued yelling orders. I spotted the emerald and clasped it in my hand. The footsteps stopped just outside the door. As quickly as my shaky hands would allow, I zipped the pocket closed and fastened the clasps together. The speaker grasped the door handle and I heard it begin to turn. I closed my eyes, shook the emerald, and threw it up into the air.

The door swung open.

"THE BREECH!" I heard the voice scream.

In the blink of an eye, the emerald exploded into a thousand green lights that swept me into the sky, blinding me before gently placing me back in my seat at Mr. and Mrs. Marty's dinner table. The map lay blank in front of me; the emerald rested innocently on top of it.

"Well what on earth happened to you?" Mrs. Marty looked aghast. My hair was still dripping, my dress was soaked, and I was shivering and panting for breath.

"Well she's just been through a Shrinks map," Marty chuckled. "Haven't you ever been in a Shrinks map?" he asked his wife.

"No I haven't," she responded. "And from the looks of this one I will count my lucky stars that I haven't! Hazel dear, let met fix you a hot drink and something to change into for the night."

"Nice backpack," Newton chimed. I shot him a grin, it was a nice backpack.

"Well?" Cowie asked. "What did you learn?"

I could hardly contain myself, "I learned that I was not alone in the map! The gophers were there and I think Schultz almost caught me in his office. Someone was there when I left, they knew I had been snooping around the castle. They said I was a breech."

Newton gasped and Cowie raised his eyebrows.

"Not alone in the map?" Marty whispered, his jaw dropped and eyes opened as large as dinner plates. "Never heard of that before. Never in my life." He looked carefully over the paper with his looking glass. "I wonder…" he said to himself, "Could it be? No… impossible… how did he do it?" He flipped the map over and over, analyzing every nook and cranny of it.

"Did you map out our route?" Cowie asked.

"I am not sure."

"What do you mean you're not sure?" Newton scoffed, "Either you did or you didn't. And from the sounds of that, you didn't. The map should have said Newton."

"Newton," Mrs. Marty scolded as she passed me a steaming mug and a heavy green cloak. "Don't talk to a lady that way. I'll tell your mother on you, I will."

Newton rolled his eyes but didn't say anything more.

Mrs. Marty turned her attention back to me, "Now Hazel, this is old but it should fit. You can use the tub room through that door. Go ahead and dry off with the towels and leave your dress in the sink. I will have it cleaned and pressed for you by tomorrow."

She shooed me into a side room with a round tub and a sink that was stacked with towels. I changed quickly into the cloak. It fit me quite well. It was fuzzy on the inside but velvety on the outside, like a warm heavy bathrobe. I wrung out my hair into the tub and left my wet dress in the sink. After a minute, Mrs. Marty knocked on the door.

"Come in," I called.

The door creaked open and she entered, smiling. She reassured me that she had talked to the boys and Newton would mind his manners now. "I'll have this dress all cleaned up for you by morning," she said.

I apologized for giving her more work and she told me to hush with such nonsense and go finish my tea. Newton looked annoyed when I returned, but he didn't say anything cross.

I retrieved my adventure book and showed Cowie, Marty, and Newton my notes outlining the way to the dungeons. Newton was horrified when I told him about the stairs. "Why didn't you just follow the directions?" he cried indignantly.

"I thought it was a mistake," I defended myself. "I looked along both and the stairs that I picked definitely went down-"

"And what is this nonsense," he said, ignoring my case and interrupting me. He was pointing to the page in the book that said to go through the door labelled 'number g.' "G isn't a number at all! I say, you must have hit your head while you were in that map."

I dismissed his remark. Cowie was very interested in the book that I had retrieved from Shultz's office and quickly buried himself in it. He sat on the floor, turning page after page, yet giving no comment on what he was reading.

Newton continued critiquing my notes and Marty kept staring at the map and saying, "Doesn't make sense, not any sense at all. How could she have not been alone in the map…"

I was feeling very left out once again. I sipped the tea that Mrs. Marty had made me, peppermint. It was quite good. Finally Cowie snapped the book shut and said, "fine job Hazel. No one could have done it better."

"What?" Newton and I both asked in shock.

"Not everything went as planned," Cowie answered. "But it turned out perfectly. Think of it Hazel, how would you have found out where the rat keeps his keys without taking the wrong stairwell? Or found the office and this book?" No one answered. He had a fair point. "You see," he passed the book back to me, "the castle is riddled with incorrect instructions so that they confuse anyone who enters without permission. It is positively littered with boobytraps so that no adventurers can get in or out without being caught. Hazel had no hope of finding the correct way to the dungeon on the first try. Instead she found the true map of the castle, the boobytrap book."

Newton grunted in disapproval.

"So do you know what we have to do?" I asked Cowie hopefully.

"Yes," he said with a smile. "I know we have to get into the castle, rescue the traveller, and get her back home."

I sighed, "But we knew all that before."

Cowie nudged my hand with his nose, "We have more knowledge than we had before. We know the way to the dungeon now. We will make a plan, don't worry."

"No sense getting caught in all the details of the plan now, you still have a ways to travel before you get to the castle at all," Marty chimed. It seemed he had given up trying to figure out the secrets of the map and turned his attention back to the group.

"Yes," Cowie agreed. "Quite a ways indeed. Speaking of which, we should all get some rest."

Mrs. Marty said she was glad someone had finally found their senses. She made up a cot in the living room by the fire and took my mug to the kitchen sink. Everyone washed up for the night and wished one another sweet dreams. Cowie, Newton, and I curled up under the blanket on the cot and listened to the fire crackle. The den was completely silent and still. I hadn't realize just how exhausting my adventure in the map had been. In no time at all I was given over to sleep, dreaming I was still wandering around Feazel's castle looking for the lost traveller.

Chapter 25

Plans

"Thirteen days," Newton announced in the morning. The fire was out, the air was chillier, and I felt very groggy.

"It's still raining outside," Marty said as he hung up his rain coat and came into the living room. We cleaned up the cot and Marty built a fire. Mrs. Marty passed me my clean dress, which had been dried and pressed that morning, and I washed up in the tub room. By the time I came out, Mrs. Marty and Newton had fixed a scrumptious breakfast of fried potatoes, pancakes, and eggs.

"Are we going to go in the rain?" I asked Cowie.

"That depends on how rainy it is I suppose. What does it look like out there, Marty?"

"See for yourself," Marty pointed to a frame in the side of the living room. Cowie walked over to it and sighed heavily, "Looks like we should wait a while."

I got to my feet and looked in the frame, which was actually a sort of window. I was not sure how it worked since we were so far in the mountain that we could not possibly see outside from here; but there it was, just on the other side of the frame. The rain beat down and puddles gathered on the ground. The clouds above looked dark and unrelenting.

"But there's only thirteen days left," I whispered to Cowie. I was growing worried about time since Marty had said we were still a long way from the castle.

"Even if it rains all day, a day spent resting and planning would be a day well spent." Cowie nudged my arm and I stroked his head. I trusted him.

"Wise words," Marty agreed. "Now come on you two, let's go over those notes again, see if we can sort anything out." We sat around the kitchen table for hours pouring over the notes and the Schultz's boobytrap book.

"Why did he tell you that eleven is Feazel's favourite number?" Marty asked, tapping a pen on his chin. The table was covered in paper that bore the scribbled marks of hours of brainstorming. "Could it be a code?" he asked, looking to our faces for approval.

Newton shook his head, "A code for what? There's nothing in the book about anything requiring a code."

Enthusiasm for planning was quickly disappearing. I looked at the paper labeled 'What we know:' I cleared my throat and read the list aloud.

"Feazel's favourite number is 11. To cross the final bridge we must look over not under. The map said to cross under the bridge. Circular entertainment devices are not allowed on shift. The rat's keys are at the bottom of the wrong staircase. There is only one way in. There are two ways out (the gate and the slide). The castle is full of false directions and booby traps-"

"Which we have the book of," Cowie chimed in.

"What's a circular entertainment device?" I asked.

Marty shrugged, "I don't know. What's the shift?"

"Perimeter patrol," Cowie said. "It's on page twenty-seven. Hyenas patrol the outer walls to scare off intruders and alert Schultz of any suspicious activity."

I drummed my fingers on the table one after another while I thought about hyenas. Hadn't I heard something about hyenas before? Where was that. I flipped through Mr. Sploot's adventure book and searched through the pages. "It's a ball!" I proclaimed, pointing to Mr. Sploot's writing: *throw the ball for the hyena.*

Cowie raised his head and looked at the note, his face split into a grin and he let out a bark of excitement, "Yes! Of course!"

Newton crossed his arms in annoyance, "Really? We were stumped by a *ball*? Geniuses we are."

"It makes perfect sense why they would be banned," Marty said. "Those hyenas are a special sort. They are so easily distracted."

Cowie flipped through Schult'z book and read a section: "The perimeter patrol work in pairs, walking along the outer walls of the building, completing one lap every ten minutes. No distractions are permitted since their attention span is that of a gnat and they are as easily blown off course as a dust bunny."

Marty laughed, "well that is one way to put it!" He sounded like my father when he said that and a small homesick ache grew in the pit of my stomach. Cowie must have noticed my face change because he pressed his head against my shoulder and looked very sympathetic.

"That is your plan to get into the castle then!" Marty clasped his hands together excitedly. I wasn't sure what exactly the plan was but apparently he was satisfied.

He rose from his chair and dismissed himself from the table.

"What if the draw bridge is up?" I asked.

"It's always down," Cowie said. "It broke years ago but no one has bothered to fix it." He showed me a section of the book which was labeled 'maintenance requests.' It seemed that many requests had been submitted and none had been resolved.

"I believe that," I said. "There are gaps in the floors everywhere. What security do they have inside?"

"Not a lot. They mostly rely on their boobytraps. The rat, Roy, is the jail warden and he is not one to be worried about. He lost interest in his job years ago and has had several warnings issued against him. Apparently he has shown up to work late many times and has frequently been caught sneaking wine and cheese out of the Feazel's kitchen," Cowie said.

"What about the W.S.S.?" Newton asked.

"The W.S.S. is kept busy with activities outside of the castle."

"And the Feazel's Boobytrap Inspectors?"

"They are activated only when a trap is tripped," Cowie explained.

Marty returned to his seat and passed me a small bag of bright yellow tennis balls. "Put these in your

187

backpack. You can use these to distract the patrol," he instructed. I thanked him and tucked them safely away.

"Do you know where the boobytraps are?" Newton asked Cowie.

"I've memorized as many as I can for now, but I'm afraid there are many more and I will not be able to remember all of them. We will have to rely on the book to double check while we are inside. There's a lot we won't know until we actually get there I am afraid."

"Aye," Marty said. "That is how adventures go. And isn't it true someone knew you were in the office, Hazel? Perhaps they will notice the book is missing and start rearranging things."

"Hopefully not," I said.

"Yes," agreed Cowie, "hopefully not."

"Well if he cares enough to have his shelves labelled I am sure he cares enough to check and see that his books are there," Newton muttered. I silently agreed with him but hoped deep down that we were both wrong.

Chapter 26

Intuition & Shortcuts

The rain let up in the middle of the afternoon and even though it was late, Cowie thought it would be best if we started moving again. "We still have a long way to travel," he said, "And there is no telling what will happen up ahead."

Mr. and Mrs. Marty agreed. Mrs. Marty packed us some snacks and hugged us goodbye before Mr. Marty escorted us back through the mountain tunnel and to the entrance of the cave.

The road from the Marty's house travelled up a very steep mountainside. The climb was unrelenting, no matter how far up we walked, there was still more up to go. Just when I thought we must be close to reaching the top, I looked ahead to see the cliff grow just slightly steeper, stretching endlessly towards the sky. I was tired. I stared at my feet and focused on putting one foot in front of the other, trying very hard not to slip backwards. The muscles in my legs burned and my backpack felt like it got heavier the longer we went on. The wind rose and rushed around us, threatening my balance and making my ears ache; still we pressed on.

"I'm really tired Cowie," I said as I was huffing and puffing for breath. I had to yell so he could hear me above the wind.

"I know Hazel," he looked apologetic and also very exhausted. "But we have to keep going. We are in the bear scouts territory right now and they are never understanding about adventurers."

We ducked into the trees where the wind was quieter and we could hear each other better. Newton collapsed on the ground breathless, too exhausted to even bother complaining.

"What do you mean?" I asked. Partly curious and partly just trying to keep him talking so we could have a longer break.

"The bear scouts patrol the woods. They are an enthusiastic lot and take any travellers to the Council Circle for interrogation. Only adventurers are supposed to go up these paths because the way is very dangerous. This is where Mitch gets stuck having to rescue the donkeys. There are always young ones that try and go through these parts and end up critically injured. It puts a strain on the rescue teams to constantly be fishing donkeys out of the ravine. Mitch worked with the Council Circle to implement travel restrictions so that, now, only those accompanied by a senior guide can take these trails. The bear scouts was an initiative of the grizzlies and black bears who wanted to give their young something to do and keep them out of trouble. They are a well intended group but can be a tad over zealous."

"Well aren't you a senior guide?" I asked.

"Yes but they never take my word for it," he said, "If they find us they will drag us away anyway. We wouldn't be in any trouble but it would be a colossal waste of time. Once we are out of their territory, we can camp at the ridge. If we keep up this pace, we can make it well before nightfall."

I mustered all my strength. I didn't want to be dragged off course by the bear scouts. "Alright," I agreed.

"I know it's hard. But dig deep inside. Find that little voice that is telling you to give up and see what happens if you tell it no."

I nodded. Newton climbed up onto Cowie's back when we started walking again. It was so steep that Newton had to keep hold of Cowie's ears to keep from sliding off and splatting on the ground.

Every step I took I could hear my legs complaining and screaming at me, begging me to give up. It was hard and I was tired. I started to feel like I should just curl up in the grass and have a nap. I could. What were the chances the bear scouts would be in this area and catch me snoozing? Wouldn't it be better to rest instead of breaking my body climbing this unreasonable mountain?

Cowie looked tired too but he kept steadily on. His persistence motivated me and pulled me forward. I tried to do what he had told me to, I listened to my legs and found the voice in my head that was telling me to give up. Every time the voice propositioned me to quit I would tell the voice, "no, it isn't time to rest yet. We are almost there." Little by little, step by step, I convinced my legs to move. Over and over I calmed down the voice that told me to give up and eventually, it stopped distracting me so much. Even as my legs grew heavier and the mountain stretched higher, I pressed on. I felt very proud of myself for not quitting.

Nearing the precipice of the cliff the path split into two parallel trails. At first it was just a blade of grass separating them left from right. Then there was a sprig of baby's breath in between the paths, then a small tree divided them, then a row of small trees grew up so you could barely see the left when you were on the right. It became clear that there were two different paths and even though they seemed to travel in the same direction, we would have to pick one or the other.

"Which way?" I asked.

"It's your adventure," Cowie replied.

I was too tired to protest, evidently Newton was too. He hung like a limp rag doll off Cowie's ears, his eyes barely open. Little hiccups sparked out of his mouth, it seemed the heights were getting to him. I took out my thing-a-ma-jig and found that it was no help. The paths were so close to the same that it was impossible to interpret whether the thing-a-ma-jig was pointing right or left. I looked around for any blue rocks, there were none. I examined the right path and the left, there was nothing I could see that made the two paths any different.

"No pressure, but we really can't waste time," Newton cautioned through hiccupy gasps.

I analyzed the paths silently. I did not feel equipped with the tools or energy to make a wise decision. Looking down the left path I saw that the incline was ever so slightly less aggressive and there were little yellow flowers growing along the trail. I had always loved yellow flowers.

"Left," I announced after a short contemplation.

"And you base that on…?" Newton opened his sleepy eyes, looking completely unimpressed. Frustration bubbled up inside my stomach. I didn't feel like Newton had the right to say anything since he had been riding on Cowie's back most of the journey. He was not as tired as I was and he was just being his usual difficult self.

Cowie hushed Newton and told him just to close his eyes. "She has to learn," he said, "intuition doesn't just come from nowhere. And please mind that your sparks aren't hitting my ears, you've already burned my neck."

"Intuition?" I asked.

"Gut feeling," Cowie replied.

"Oh," I remembered hearing Mother and Father talk about their 'gut feelings.' Mother said she could tell lots of things by her gut feelings: how much flour to put in cookie dough, whether we needed to take an umbrella to the store, or if Richard had to go to the clinic.

Frustration with Newton gave way to sadness. I missed Mother, Father, and Richard.

Sadness made me want to give up travelling again, but I couldn't give up now. I shut that door in my mind and started walking down the left path without acknowledging the others. White aspen trees grew up around us. They were clothed in bright leaves that made the whole forest glow green. The wind subsided. Flowers were everywhere: yellow, orange, and white. A purple butterfly flew by and I thought I had never seen anything more perfectly delicate. The ground was a maze of tree roots and pieces of mountain poking through the dirt. I had to be very careful not to trip but it was still easier than the path we had climbed before, not nearly as steep. I liked this trail, it was smoother and easier. My legs thanked me for choosing this path.

We walked a very long time before I realized that we didn't seem to be going anywhere. We weren't going up and we weren't going down. I didn't feel any nearer to the peaks. I stopped and listened to my gut. I started getting an eery feeling like I was being watched. I spun around and looked at Cowie, "I think I'm having an intuition."

Newton rolled his eyes but Cowie hushed him before he could start criticizing.

"You always have intuition," Cowie corrected, "your intuition is just talking to you now. What's it saying?"

"I think that I picked the wrong road."

"What makes you think that?"

"I don't know. There are no blue stones or any other signs that this isn't the right trail. I can't find anything in Mr. Sploot's book or any instructions from Wordy that tell me that we are walking the wrong way... I just *feel* like we are. My conscience agrees with my gut."

"Did you check the thing-a-ma-jig?" he asked patiently.

I pulled it out of my backpack and opened it. The arrow swung to and fro for a moment before pointing straight behind us.

"Great. Now I made us lose time and we have to walk all the way back to the split in the trail and go back up the right way."

Frustrated tears threatened to start leaking out of my eyes. I didn't blink and did my best to hold them back. I was not prepared to waste more time by crying.

"Well let's turn around then. You can lead us back and take us the right way. It's alright," Cowie sounded patient and his calming voice made me feel slightly less awful.

I criticized myself silently the whole time we began walking back to the place where the trail had split in two. The only reason I had picked the left road was because it looked easier. That had not been a good reason to pick the road. Now I had wasted everyone's time. Why hadn't I checked the thing-a-ma-jig sooner? I wondered if Cowie had known all along that I was wrong and why he hadn't said anything if he did. I was so lost in my guessing games that I didn't pay attention to how far we had walked.

I stopped dead in my tracks and looked back to Cowie, "Have we passed the split in the trail?"

"You're leading," he shrugged.

Panic clenched my chest in its hands. I felt my heart pick up speed and my breath start to waiver. I looked around. Had we passed the split? Everything began to look the same, equally familiar and foreign. There was a tree with a funny marking in it, I knew I had seen that at the place where the trail split… but this mark looked more round than the other had… it must have been a different mark. Now that I was thinking about it, the mark on this tree didn't look anything like the one I had seen at the trail split. We had walked too far.

"We passed it!" I yelled, hurrying around Cowie and Newton, and running back up the trial. I ran until my legs couldn't keep up to my ambition any longer. I tripped on a tree root and collapsed on the road. I heard a rustling in a bush and a low voice coming from further ahead. I looked up and saw a furry face turn a corner far in the distance. It was a young grizzly bear. He was very large with a great hump on his back and paws the size of dinner plates. He walked along slowly and swayed to the rhythm of the song he was singing loudly and painfully off key. Thankfully he didn't seem to have heard me fall.

I signalled to Cowie behind me and whispered, "Back back back! There's a bear."

Newton turned an odd colour and ducked behind Cowie's ears, trembling. As quiet as we could, we crawled back along the trial. We passed by the tree with the funny mark on it again. I wasn't sure where the bear was and I was feeling very nervous that we would soon be apprehended. Tiptoeing into the thicket, I whispered to Cowie, "Here, this way."

"This isn't a trail," Newton protested.

"Shhhh! Do you want to get caught?" I hissed, "The trail is right over there. This is just a shortcut."

"I don't think-"

Once again Cowie hushed Newton. Newton crossed his arms and started grumbling about how nobody valued his opinion and he should not even be on this adventure if no one was going to take him seriously.

We walked into the thicket. The grass grew up to my ankles, then up to my knees, and soon it was reaching all the way up to my waist. Stubbornly I pushed my way through the mess. Soon we were tangled in bushes and unable to wade through the thick grass anymore.

"Are you ready to quit it yet?" Newton asked when I got my hair stuck in a tree that was dripping sap. I hung my head and tried to pick the sap from my hair, managing only to spread it along my fingers, on my dress, and onto Cowie's nose when he nudged my hand.

My lip quivered and the dam of tears broke, letting my sorrow run freely over my cheeks and splash into puddles on the ground below. "I'm so lost!" I cried.

"Why all the fuss?" Cowie asked, licking my cheek.

Through sobs and gasps I told Cowie how everything was ruined and it was all my fault. We weren't just lost, we were destitute. We were never going to make it to the castle in time to rescue the traveller and we were never going to get home. We would be trapped on this mountain forever until the bear scouts picked us up and took us to be punished at the Council Circle. I lay on my back on the forest floor in embittered resignation. "I did it. I trapped us all and ruined everyone's lives," I lamented.

I was staring up at the sky contemplating how long it would take anybody at home to notice I was missing when Cowie walked over top of me and looked at me in the eyes. His face looked funny upside down and I nearly laughed (but I didn't because I was determined to be miserable).

"Well I daresay Hazel, this is quite a production. The Council Circle would not punish us, I already told you that. And I daresay that you are giving yourself far too much credit," he sounded rather amused.

I sat up and wiped my tears away with my dirty hands. I wasn't sure if I was offended or relieved by his tone, "What do you mean?"

"How could you have possibly ruined everything?"

I explained once again that we were so lost that everything in life was now hopeless. My face contorted in disgust when he actually laughed at me.

"Hazel, you haven't ruined a thing. You've only *learned*."

I glared at him but he only sat down and smiled at me.

"First of all," he continued, "You learned that you should trust your intuition. Your gut told you that you had chosen the wrong trail and you listened to it."

"Why didn't my gut tell me to go down the right trail in the first place?" I interrupted.

"It takes intuition time and practice to develop. You need to *learn* to listen to it. Learning unfortunately involves making many mistakes. Choosing which way to take was a very hard decision and you did your best. You made the wrong choice but when you realized that you had, you admitted it, and tried to correct it. You were just a bit hasty with your method of correction."

"And I got us hopelessly lost," I said in one last effort to be inconsolable.

"Well that's because you believed a lie."

"I did?"

Curiosity got the better of me. I stopped feeling so sorry for myself and began asking questions again.

"Yes you did. You believed there was a shortcut. The truth is, there are no such things as short cuts."

"There aren't?"

Cowie shook his head solemnly, "There is only one way through and it requires immense amounts of patience and perseverance."

I contemplated this new information. I did not know if I had really believed that my 'shortcut' would lead us to the trail. I was just afraid of getting caught by the bear and in a hurry to get up the mountain. I looked at Cowie's face and realized that he did not look the least bit hopeless or distressed.

"Are you lost?" I asked him.

He lifted me onto my feet and shook his head. "Stick close," he said.

I kept a hand on Cowie's neck as we walked back through my pretend shortcut, back to the split in the road, and all the way up the right trail. It took hours to undo my mistake but we finally took the last steps up onto the peak. The sun was just slipping behind the horizon and the sky was a vibrant celebration of colours and clouds. We built a toasty fire and all huddled around it. I wanted to sleep right away but Cowie reminded me I had to write down my lessons so I wouldn't repeat my mistakes.

I found a blank page in my adventure book and wrote down the lessons: *Trust my intuition.* And *THERE ARE NO SUCH THINGS AS SHORTCUTS!!!!*

My adventure book erased the large letters and put them back in my regular writing, neatening my sloppy hand. Newton clucked his tongue when he saw the book erase itself.

"Adventure books don't like to be yelled at," he chastised, sticking his nose in the air and shaking his head.

I shot him an annoyed look but said nothing. I placed my book on the ground and leaned against Cowie. As I closed my eyes I listened to the forest behind us. There was no wind and yet the leaves were rustling in distinct rhythms creating a gentle melodic whistle that drifted along the forest.

"What's that sound?" I asked sleepily.

"It's the trees speaking," Cowie said.

"The trees talk?" I listened carefully to see if I could interpret the language of the forest.

"Well of course they do. What do you expect they just sit around all day watching the whole world go by and saying nothing?" Newton retorted.

"How come trees don't talk in our world?" I asked Cowie with a yawn.

"What makes you think they don't?" he replied.

I had never thought about that. I would have to listen to the trees back home more carefully.

The One That's On Top

When I woke up, the dew was heavy on the ground and everyone else was still asleep. The air was chilly. I got up quietly and walked around the ridge. I could see clouds resting low over the mountain side that we had climbed up last night. I watched the clouds stretching out below us like a white cotton blanket. I looked down the other side of the ridge and saw, so far off in the distance that it was barely visible, another mountain peak reaching out from the white cloudy blanket.

I giggled with delight, "Cowie wake up! We are *above* the clouds!"

Cowie rose to his feet and stretched his legs.

"Twelve days," Newton uncurled his tail from around his body and yawned. He blinked several times and rubbed the sleep out of his eyes before he looked around and saw the clouds beneath us. Screaming, he leapt straight into the air and jumped behind a nearby rock. There he lay with his hands over his eyes and his whole body trembling.

Calmly, Cowie walked over and prodded Newton with his paw, "Come on. It's alright. We are nowhere near the edge. You are safe."

Newton's side seized with hiccups and tiny flames shot out from his mouth.

"It's too high, it's *too* high, it's TOO high," he said over and over in a high pitched crackly voice.

"How high are we?" I asked.

"TOO HIGH!!" Newton squealed.

Hiccups were shooting out of his mouth in rapid succession. He groaned in pain. Cowie tried to console him and I looked back over the edge of the ridge. The clouds slowly rolled away and I saw just how high up we were. Miles beneath us I saw purple cliffs jut up and down, a river travelled between them, looking no bigger than a string of blue thread. I gulped. I had never been afraid of heights, but mind you I had never been this high either.

"Wow," I gasped.

Cowie turned his attention to me for a moment. "This is the tallest mountain in this world," He said calmly. He lifted a paw and pointed to the distant peak I had spotted earlier, "That is the second highest mountain and that is where we are going."

"How are we going to get there?" I asked. Cowie only smiled in response.

Poor Newton was groaning in pain and repeating his mantra that this was all *much* too high.

"It's alright Newton, you will be okay," I patted him gently on the back and tried to comfort him but it was no use, Newton was paralyzed with fear. Neither Cowie nor I could convince him that he could take a step away from the rock. He just trembled on the ground, stiff as a board, and shaking his head back and forth. Cowie and I brainstormed how we were going to take Newton along.

"He can ride in your backpack," Cowie stated.

A stream of fire shot out of Newton's mouth and I stared doubtfully. I liked my backpack and I didn't want Newton to turn it into a pile of ash like he had done to Priscilla's hat. "Won't it catch fire?" I asked.

"Hmm," Cowie muttered, "unless…"

He walked over to the trees and started turning over leaves on the bushes looking for something.

"Ice berries," he announced, pointing to clusters of berries. Little blue raspberries hung in bunches of six or seven. I pulled them off the branches and cupped them in my hands. They were cold to the touch and shimmered like a blue jewel. We walked back over to the rock where Newton had been hiding but he wasn't there.

"Where did he go?" I asked.

A flame shot out from under a nearby rock.

"Found him," chuckled Cowie, "he hates ice berries."

Newton put up an elaborate fuss over the berries. He shook he head, clutched his hands over his mouth, and hissed at Cowie.

"They," hiccup, "make my," hiccup, "stomach" hiccup, "feel funny!" he argued.

"Well if you don't want to eat the berries and you don't want to walk, I suppose we could just leave you here," said Cowie.

Newton glared at him and muttered insults that I didn't understand but he inevitably surrendered to the remedy. One by one he took the berries from my hand and popped them in his mouth. He grimaced when he chewed them and I watched as they turned his tongue electric blue. A sizzling sound escaped his throat every time he swallowed. His hiccups didn't stop but the flames grew shorter and shorter and finally disappeared completely. The last berries were swallowed with much gagging and sputtering after which tiny snowflakes escaped in a flurry whenever Newton hiccupped. I laughed and caught one of the flakes on my hand. Newton glared at me.

"This is," snow flurry, "not," snow flurry, "*amusing*," his voice was higher pitched than normal and sounded squeaky from the ice berries.

I apologized, opened my backpack, and let him crawl inside. Tiny bursts of snow escaped through the seams of the backpack as he hiccupped and I felt the cool breeze with every flurry.

"Right," said Cowie, "now down to business."

He led me to the very edge of the ridge and my stomach did a flip underneath my skin when I peered over the edge. I swallowed my nerves and thought maybe it was best not to look down. After a few minutes we arrived at the base of the largest tree I had ever seen. The trunk looked about the size of the base of the Feazel's castle. Long branches stretched past the edge of the cliff and into the distance. Clouds were rolling back in and I couldn't see where the branches ended. I hoped desperately that we would not be climbing over a tree branch to get to the other peak.

"The Swing Tree," Cowie announced.

It was a very tall tree with thick limbs that stretched into fine branches covered in white flowers. I froze in my steps. This couldn't be what Wordy was talking about when he talked about swings. I reached into my backpack for my adventure book to double check Wordy's letter. Newton was still shaking in the bottom, covering his eyes and complaining. He was now laying on a small pile of snowflakes that had gathered underneath him. I retrieved the letter from under the snow and read the instructions: *go straight up the mountain,* we were at the top, *and cross the purple cliffs,* I looked over the edge and saw that the cliff below us were undeniably purple. And: *when you get to the swings take the one that's on top.*

"This can't be right," I said and showed Cowie the instructions, "Surely he didn't mean to tell us we had to swing across the purple cliffs. That is much to dangerous."

"Is it?" Cowie asked.

"YES!" Newton screamed, poking his head out from the backpack. He took one glimpse of the tree and immediately fainted backwards.

"Hmm," Cowie sat and looked at me with a twinkle in his eye, "Has Wordy steered you wrong yet?"

I thought carefully. We had gotten lost in the woods, but that was my fault. We did get betrayed by Priscilla for following Wordy's instructions, but then again it was I who had invited her. I did get hurt when I ran into Francis in the woods, but again I had gone wandering off the path when I knew better. Wordy had said nothing about inviting a confused goose on the journey or galavanting after magical lights in the middle of the night. I flipped through my adventure book before placing it back in the backpack. Wordy had not steered me wrong, everything he said had been true.

"You have a choice to make," Cowie looked at me seriously, "You can have faith that Wordy's instructions are good and true, or you can take your own way and find another path across the cliffs."

Lori-Anne's lesson came to mind, *Faith is the choice to trust that, what we cannot explain, is still real.* I couldn't explain why Wordy's instruction were good even when they didn't make sense, but I had to believe that they were. I had to have faith that this instruction was good.

"Are you prepared to abandon his instructions now just because they look different than you had expected?" Cowie encouraged my thoughts along.

I shook my head, "No, I have more faith than that.

"Good," he smiled, "Then let's go."

210

Cowie gracefully leapt up onto the first low hanging branch. I followed. A few branches up there was a sign with an arrow pointing up labelled "the one that's on top," and another arrow pointing out to the right, "not the one that's on top."

I knew which way we had to go. I followed Cowie carefully as he led the way up the tree, jumping from one branch to another. As we stepped on the branches, white flower petals shook off and floated down like snow. I wondered how Newton was doing in my backpack.

The limbs got smaller and smaller as we climbed higher and higher. I didn't look down, I didn't want to know how far above the ground we were. We climbed so high into the tree that I could see the very last branches. Cowie paused and turned around and said, "We can only go one at a time."

"Go where?"

"Across the cliffs," he stated before tiptoeing out on one of the smaller branches. He turned to look back at me, "Watch what I do very carefully so you know what to do when the swing comes back."

"Are you sure we can't go together?" I didn't know where we were going but I knew I did not want to go alone.

"I am sure," he said, "Chin up. You can do this."

He tiptoed a little further down the branch and reached into a cluster of white flowers where a swing rested. This was not like an ordinary swing that I had seen at the parks back home, this was a large wooden bowl attached to a thick green leafy vine.

"Where is the vine tied to?" I asked, full of concern.

"The moon I believe," Cowie replied as he carefully placed his front paws into the bowl. I didn't know if he was being serious but I didn't ask anymore questions.

"As soon as I jump into the swing, come stand where I am now. You will need to catch the seat when it comes back. Do not get distracted, you do not want to miss it."

I nodded, steeling my determination. Cowie grinned and jumped gracefully into the large seat. I watched the swing drop quickly down and away as it disappeared into a cloud below.

"I should have asked where the swing leads to and what to do at the other side," I criticized myself. I tiptoed along the branch and stood where Cowie had been. The wind rustled the leaves and I wondered what the tree was saying. I held onto a branch to keep my balance and let out a heavy sigh, fixing my gaze on the cloud the swing had carried Cowie into. There was nothing to do but wait.

Chapter 28

Across Purple Cliffs

Minutes felt like hours. I tried to remember to breathe. I hardly dared to blink, I was so concerned that I would somehow miss the swing coming back and get trapped on this side of the cliffs. How would I get to Cowie without the swing? How would I find my way across? I didn't even know my way around. Or would he find me? I shook the thoughts from my mind and reassured myself that I would not miss the swing and everything would be just fine.

"You know," a singsongy voice spoke from a branch below me, "You could just take the lower swing. It's safer."

"Hello? Who are you?" I called, worried I was going mad and hearing things.

"Oh Hazel, don't tell me you've forgotten about me already," I recognized the voice as it grew closer, Francis. He jumped up on the branch behind me, flashing his perfect smile.

"Francis!" I gasped, steadying myself against another branch, "Get away from me."

He clicked his tongue and curled his tail around his feet. "That isn't any way to greet a friend," he said, "What have I done to you?"

"You tried to trick me out of an adventure! You tried to turn me into a silver tongue with your fruit and then you chased me in the woods!"

"Did I now?" he pressed a paw to his chest, "I only remember offering you wisdom and trying to have a conversation with you when you came to me in the woods. I was only running to catch up with you. I was not chasing you." He shook his head. "And I would never try to turn you into a silver tongue, honestly. Where have you gotten these horrible ideas about me?"

His eyes grew wide and he blinked at me imploringly. I almost believed him but I remembered that he could only tell lies. I glared at him and looked ahead so I would not miss the swing. I could not let myself be distracted.

"All this nonsense about a silver tongue," he continued undeterred by my silence, "Seems that dog has been filling your head with nonsense. See for yourself, I don't have a silver tongue."

Curiosity got the better of me and I glanced backwards. Francis was sitting closer to me, his mouth open. He stuck out a pink tongue and I was shocked. My surprise must have shown on my face.

"Oh did they tell you that I was a silver tongue? Silly creatures. It's just jealousy. I am, after all, in charge of the tree of wisdom and they were always cross that I had been trusted with it and not one of them."

That didn't sound right. My intuition told me to turn around and ignore him and so I did just that. Once again, I fixed my eyes on the path of the swing.

"It will be a while before that swing comes back," Francis chimed again, "It couldn't hurt to go down and *look* at the other swing. Explore your options."

I didn't turn around this time.

"Wordy said to take the one that's on top," I said as stubbornly as I could, wishing Francis would go away and leave me alone.

"Why listen to Wordy all the time?" he asked, "Why do what he says just because he said it? Seems rather foolish to trust a bumbling bird."

"It's what the book said and the book can only accept the truth."

"Why believe such folly. A book cannot be wise, it is just a thing and has no mind of its own. How could a book possibly know what is true," he scoffed. "Here's a truth for your book, it is *always* best to explore *all* of your options."

I paused, that statement actually made sense. Why wouldn't I want to explore all my options? Why was I letting everyone make all the decisions for me? But I wasn't, I was making my choices. Cowie let me choose whether to come up the swing or not, I chose to get lost in the woods, and I chose to say yes to the invitation of adventure. Francis was wrong, no one was choosing for me. But still, I couldn't shake the tempting notion of exploring all of my options. Carefully I slipped my backpack off my shoulders and retrieved my adventure book. I tried writing down Francis's words and the ink instantly vanished from the page. I tried once more just to make sure and the book again erased my writing.

"You're wrong," I said defiantly and placed my book back in my bag. Newton was still passed out in the bottom on top of his ever-growing bed of snowflakes. I closed my backpack and shot Francis a steely gaze, "I don't think there's one bit of truth in you, now please leave me alone."

When I turned to face the clouds, I heard a swooshing wind and saw the great wooden bowl swinging towards me. Francis walked swiftly behind me and grabbed my hand with his paw, "you have no idea what's on the other side of that swing. You don't want to take it."

His lies had no affect on me this time. I shook off his paw, "Go away!"

The swing came closer and closer.

"You're being incredibly foolish," he clucked. "You haven't looked this all the way through. You have blindly accepted the orders of an owl and an oversized drooling dog-"

I ignored him. I had to keep my focus on the swing. Just a moment more and then I would be free from Francis.

"- and that slithering hot headed lizard-"

The swing rushed into the tree and I took hold of the basket with my hand.

"He's a dragon," I glared at Francis, grasped the rope, and jumped off the tree.

217

"No!" Francis lunged forward and grasped the strap of my backpack in his teeth. He dug his paws into the branch and tried to pull me off the swing. I kicked and screamed and fought with all my might. Francis yelped when my foot met his eye.

Newton's head appeared out of the backpack, "Call me a lizard," he said woozily, "I'll teach you!!" He spat out a snow flurry so intense that it frosted Francis's whiskers and fur. Evidently the surprise of frosty snow was enough to startle Francis into letting go of the backpack. The swing plummeted through the branches and down into the open air. Immediately I pulled my feet into the seat and squished myself into the bottom of the bowl. Wind rushed as I felt the swing fall downward.

Newton's heroic gesture gave way to extreme fear and he stumbled back and fell limply into the bottom of my backpack. I took the bag off my shoulders and hugged it to my chest. "I love you Newton," I whispered, hoping that he would be alright.

When I felt the dropping of the swing level, I found my courage and curiosity once again. I placed the backpack on my shoulders and carefully peered over the edge of the basket. Purple mountains flew by beneath us. We had been carried so low that the river, a mere thread from the top of the mountain, now looked like a raging and powerful beast. I could see clouds above us and the rocky cliff behind. It was breathtaking. I relaxed and started to actually enjoy the ride. I held onto the rope and stood in the seat and let the wind rush by.

"Wooohooooo!" I yelled at the top of my lungs, feeling like I was flying.

Down by the river, a brown speck caught my eye. We zoomed closer and closer and I saw that it was an owl! An owl with big bushy eyebrows and a monocle. Wordy! The swing passed him in a blur and I whipped my head around to see if it was him. Was it? I couldn't tell. I waved furiously in that direction hoping that he would see me, if it was him.

The swing pulled up and I stumbled back a step. I held tight to the rope to steady myself and looked forward. We raced up through a cloud, across a dark purple mountain, and over a waterfall. We were so near the falls that the mist from the water splashed my face and soaked my hair. I laughed loudly.

The swing started slowing down as we rose into another cloud which was so near the sun it shone a warm gold. The swing slowed more and more until it seems to hover in mid air.

"Hazel!" I heard Cowie call. "Jump!"

The cloud was completely obstructing my vision. I couldn't see anything but gold shimmering light. "I can't! I can't see!" I cried.

"Jump now!" he called again.

I couldn't tell where his voice was coming from. It sounded far away and then close beside. Was it below me? Or above me? Where was the ground? Where was he?

"There's no time!" He barked loudly.

I felt the swing pause briefly before gravity began to pull it down again.

"Hazel!" Cowie brayed.

I snapped back to reality. There was no time to waste. The swing was sinking down faster. I inhaled a deep breath, grabbed the straps of my backpack, clenched my eyes shut, and leapt out of the swing.

Chapter 29

Height Hiccup Healing Herb

I plummeted through the sky like a rock in water. I still couldn't see the ground and I squeezed my eyes shut and called for Cowie. I heard him howl before something soft caught me in the air. I opened my eyes, it was the cloud! The gold cloud swirled around me and guided me down to the ground where it gently set me on my feet.

"I saw Francis!" I cried as I ran over to Cowie and buried my head in his neck, "he tried to pull me out of the swing."

Cowie calmed me down and gradually got me to tell him the story of Francis at the tree, Newton's valiant defence, and flying across the cliffs.

"Showing some grit," Cowie grinned, "Well done."

By the time I had relayed the whole ordeal to Cowie, Newton had woken up. With a great coughing and sputtering he tumbled out of the backpack which was now stacked with snow. I took my things out and emptied the backpack, shocked to find that everything was still dry.

"Terrible! Awful!" Newton panted, "Francis… falling… ice berries!" His hiccups had ceased but he was a much paler orange than usual and his eyes stuck far out of his head.

"You're fine and you did well, Newton," Cowie said. "Now I think that's enough of a production for now, don't you?"

Newton glared at Cowie but made no reply. He took shaky steps forward as we began walking up the trail. It took him well over an hour before he finally relaxed and became his pleasantly indignant self. He lamented that the ground was too rough and the trail too wide, the sun was too bright and the clouds too puffy, adventurers were too fragile and Cowie was too fast, I was too tall and he was too short, and on and on he went.

"It's good to see you're feeling better," I smiled at him. He looked confused but smiled back.

Early in the afternoon we came to a place where the ground dropped steeply down into a great pit.

"Another cliff," I said in dismay. It seemed after our endless climbing up the day before, we were going to spend today climbing down. I saw that a different path stretched along the cliff's edge and seemed to go down eventually, just not as abrupt. It had to lead to the bottom.

"Can we go around?" I asked, "Maybe there is another way instead of going straight down."

"I would very much like to go around," Newton nodded his head in agreement.

"You know we have to go down,"Cowie chimed.

Newton's face fell, "I have had enough climbing cliffs for one adventure and don't want to go down. I know what's at the bottom of this cliff and I am not interested in going to the Crows Net Pass right now."

"The Crows Net Pass?" I quaked.

Newton nodded emphatically, "A long stretch of trail that takes a day and a half to walk through. A path between cliffs that is home to the crows. They fly around with their nets, picking up anything that catches their fancy. I've heard they've carried off other creatures before."

"Is that where the traveller got caught?" I whispered.

Newton nodded solemnly. If he was trying to scare me away from the pass, he was succeeding.

"That sounds dangerous," I turned to Cowie, "Shouldn't we try and go around it if we can?"

"Check the book," he replied.

I flipped through my adventure book and saw Wordy's instruction: *Avoid paths with blue stones*. Frantically I scanned the path down for any blue stones, there were none. I thought I saw a tiny blue stone on the path that went around, but did that really count? I checked the thing-a-ma-jig and the arrow pointed ahead, down the cliff. I closed it without telling anyone where the arrow said to go. Desperate to find a reason not go through the pit I flipped through Mr. Sploot's book. I scanned the pages for any cautionary messages involving steep cliffs or the Crows Net Pass.

"What does your book say?" Cowie interrupted my search.

"I'm checking. I want to look at things all the way through," I did my best to sound rational and convincing. When Cow looked at me suspiciously I defended my stance, "I think that going all that way down and all the way through the pass might take too much time. We don't want to waste anymore time, right?"

"Like a shortcut?" Cowie grinned.

"No," I said. "Just, an *efficient* cut."

Even I thought that sounded ridiculous when I heard it come out of my mouth. I turned the page in Mr. Sploot's book and saw the words: *There is no way around the Crows Net Pass.*

Newton was laying on Cowie's back in distress, "Please tell me there's a way around."

I sighed heavily, "Mr. Sploot's book says there isn't."

Newton shuddered.

"Underground Postal Service!" A smiley young gopher beamed as he scrambled up from the side of the cliff, "A delivery for Newton and Hazel."

He passed Newton a small parcel, which I hoped was squares from his mother. I was given a small envelope that contained a note written on soft pink paper.

"Hazel,
I know the cliff looks daunting but again you have to choose,
To cling to what you know & take the road you know is true.
I realize that you are searching for a way around in fear,
But there is a lesson to be learned, one you should keep near.
Hazel…
There is no way around - there is only the way through,
And things always take just as long as they do.
Best wishes,
Wordy."

I took out my adventure book and copied the lessons onto the blank pages. Before I put it back, I wrote in the very front cover: "the only way through is through and things take as long as they do." I had a feeling I would need to look at that lesson more often than others.

"What did you get?" I asked Newton hopefully.

"An eye mask and some medicine," Newton looked unimpressed. Cowie looked amused. Newton passed me a dull brown bottle with a white cap on it: "Height Hiccup Healing Herbs," I read aloud. "From the Sweet Grass forest. Lasts for four hours."

"It will help him relax when we go down the pit," explained Cowie.

"What's the eye mask for?" I asked.

"Apparently I will feel much better about the whole thing after I have a nap," Newton snarked, looking more annoyed than ever.

"What have you decided?" Cowie asked me.

"We have to go down," I pointed to the cliff, "I'm awfully sorry Newton... you better take some of your medicine."

"I don't need it," he protested at first, but as soon as we neared the edge of the cliff, his hiccups flared up with a vengeance and he asked for help taking the herbs. I helped him drop some of the brown liquid in his mouth as we began the descent. We had barely started walking when it took effect. Newton hung limp across Cowie's back in complete relaxation. He wore a dopy smile on his face and hummed a sleepy tune. The narrow path turned into tiny stone steps, so small that only one foot could fit on at a time. Ordinarily Newton would be hiccuping fire like a volcano but thanks to the medicine, he now he slid back and forth on Cowie's back giggling contentedly.

"You know," he began, "I really love this adventure. You're doing such a fabulous job, Hazel. I'm so proud of you. I wasn't nearly so capable on my first adventure. I went straight off the trail and got tangled with a crowd of Raccoons who spent all their time in the gully by the Murky Lake drinking old cranberry juice. You are just doing so well," he almost looked emotional while he spoke.

"Why don't you put on your eye mask?" Cowie encouraged Newton.

"What an excellent idea Cowie, it's no wonder you're a senior guide," Newton's voice was full of sincere adoration. "Hazel, might I ride in your backpack?" He asked before he placed the mask over his eyes. It was a very silly mask with bright orange eyes that had long eyelashes. I helped Newton nestle into the bottom of the pack and in no time at all he was snoring away.

With Newton snoozing safely and Cowie walking before me, I dared to look down the cliff. I couldn't see the bottom and I gulped. I looked up, I couldn't see the top of the cliff either. I felt trapped and I froze in horrified fear. Cowie's foot landed on a loose stone that nearly made him slip. The stone echoed eerily across the earth as it bounced down, over and over, never seeming to find rest on solid ground. This was terrible. I stood rooted in my place, too afraid to move. I didn't want to take another step for fear of slipping and falling down the pit.

"It's alright Hazel. Just take one step at a time," Cowie coaxed.

I shook my head. I couldn't speak and I couldn't move. I thought this must be how Newton had felt on the top of the ridge. I wondered if I could take some of his medicine.

Cowie interrupted my thought process, "You can do it. Just one step at a time. Every step you take is one step closer to getting out of here."

I fought the tears that attempted to spring from my eyes. I had to go forward. What else was there to do?

Stay scared on the side of the cliff forever? Taking slow deep breaths I took one shaky step forward.

"Good!" Cowie encouraged, "Now just keep going."

Just keep going - he made it sound easy. It wasn't easy.

Again, I forced myself to take a step, and then I forced another, and another after that.

Step

    Step

        Step

            Step

Over and over.

Step

    Step

        Step

            Step

Finally, the bottom of the cliff was visible.

Step

    Step

        Step

Cowie was at the bottom!

Step

    Step

        Step

"You're so close," Cowie said, "you can take the leap now!"

I collected all of my last nerves and jumped as far away from the cliff as I could, landing with both my feet planted firmly on the ground.

"We did it!" I cried. Cowie laughed and I heard Newton call "Hooray!" very sleepily from the backpack.

Chapter 30

Crows Net Pass

I let out a squeal of delight when I turned back and saw the cliff we had descended. Never would I have ever believed that I would be able to climb down such a great height - but I had. I checked on Newton who was back to snoring blissfully in the backpack.

Looking around our new surroundings I noticed an odd thing, there was no wind. Everything was as still as a statue. Towering mounds of twisty rocks created a labyrinth ahead of us. You could barely see the sun behind the cliffs.

"The pass," Cowie whispered quietly beside me.

"The only way through is through," I said more confidently than I felt.

"And things always take just as long as they do," he replied, "Shall we begin?"

"Yes."

We walked into the maze. Towering rocks created an echo chamber that reflected every footstep, every word, and every crow caw. Great birds with black feathers and white nets flew from rock to rock, swooping down to grab things with their beaks.

"What're they doing?" I asked Cowie.

"Cleaning up the forest," he replied. "Or at least that's what they think they are doing. They take anything that catches their fancy and carry it away in their nets. They're really quite well intending."

A fog rolled in and everything felt a few degrees colder and a good deal more frightening. I pet Cowie's neck as we walked, feeling safer when I was close beside him. A shadow flashed across the path and I jumped.

"It was only a mouse," Cowie comforted.

I grimaced. I didn't find that fact very comforting, I had never liked mice. A party of crows flew by loudly yelling at one another and Newton poked his head out of the backpack.

"Blasted no good crows," he shook the eye mask off his face and took his usual position on Cowie's back, yawning and stretching limbs. "You better remember to keep the thing-a-ma-jig safe," he reminded, "I've heard

232

that crows can sneak in and out of a backpack without you even noticing."

"Where did you hear that?" Cowie retorted, but Newton gave no answer. A crow swooped down and picked at the clasp of my backpack and I shook him away. I reached into the zippered pocket, retrieved the thing-a-ma-jig, and clutched it protectively in my hands. I would not let the crows get near it.

The sky grew dark, the air turned chilly, and soon everything succumbed to the blackness of night. We stopped for the night in a small crook of the rock on a smooth stone slab. Newton built a roaring fire and the three of us packed closely together. Soon it was plenty warm and much less frightening. With crows swooping around us and calling back and forth across the pass I grew increasingly worried about my backpack and thing-a-ma-jig. I told myself it would be safe if I just kept it tucked in my hand. With all the action going on I wasn't sure I was going to be able to sleep. Newton suggested I take some of his medicine but Cowie said that the medicine must only be used to treat height induced hiccups and not merely for sleeping.

I closed my eyes and tried to rest. Hours went by before I finally fell asleep. I dreamt all night I was trapped in Feazel's castle surrounded by crows who were trying to get at my thing-a-ma-jig.

Before I knew it Newton was shaking me awake.

"Eleven days," he said when my eyes finally opened.

I felt stiff from sleeping on the ground.

"Did you say eleven?" A panicky voice shouted. We all turned to see a very tall bird standing behind us. It had a long neck, beady eyes, and a plump body stacked precariously on top of very thin legs.

"Not eleven!" cried the bird, "Eleven is the unluckiest number."

"It is?" I asked.

"Luck is such nonsense," Newton immediately began criticizing.

"Yes!" she wailed, flapping her arms and leaping from one foot to another, "It is the unluckiest of numbers because it is the same backwards and forwards. Madness. It's completely off it's head."

"Lots of numbers are the same backwards and forwards," Newton said sassily, "like 22, or 77, or 1991-"

The bird jumped even faster and bobbed her head up and down, "not any of those number are so bad as the number eleven. Number eleven is the number one worst number because it is the number one two times!"

She whimpered in distress, "Besides, it's the Feazel's favourite number and he's just terrible to us emus. He likes our feathers for his quill pens. Imagine, my feathers as a pen," she trembled.

"But 22 is 11-"

"That's enough Newton," interrupted Cowie.

"They've all been following me," she cried, "the crows, trying to pluck out my feathers to win favour with the Feazel."

A crow cawed in the distance and the emu leapt into the air with a screech. "Run away!" she screamed in my ear while she pushed me back down the trail with her wings.

"We have to go this way," I brushed her aside, "We have to get to the castle. We're on an adventure."

"You can't go on an adventure now! Not on a day that has an eleven in it. Don't you know that it would be the very unluckiest thing to do? Disaster awaits I tell you - disaster awaits! Follow me, follow me, I will get you out of danger!"

When she finished her speech, she turned and ran straight into the side of one of the twisty cliffs. Regaining her balance, she shook her head side to side rapidly and sputtered something about the number eleven.

"We have to go this way," I said, pointing down the pass.

"You are mad! You will be turned over to the Feazel by the crows! That's what happened with that traveller."

"You know about the traveller?" I asked.

"Oh *everyone* knows about her. Dropped right into one of the nets! Spotted by the W.S.S. falling right out of the sky and taken immediately to the castle. If you go this way, you are sure to be captured."

Even though I doubted the emu's sanity I found myself considering her argument. I didn't want to end up caught in the nets of the crows and carried off by the W.S.S."But we have to go this way to get to the castle," I said feebly, trying to convince myself more than her.

"No you don't! There's another way. If you follow me I will take you there."

"Really?" I turned to Cowie, "I think we should go with her and scout it out then."

"You have gone crazy," Newton muttered, "You *know* what the book says about that."

Yes of course, Mr. Sploot had said it was not wise to follow the emu and that there was no way around the pass... but still... walking through a treacherous pass of menacing crows didn't seem any wiser.

"Come now, there's no time to lose!" The emu turned and started running out of the pass.

I took a hesitant step after her.

"Where is your thing-a-ma-jig?" Newton asked, pointing to my hand. I gasped when I realized I didn't have it anymore. Frantically I searched my backpack.

"It's not here! Oh no, oh no, oh no!" I ran back to the place we had spend the night. Cowie and Newton followed close behind. The emu ran after us, yelling. We scanned the rocks all around, but the thing-a-ma-jig was nowhere to be found.

"How could I have lost it?" I moaned.

"It's those crows. That's what I've been telling you - you aren't safe here!" the emu flapped her wings and hissed wildly as one of the black birds made a dive for her feathers.

"What are we going to do?" I asked Cowie quietly.

"We're supposed to keep going," he winked, "All is not lost."

"How can we move on without the thing-a-ma-jig?" I cried, "It shows us the way to go."

"See, disaster has already begun! It is hopeless! Turn back while you can!" the emu was getting more agitated by the second.

"We already know which way to go," Newton argued, "through the pass and *not* with the emu."

A crow cawed and swooped down low, making yet another snatch at one of the emu's feathers.

"Stay behind and get captured if you must, but I refuse to be part of this craziness!!" The emu squealed before diving her head downward. There was a dull knock as her face collided with a rock. She stood up for a minute before wobbling side to side and collapsing in a feathery heap on the ground.

"Poor dear," Cowie shook his head.

"Poor dear?!" Newton gasped.

"She can't help herself. Emu's just are the way that they are," Cowie said. A crow made another dive at the emu and Cowie scared it away with a bark, waking the 'poor dear' back up. Her wobbly legs swayed back and forth as she collected herself off the ground. She looked forwards and backwards, and then took off down the way we had come, flapping her feathers madly.

"What a nut," Newton said.

"I can't believe I've lost the thing-a-ma-jig," I sat on the ground with my head in my hands.

"I can't believe you nearly followed an emu," Newton retorted.

Chapter 31

Rumbly-Tumbly River

Cowie picked me up by my backpack and stood me on my feet. He brushed the dust off my dress with his paw, "Come on now Hazel, that's enough."

I was determined to pout, "But I've lost the thing-a-ma-jig."

"Well then," Cowie said, "I suppose we will just have to pick up the shattered pieces of our adventure and move on. Chin up and eyes forward."

I relented and walked along the trail with my hand resting on his neck and a determined pout on my face. We hadn't walked far when a voice called to us from up ahead.

"Well hello there travellers."

A great lumbering panda was walking towards us.

"Hello," I responded cautiously. I had not expected to meet so many creatures in the pass.

""Who are you?" he asked.

"Hazel," I replied, "Who are you?"

"Noodles," he sat down beside us and smiled broadly, "Where are you going?"

"To Feazel's castle," I replied.

"Well that explains why you look so sad," he pointed to my face. "That is not a very happy place to go and it's such a long ways too. I would be very sad if I had to walk that far."

"I'm not sad because I'm going to the castle," I said more sharply than I meant to. "I mean, I'm happy to go to the castle because it is part of my adventure. It's just that I've lost my thing-a-ma-jig and so I am worried."

"You had a thing-a-ma-jig?" Noodles asked excitedly. "I've heard of those!"

"Yes," I said. "I had it but now I've lost it."

"I bet you haven't really," Noodles replied very cheerfully. "I bet the crows picked it up last night. Didn't anyone tell you to keep it away from the crows? They'd be all over a thing-a-ma-jig."

Newton chuckled in a matter that let me know he had told me so.

"I tried to," I defended. "I slept with it in my hands so they wouldn't be able to take it without my knowing."

Noodles shook his head. "Those crows are a crafty lot when it comes to taking things, especially shiny things. They'll take anything really, but the shinier the better. I bet they had never seen a thing-a-ma-jig before - those are so rare. They probably fiddled with it too, darn things, they love gears and arrows. Be careful if you find it, they probably tampered with it and broke something. But you should really check with that old Platypus that keeps track of *all* the things."

Suddenly I remembered, "The platypus Fritz?"

"How did you know?" Noodles grinned widely. His ears twitched back and forth and he grabbed his toes and rocked onto his back.

"Wordy the owl!" I answered excitedly. "Do you know where he is?"

Noodles sat back up and shook his head, "Haven't seen Wordy in a while I'm afraid. Doesn't tend to frequent these parts. He's a good fellow though, very wise I hear."

"I meant Fritz," I corrected.

"Well of course I know where Fritz is! He's in his office!"

Noodles rose, walked over to a bush, picked off a leafy branch, and chomped on it slowly.

"Can you take us there?" I asked.

"No, it is too far for me," Noodles replied, "I would get very sad if I had to walk that far. I would have to skip one of my naps and that would never do. I can tell you the way though," he offered.

"Yes, please!"

"Follow the path through the twisty rocks until you reach the Rumbly-Tumbly River," Noodles said this all very slowly between mouthfuls of the bush he was eating. I waited anxiously for him to continue. "Follow the purple stones until you reach the dock," he paused to pick another branch off the bush, commenting on how the ones that were smaller and more yellow were the ones he preferred since they had a slightly sour flavour. I nearly burst with anticipation waiting for the rest of the instructions. "Anyway," he finally continued, "after the dock, you need to take the cobbled path and stay on it until the water runs green, green-green not blue-green, then ring the bell."

"Thank you!" I gasped, relieved he had finally gotten all the way through the directions. He smiled and wished us well. We bid him goodbye and continued on our journey.

"We are really wasting a lot of time if we go to the office," Newton complained.

I looked to Cowie, "Should we not go?"

"What does your intuition say?" he asked.

I stopped and stood very still. I closed my eyes and tuned my ears to my gut.

"I think we should go," I answered.

Cowie nodded, "Then we will go."

A colourful parrot flew ahead of us calling, "Disaster ahead! Disaster ahead!"

I looked nervously at Cowie.

"Must have run into that emu," Newton rolled his eyes and I remembered the instructions: *Don't trust the parrots because they repeat whatever they hear.*

It turns out the Rumbly-Tumbly River was on the other side of the Crows Net Pass and we reached it just as dusk fell. I wanted to go all the way to Fritz's office but Cowie said it was too late to continue.

"We can camp here tonight and then go to the office tomorrow," he announced definitively.

"Can't we go now?" I protested.

He shook his head, "It isn't safe to travel the river in the dark. Besides, it would do no good. Fritz is very particular about his office hours and will not answer the bell after sundown. Let's get a good rest and an early start tomorrow."

Reluctantly I surrendered to camping by the river. A turtle swam by while we were building the fire. It had a red stripe on its side. I waved at it, it waved back. I wondered if this was the river where I had met the gold fish.

The evening spent by the river was much nicer than the night spent in the pass. Soft grass made sleeping much more comfortable and there were no rock towers blocking the moonlight. Brilliant stars lit up the sky and green and purple lights danced across the horizon.

"The Northern Lights," Cowie pointed to the glow.

I sat in awe. They were beautiful. Suddenly in a great cawing ceremony, hundreds of crows flew up out of the pass. They were each carrying a small white net and were headed down the river. The swoosh of their wings created a powerful wind that blew my hair and fanned the flames of our fire.

"What was all that about?" I asked Cowie when the last crow had disappeared.

"They're taking their treasures to the office," he replied.

"They do that every night," Newton explained, "They clean up the pass and take everything they find to Fritz."

I couldn't fathom how they could find so many things in the pass every night, the nets they had been carrying were bulging. I wondered what Fritz's office must look like if he was receiving so many items every day. I supposed I would soon find out. I closed my eyes and let the bubbling of the river lull me to sleep.

Chapter 32

Office of Procurement

"Ten days," announced Newton at the crack of dawn.

My stomach tied itself into several little knots. We were running out of days. I felt incredibly guilty for wasting time going after the thing-a-ma-jig when I should not have lost it in the first place. Yet, my conscience and my intuition still agreed that we should go the office.

I walked behind Cowie to the edge of the river. Noodles had said to follow the purple stones but I didn't see any. I was about to ask Cowie where the stones were when a great purple boulder jumped up out of the river with a splash. I nearly jumped out of my skin when it landed in the middle of the water not far from the bank.

Newton chuckled at my startle. "I think I'll take a swim," he said before he leapt into the water and began splashing his way down the stream. He splashed so wildly that it looked rather frantic, I grew worried until I saw him puff up his stomach and float on his back.

Cowie jumped from the river's edge to the purple stone, "Come along, Hazel!"

I leapt from the edge and barely made it to the rock. As soon as I landed, another boulder jumped out of the water just in front of us. We leapt onto that rock and the one we had been standing on disappeared under the water with a great SPLOOSH. All along the river the cycle repeated, a boulder appeared in front and a boulder disappeared behind. A purple road rose up to meet us as the river took us around twists and turns.

The river grew very narrow and then very wide, eventually splitting into two. Around a bend we had to jump down a small waterfall. Newton didn't see it coming and tumbled down with streams of fire cascading out of his mouth. At the bottom of the falls there was the small brown dock that Noodles had told us about. We all clambered up onto it, Newton dripping and panting for breath.

"Forgot how long of a swim that was!" he said as he climbed up onto Cowie's back.

At the end of the dock the cobbled trail began. Like the river stones, the cobblestones were purple, though much smaller than the ones in the water. As I skipped over them I noticed how similar they were to the rocks that I had accidentally thrown on the gold fish's spinach garden.

We walked along the road and I kept careful eye on the water hoping to catch a glimpse of the fish. The water had turned from clear blue to a blueish green. A little further down, a small and very distinctly green stream stemmed off the main river.

"Here we are," Newton announced, climbing off Cowie's back and scampering down the road. I looked around the green water for the fish but didn't see him. I took a purple stone and tossed it in the river.

"What on earth are you doing?" Newton scolded.

"Just checking," I shrugged my shoulders.

A short wooden sign was pounded into the ground at the end of the path: "Office of Procurement. Please ring bell for service." A small brass bell hung from a purple cord. Cowie nudged it with his paw and it jingled a merry ring. There was a bubbly splashing for a moment and the river churned excitedly. The water split and stocky platypus walked up small steps that were set in the bank. He was carrying a very thick book and had large round spectacles resting on his bill which made his eyes look about ten times too big for his face.

"Greetings my friends," he said. He flipped a short table out from the side of the sign and rested his book on it. "What can I do for you today?" He glanced up at our faces and then squinted, "Ahh Cowie! And Newton - how is your mother? I was just about to send her a package this morning but the post hasn't arrived yet."

"She is well," Newton was yelling very slowly, "Yes the postal service, quite backed up these days."

"I am so glad she is well. She was worried about you last time I spoke to her. Said you were on an adventure and she had sent you some squares but hadn't heard back from you. I shall have to let her know you are alright. You can slip a note in her parcel today if you would like."

Newton said he would like to and Fritz passed him a pen and paper before turning his attention back to Cowie and I, "Now who has an inquiry for me this fine sunny morning?"

Cowie nudged me forward with his nose.

"I lost something," I mumbled.

"What?" Asked the Platypus loudly.

"I lost something," I said a bit louder.

"What?" Called the Platypus again. "You must speak up my dear, I have done this work for nearly a hundred years, the hearing tends to go after a while."

"I've lost something!" I said as loud and as clear as I could.

"Yes of course of course," He flipped open his book, "What day did you lost said 'something?'"

"The night before last I suppose. I noticed it was gone yesterday morning."

Fritz looked like he was trying very hard to hear me.

"You need to speak clearer," Cowie whispered in my ear. I leaned close to Fritz and repeated myself, yelling as loud and as slow as I could manage.

"No need to shout. I'm not deaf you know," Fritz said with a wink. He flipped open his big book and thumbed through the pages. His hearing may have been bad but his eyesight must have been spectacular for the writing on the pages was so small that I could not read it at all. It was evident he could as he looked through the scribbles knowingly.

"Hmm…" he said as his finger slid slowly down the selected page, his eyes scanning back and forth as he went. He whispered out items as his finger passed them: "this thing, that thing, up thing, blue thing, no thing, top thing, ripped thing, thumb thing" and on and

251

on for pages he went, reading out the different 'things.' Once he had flipped three pages, he shook his head with finality, "No, I'm afraid there were no 'somethings' turned in yesterday."

I sighed heavily, "Not a something, a thing-a-ma-jig."

"Well why didn't you say so!" he laughed, his round belly bouncing up and down. "These new adventurers. Always forgetting about the details. Don't you worry dear I know just the one you are after. I thought it was odd that they brought me one as there's only two in the whole island and Wordy is usually very careful with who he entrusts them to."

I felt the familiar pang of guilt.

Fritz left his book open on the table and dove under the water.

"I didn't mean to lose it," I muttered to Cowie.

"I know. It's alright."

Fritz returned a moment later with a big green bag on his shoulder and the thing-a-ma-jig in his hands. It had small dents in the top.

"They were fiddling with it I'm afraid," he said as he passed it to me.

I opened it up and saw that the arrow was broken off, leaving a black stump that swirled around back and forth before pointing right.

"It still seems to work," I said.

"Yes, it *seems* to doesn't it," Fritz smiled, a twinkle flashed through his bright aged eye.

"I've finished my note," called Newton.

Fritz took it and folded it up, "Perfect."

He took the green bag off his back and peered inside. He reached so deep into the bag that his feet came off the ground and he nearly fell completely inside. He pulled out a small box with a tin lid in which he placed Newton's letter. "I'll just send it along with the yarn that she ordered," he said. "Your mother, she's always working on some project isn't she?"

Just as he closed the tin lid, a gopher leapt out of the ground. "Good morning Fritz," he yelled with a cheery wave.

"William," Fritz said, "running behind this morning I see?"

"Hold up at the beaver dam," William replied, "they needed my help on a project."

The gopher passed a small envelope to Fritz which he placed on his big book. "Don't they always," he clucked.

I watched as the gopher held his mail bag open and Fritz placed several packages inside. I couldn't see the names that were written on them but I was very curious to know where each one was going. One by one Fritz piled parcels into the carrier. Some were as large as himself and others were as small as Newton's toe. Somehow each time he added another package, the gopher's mail carrier grew large enough to accommodate it. By the time Fritz had placed the last parcel in the carrier, the sack was bulging, and mail piled out of it in a precarious tower that stood much taller than William himself.

"Is that all?" the gopher asked. He took the handles of the mail carrier looking completely confident, I wasn't sure how he was going to be able to lift it.

"Yes," Fritz scanned a list in the back off his book, checking things off as he read. "It is a rather light day, isn't it?"

The gopher agreed and gave the mail carrier a shake and the sack returned to its normal size, all of the parcels collapsing inside. He slung it over his shoulder easily, tipped his cap, and disappeared down the hole. I stared, dumbfounded. I wished my backpack worked like that.

Fritz opened the envelope the gopher had given him and read it very carefully. "Interesting," he muttered and shifted his gaze to look at me. "So you're headed to the castle you are?"

I nodded.

"Well I have something for you in that case," he reached into his green bag and pulled out a small rock. He placed it in my palm and cupped my fingers around it gently. "Do not lose this," he said, closing my fingers around it.

"What is it?" I asked.

"The time will come for that question to be answered - but it is not now. You must be headed back."

Once again he reached into his magical green bag, which was making me feel as curious as Mr. Sploot's briefcase had, and took out a very small jar that was painted a glittery blue and had drawings of stars on the side. At the sight of the jar Newton leapt into the backpack and began scrounging for his medicine.

"Hold onto Cowie," Fritz instructed. I wrapped my arms around Cowie's neck and Fritz unfastened the jar's lid.

Chapter 33

Up or Down

There was a great whoosh and water leapt out of the jar. Before I could see what was happening Cowie, Newton, and I were swept into the air on a gigantic wave. The wave carried us back through the river and to the spot we had camped the night before. It deposited us in a pile on the shore, me clinging to Cowie's neck for dear life, and Newton trembling in the backpack.

"Is it over?" He emerged, "I couldn't find my medicine!"

I smiled, "It's over."

I was surprised that we weren't drenched.

"Let's get a move on," Cowie prodded me with his nose.

We walked along the road. The sun was shining, the birds were singing, and I thought about how grateful I was to be walking in the fresh air and not amidst the rock towers. Trees stretched out around us and flowers poked through the ground. The road was smooth and the going was easy.

"I wish it could be like this all the time," I said.

"No you don't," Newton retorted. "If all roads were smooth then no roads would be."

"What?"

"He means," explained Cowie, "That it's by walking rough roads that we learn to appreciate the smooth roads. If you hadn't been through the pass, you wouldn't appreciate where we are now. If you hadn't had difficult days, you wouldn't enjoy the simpler ones."

That made sense to me.

A little ways up the road and down a small hill there was another fork in the road. This time the forks were distinct. One dropped sharply down the mountain and one rose up. I looked along each road for any clues about which way was the correct path. I didn't feel the need to take my adventure books out of my backpack, I had so many of the instructions memorized. I didn't see any blue stones and I didn't have any special gut feelings. I checked the thing-a-ma-jig and it pointed down.

"Down we go," I said.

"Why?" questioned Newton.

I showed him the thing-a-ma-jig.

"What are you complaining about anyway? I thought you would be grateful to avoid climbing up another mountain," I teased.

Newton dismissed my argument with a wave of his hand. "Should you really be trusting that thing after the crows have been messing with it? Didn't Noodles say they like playing with gears?" he sounded very skeptical.

"It hasn't steered us wrong so far," I defended the thing-a-ma-jig, "Besides what does Noodles know about thing-a-ma-jigs and crows."

"Well he lives around the crows," Newton retorted.

I didn't understand why Newton was defending Noodles and arguing so strongly against going down the easier path.

"We're going down," I said defiantly and started walking along my chosen path. Newton scampered off Cowie's back and started scrounging in the bushes.

"Ah hah!" he yelled after a minute of searching. A blue rock in hand, he bounded over to us. "A blue stone," he announced, dropping it in front of me.

"That doesn't count," I said.

"Why not?"

"Because it wasn't on the path," I said. "It was in the bush. Wordy said avoid the *paths* with blue stones, not the bushes."

Newton looked aghast and turned to Cowie, "*do something!*"

"I'm afraid I can't. This is Hazel's adventure, her story to write," he shook his head. Newton crossed his arms and took his position on Cowie's back, muttering arguments that I blocked from my ears.

Stubbornly I pressed on. As we walked, I noticed a small blue stone in the path. Newton pointed it out but I showed him that it really wasn't quite that blue, it was more of a teal or a green.

"That's what Priscilla said too," he mumbled. I pretended not to hear him. How dare he compare me to that goose!

Several minutes later, I noticed another stone in the path. This stone was undeniably blue. There was another shortly after, and another beside that one, and all of a sudden I found myself standing on a beach of small blue stones. I swallowed the lump that rose in my throat as Newton stood with his arms crossed, tapping his foot on the rocks, "These blue enough for you?"

I didn't acknowledge him. He rolled his eyes and turned around to head back up the path. "Time to go back up!" he said.

"We can't leave yet," I reached out and grabbed his tail to stop him from leaving.

He gasped and shot a ring of fire towards my hand, "Disgraceful behaviour! *Never* grab a dragon's tail!"

I muttered an apology. I genuinely felt sorry for grabbing his tail but I didn't want to leave yet. Something rebellious and defiant had taken over me and I wanted to *be* right more than I wanted to *do* right. I didn't want to be wrong again. I was tired and I didn't want to go all the way back to the fork in the road and then climb up the other path. I had wasted enough time already.

"Why can't we leave?" Cowie asked.

"Because," I shrugged casually, "we just got here."

I searched the corners of my imagination for an excuse. Cowie gave me a quizzical look and Newton rambled on and on about how Cowie should be *doing* something. Gentle waves lapped up against the pebbly stones. Tentatively I walked to the shoreline and peered into the water. It was a sandy grey water that reflected a muddy picture. I couldn't see the bottom.

"Murky Lake," Cowie said, coming to stand beside me.

"Where the weasels hide their secrets?" I asked, my heart stalling for a moment. If this was the murky lake, we definitely went the wrong way.

He nodded.

A splash came in the distance. I looked up to see a towering black stone rising out of the middle lake. My eyes traced the stone up and I saw a draw bridge span from the top of the rock to the mainland.

"Feazels' castle!" I whispered.

"Yes," Newton both looked and sounded annoyed. "The castle with the imprisoned traveller inside that we are supposed to be *rescuing.* But instead we are wasting time staring at the dumping grounds of the bad guys."

"We have ten days," I crossed my arms and glared at him.

"Yes," agreed Cowie. "Ten days to get into the castle, down to the most secure dungeon which we don't completely know the way to, free a prisoner who we don't know, and get her back to her own world that we don't know exactly where it is."

"Yes," mocked Newton, "ten days is plenty of time. Pardon me, I don't know what I was worried about."

The wind blew a cold chill across the water. I shivered and a weight sunk in the bottom of my stomach as I realized what I was doing. An innocent traveller was trapped in a terrifying castle dungeon and I was wasting time taking a side trip to the murky lake. Another splash interrupted my thoughts.

"What is that?" I asked.

"Rubbish," Cowie replied. "The weasels put all the evidence of their wrongdoings in a rubbish bin, box it up, and throw it out the castle rubbish chute."

Splash after splash hit the water and I wondered how many terrible things the weasels must be up to to have so much rubbish. I shuddered to think of what the Feazel was like if he was in charge of the whole operation.

"We have to get to the castle," I said quietly.

"Going to the castle are you?" called a voice behind us. "Why don't you just take the boat?"

Chapter 34

Boatride

I spun around to see who was talking. Newton yelped, a small flame jumping out of his mouth, Cowie growled. A lanky raccoon was sitting in a hammock reading a book and sipping red liquid out of a tall skinny glass.

"What did you say?" I asked him.

Newton hissed, "Why are you talking to him, raccoons are bad news."

"Just take the boat," the raccoon said. He put down his book and jumped out of his hammock, "My apologies. I couldn't help but overhear you saying that you want to go to the castle. We have a boat that can take you there now if you're in a hurry."

I was in a hurry. My mistakes had cost us enough time already, "Well we do need to get there soon."

"Careful Hazel," cautioned Cowie.

The sun was starting to sink down and everything was growing dimmer.

"I'm being careful," I said, "I'm just trying to get us up there faster."

"You're not being careful at all!" Newton argued.

I pointed to the castle, "Do you want to walk all the way up?"

"I'd rather walk all the way up than tangle with the raccoons!" Newton hissed, ducking behind Cowie's leg.

"Newton, old scallywag!" the raccoon called. "So, the rumours are true, you are back by the murky lake. I have to confess I didn't believe it when I heard the news. I thought you had bent yourself too straight to hang with us anymore."

Newton puffed his beard at the raccoon, "I'm not back. I'm just passing by. I'm on an adventure."

The raccoon laughed out loud, "imagine that. Newton on an adventure."

"How fast can we get there by boat?" I interrupted the reunion.

"You could land at the castle tonight," the raccoon said coyly.

It had taken us an entire afternoon to climb down the wrong path and we didn't know how long it would take to climb the trail that led to the castle gate. Backtracking would cost us an entire day - at least.

"Don't be mad at me," I whispered before I turned to face the raccoon. "Where's the boat?"

The raccoon smiled a set of flashing white teeth, "I'm so glad you asked."

Newton clung to Cowie's leg horrified. Cowie grumbled and growled a good deal but came along without any other protest. We followed the raccoon along the beach to a weathered brown rowboat that had no oars.

"Where are they?" I asked, pointing to the oarlocks on the side.

"This boat doesn't need oars," the raccoon replied. "It's a magic boat."

I looked at the rickety structure with suspicion, it didn't look very magical to me. My conscience was starting to bubble and my intuition was rearing its head and telling me the boat was not a safe option. I squashed them both down and listened instead to desperation.

"Alright," I nodded towards the boat.

"You can't be serious!" Newton cried.

The raccoon grinned, "Oh she most certainly is."

"What's the catch?" I could tell Newton was fighting the hiccups as he turned to face the raccoon. "Everything has a cost with your lot."

"Why don't we settle it later, old chap. Consider it a favour from a friend - for the time being," he winked and pushed the boat down the pebbly beach and into the water.

Committed to my choice, I climbed inside the decrepit vessel. Newton let everyone know how disgusted he was by this expedition but declared he would rather be stranded in the middle of Murky Lake with us than left on the beach with the raccoons.

"Suit yourself," the raccoon shrugged and shoved us off with a wave. "Follow the light," he called, "it's the outer entrance."

It was true, the boat didn't need oars. It glided noiselessly along the surface of the water. Everyone kept silent. The sun sunk completely below the horizon and the lake was swallowed in blackness. The pale moon hid behind the black tower, making the whole scene even more dull and grim.

Newton looked greener than grass and clung to the side of the boat looking as if he would vomit at any moment. Another icy chill came from across the lake and small bumps rose along my arms. I heard a soft

266

hissing coming from underneath us. The hair on the back of Cowie's neck bristled up and he looked the most uneasy I had seen him on the journey so far.

"What is that?" I asked. No one answered.

The hissing grew to whispers. Voices sounded underneath the boat, beside the boat, and then in front where something splashed the water. I was starting to get scared, recalling Newton having mentioned something about a monster. Relief swept over me when I saw a small light hanging in the distance.

"The entrance!" I cried, pointing to it. No one shared my celebration. Cowie growled quietly and Newton started hiccuping large flames.

We got closer to the light every moment. Or was the light getting closer to us? I couldn't see a door that it was hanging from. I strained my eyes. It looked like it was rocking back and forth. It disappeared underneath the water for a moment and then suddenly reappeared right beside us. Something was definitely wrong. The light was no bigger than my fist and hung on the end of a stick that was swimming circles around our boat.

"What is that?" I asked fearfully.

"Don't you know?" Newton hiccuped.

"It's the Murky Lake Angler - Angus," Cowie said solemnly.

"Angler?" I asked with a squeak in my voice. I didn't know what it was but it sounded awful.

"You mean," hiccup, "*monster*," said Newton.

A deep chuckle sounded as an ugly fish peered it's head out of the lake. It's eyes glowed blue as it looked at me.

I screamed.

Angus let out a menacing cold laugh. He dropped his face under the water and blew bubbles that swirled around the boat and made it spin in circles.

"Angus is the King of the lake," Cowie called over the bubbling and thrashing of waves.

I clung to his neck, "What's he doing?"

"Calling the eels," he replied.

"Eels!?" I shrieked.

Newton dove into my backpack. I pulled him out before he could start anything on fire.

Cowie continued his explanation, "Angus and the eels feed off the rubbish from the castle... and adventurers who fall for the traps of the raccoons."

"He feeds off adventurers?" my voice escaped in stammers.

"I'm afraid so," Cowie said. "He pays the raccoons to lure adventurers into the boat."

"Why is he calling the eels?" if I was about to be eaten by an ugly glowing fish I would sooner have it over with quickly than dragged out.

"Have you ever seen a cat with their food?" Newton yelled between volcanic hiccups.

I didn't answer. Before we had moved to Blufferton way, I had seen our neighbour's cat take great pleasure in playing with mice before she devoured them. I knew what was about to happen.

Clouds rolled in front of the moon and rain started pouring down on us.

"What do we do?" tears began to stream down my face. I felt a knock on the boat. A second one followed, more forceful and rocking us back so water splashed into the bottom of our craft. A rush of knocks came as eels pushed on every side of the boat, making it teeter up and down. I knew it wouldn't be long before we were lost to the lake.

"I'm sorry, I'm sorry!" I called. "I did this, I'm sorry! I should have listened."

Streams of water poured into the boat as it finally began to tip over. Newton ran over and tucked himself onto my shoulder, I wrapped my arms around Cowie, and buried my face in his neck. We were going down.

Chapter 35

Liquid Sunshine

I thought all hope was lost. Cowie threw his head back and let out a powerful howl. Suddenly the eels stopped knocking on the boat, the light of the angler fish disappeared under the water, the rain stopped, the clouds parted, and the moon shone down. A twinkling light glowed above us, it was a soft pink cloud that came down from the sky. The cloud rested on the water and wrapped itself around the boat. As Cowie howled again, the cloud lifted the boat up out of reach of the eels and carried it away from the lake.

I peered over the side of the boat and watched the swarming eels below sink into the depths and the glowing outline of Angus grow smaller and smaller. Back on the beach, I saw the dark shadowy figure of the raccoon, staring up in disbelief. Apparently he hadn't realized how magical the boat really was.

We rose until we were level with the castle gates, the roof, and then the rainclouds themselves. Up and up the pink cloud carried us, taking the boat to rest in a sea of billowing pink mist that gathered just underneath the stars. A tree was standing in the middle of the clouds and Wordy was sitting on one of the branches.

"Good evening Hazel," he said when the boat stopped moving.

I hung my head low. My shame kept me from looking him in his eyes.

Wordy cleared his throat:

"I do think it's time, we have a spot of tea
Relax all the nerves, put the mind at ease."

Tea? Now? I had just nearly killed everyone in the boat and Wordy wanted to have tea. I was shocked. Where were we even going to get the tea from?

Wordy hopped off his branch and walked across the clouds. They swirled under his feet as he kicked up little tornadoes with every step. He took a step over the edge of the cloud and another leapt forward, rising to form a staircase. Wordy looked over his shoulder and waved a wing at me, *"come along."*

Cowie nudged my back and I stepped out of the boat. I had never walked on a cloud before. It felt like walking on nothing. I kicked at the mist underneath my feet and wisps flew in every direction. Cowie touched my back with his nose and encouraged me to go forward. Wordy had already climbed the mystical stairs to the moon. I raced up behind him and arrived just as he was dusting some dirt off the moon's surface with his wing. I gasped as I saw a thick vine hanging from a hook on the bottom.

"The swing!" I whispered to Cowie.

"Did you think I was joking?" he smiled.

Wordy reached into a little crater on the moon's surface and flipped a latch. There was a churning of gears as the moon swung open. Inside there were wooden shelves storing all kinds of things: books, feathers, watches, round containers, square containers, glittery swirling glowing balls of fire, and an assortment of stars. I never would have guessed that the moon contained so many extra things. I supposed extra stars had to be stored somewhere. Wordy held the moon open and started whistling a tune. My jaw dropped as I watched a table walk itself out from amongst the shelves, followed by four chairs - one with a very small seat and very tall legs, one with a very long seat and quite short legs, and two with medium sized legs and medium sized seats. The table stopped on a silvery cloud that drifted up from below. The chairs took their places around the table, one on each side. Wordy kept whistling his tune and a china tea pot floated out of the moon accompanied by four tea cups, four saucers, and four tiny spoons. Wordy walked over to the table, humming quietly as the teacups clattered onto the saucers and the tea pot floated to each setting and poured out steaming hot tea. The tea was bright blue and smelled like lilacs. Wordy sat on the end of the table, in one of the chairs with the medium legs and medium seat:

"Sugar in yours? I take some in mine.

Real star sugar - makes tea simply divine."

I nodded 'yes please' and followed him to the table. Cowie climbed into the chair with the short legs and large seat and Newton scrambled into the tall chair with the small seat, somehow the height of the clouds didn't seem to be bothering him.

Wordy reached up and took a shining star out of the sky. He tipped it on its side and tapped it gently. Shimmery star dust swam its way through the air and into the purple tea. He sprinkled some in my cup and offered some to Cowie and Newton who both accepted. I swirled the sugar around with my spoon, which looked more like a small rose than an utensil, and watched the star sugar sparkle as it dissolved.

Carefully, I placed the spoon on my saucer and took the cup in my hands. The tea was delightful. It tasted like a rainstorm or a hug or the best feeling in the world somehow transformed into shimmery blue drink. I had never had anything so calming and refreshing; I had almost forgotten about the disaster at the lake. But then Wordy reminded me.

"Why don't you tell me what happened," He said calmly between sips of tea. I ducked my head and stared into my cup. For a moment I contemplated how wonderful it would be to disappear. I could abandon the adventure and not have to own my wrongdoings in front of Wordy. Maybe this had all been a bad dream and I was just about to wake up! Yes, that could be it. I closed my eyes and clenched my fists, willing the dream to be over.

I opened them…I was still in the sky…

I had to answer Wordy .

I dug deep into my courage and glanced up at his face. I saw in his eyes that he already knew everything that had happened. Tears brimmed and my vision blurred. Cowie placed a paw on my knee and Wordy passed me a soft yellow handkerchief. Patiently, Wordy encouraged me to tell him the story. Regaining my composure I took a deep breath and recounted the events. I told him everything: how I had chosen the path down because I wanted the easier road, how I ignored the signs that Newton pointed out and the ones that I saw on my own, how I watched the rubbish be thrown into the water and realized we had to go immediately to the castle, and how I accepted the raccoon's trap of a shortcut. When I came to the part about the angler and the eels Wordy gasped and said, "tut-tut," many times. I finished my story and he said terribly quietly, "*How desperation can blind the wisest of minds.*" I blew my nose into the hankie. Wordy fell very silent. I watched while he finished his tea slowly and put his cup down on his saucer. He folded his wings in front of him and looked completely lost in thought. It felt like an eternity later when he finally broke the tense silence that hung around me:

"*I am truly sorry for the day that you've had,*
And it's quite plain to see that you feel very bad.
There are lessons to be found in every mistake,
So let's talk about the lessons you learned at the lake.
You knew what was true but you left it behind,
The moment you decided to push right from your mind-"

Defensiveness rose up inside me and I interrupted Wordy, "I didn't *decide* to push right from my mind."

275

Wordy was unbothered by my outburst and simply asked, "*Well what did you decide then?*"

I looked to the bottom of my tea saucer for answers. I didn't find any. I knew that I had decided to go down the easier road because I was tired, then I chose to ignore Newton because I wanted to be right, and finally I chose to take the boat because I was desperate and it was easier than walking all the way back.

"I suppose I chose easy," I admitted quietly. "I didn't want to be wrong and then I didn't want to go through the trouble of climbing all the way to the top."

Wordy nodded. Cowie and Newton remained silent, sipping at their tea and staring at the table.

"*The easier way is always easier to take,*
But more often than not… easier is a mistake.
There is nothing worth doing that is without trouble,
Resilience is needed to grow through the struggle."

"It just seems like it has been a lot of struggle and not very much fun," I said meekly. "I was tired of trouble. I don't particularly want to struggle anymore. Haven't I grown enough?"

"*Of course you could choose to face nothing at all,*
Take the easy way out and ignore adventure when it calls."

I nearly jumped out of my seat, "I don't want to ignore adventure!"

Raising his wing to calm my protest, Wordy continued:

"So when things get tough,
You must show things you're tougher;
When it takes all your strength,
All your strength you must muster.
Be stubbornly truthful and ferociously aware,
Of the signs of what's true,
For the signs, they are there."

Swallowing the guilt in my throat I looked Wordy in the eyes and told him I understood. Wordy tapped a feather on his chin, took out his pocket watch and stared at it for a long time.

"Ten days left... but essentially nine...
My my this will be tight... still, I've faith you will be fine."

He stared at me very intensely.

"Never again make a decision for the sake of your pride,
For that made you forsake the friends by your side.
There's no changing the past, the wrong choices you made,
There is only to learn and choose a different way.
Ask for forgiveness and then let's move on.
For we must be off, I have to light the dawn."

Wordy looked at me expectantly and I realized he was waiting for me to ask for forgiveness right at that moment.

"Newton," I started, "I'm sorry I didn't listen to you when you tried to show me I was wrong. Can you ever forgive me?" I swallowed tears.

Newton nodded regally and said, "All is well."

"I'm sorry I put us in danger, Cowie."

Tears escaped my eyes and flowed down my cheeks. I wished that I could bury my face in his neck and hide from the three sets of eyes that were staring at me but I couldn't. I couldn't find the words to ask him for forgiveness either. I just sat at the table and cried with my head down.

"All is forgiven," Cowie said graciously.

Wordy hopped off his chair and strolled over to me. He took my hand in his wing and brushed tears off my cheeks. His face was full of compassion when he looked at me.

"One day someone will do wrong,
And need forgiveness from you,
Then you can remember this day,
And how you were shown forgiveness too."

He led me off my chair and down the stairs of clouds. I turned back to see the tea set, cutlery, chairs, and table walk themselves back in the moon, the largest chair pulling the moon closed behind it.

When we were all down the stairs and standing beside the boat, Wordy reached into a pocket under his wing and took out a small vile. He hopped up onto the side of the boat and filled a dropper with shimmering swirly light that glowed from inside the vile. He held it up to his eyes and looked through it, shaking it up and down several times.

"Liquid sunshine," Cowie whispered in my ear.

Wordy was muttering to himself again, *"Just a drop maybe two, yes I think that will do."* He squeezed the dropper and a gleaming orange drop splashed on the bottom of the boat, followed closely by a pink one. The rickety old boat shivered and shook. The soggy brown wood started glowing and shifting in colour. It turned from brown to deep yellow, to orange, to pink, and finally to a deep red wood.

"Now for the dawn, the rise of the sun,
Oh painting the sunrise, really is the most fun."

Wordy giggled as he poured out a stream of liquid sunshine onto the cloud beneath his feet. The clouds flashed and glowed as he gently swirled the tip of his wing around to mix the sunshine in. Floods of colour raced across the sky. Wordy checked his watch, clicked his tongue, and whistled several times to the East. I watched the sun creep over the horizon, bathing the clouds in its warmth. Little flashes of light were racing towards the sun and I turned to watch an army of Grynns fly towards it. It seemed they were lining up to fill their cases with liquid sunshine which came out of a little tap on the right side of the sun. As I watched, I felt Wordy drape a fine chain around my neck before saying:

"Now into the boat for it is time to go,
Do not forget, the things you now know."

Cowie lifted me into the boat and Newton scrambled in after. Wordy swept the clouds forward with his wings and flew back to his tree. I waved goodbye. The clouds poured down in a misty river that carried us past the rising sun and back to the ground. Cowie hopped out of the boat and I followed him. We were next to a path, though it was not one that I had seen before.

"Where are we?" I asked.

He lifted his paw to silence me before signalling to follow him. Newton and I crept behind Cowie as he led us through the forest and to the edge of a great chasm, Newton looked faint when he saw the edge. Directly across our post, a gloomy black castle rose out of a pillar of stone.

"The Castle of Feazel," I whispered in awe.

Chapter 36

The W.S.S.

The castle was breathtaking in the morning light. I could see where the slide ended and where the drawbridge met the gate. I looked up and saw the black mass towering higher than the clouds. Though there was something quite crude about the castle's architecture, it was impressive nonetheless. A pair of hyenas came into view as they walked around the wall and towards the gate, they looked much bigger than they had in my imagination. I glanced back at the castle, noticing that it looked much larger in real life than it did on the map. As the hyenas drew closer, I could hear them talking:

"Schultz has gone really nuts since that break in hasn't he," said the first one.

"Tell me about it," said the second.

"Making us walk double duty. The *enhanced* inspections," the first replied.

"I know! Why is it even called an enhanced inspection. We just have to walk by his door every other lap. It's a waste of time."

"I hear ya."

The first hyena jumped up onto the net of the slide and started bouncing up and down on it like a trampoline.

"Schmidt! Nelson!" I heard a voice call from inside.

The hyenas panicked and raced to the draw bridge, tripping over one another as they wrestled to stand at attention. "Sir!" they screamed in unison.

A cackle went up from the door and a third hyena tumbled out laughing.

"Linus!" the other two cried.

"You should have seen your faces!" Linus stumbled over to the others, his loud laugh echoing across the chasm. The other hyenas swatted him with their paws and he stopped his giggling.

"Schultz wants you to add an extra inspection to your day," Linus said.

"What?!"

Linus nodded. "He said until we figure out the breech he is taking no chances."

"I need a new career," the first hyena said scowling. "This is ridiculous."

The three of them started taking a lazy lap around the castle, complaining about how hard guard life was. They disappeared around the corner.

Cowie started walking toward the bridge. "It's time to go," he said.

"Shouldn't we make a proper plan first?" I asked fearfully, stalling in my tracks.

"We have one," Newton reminded, "and it's the only one we have time for."

Cowie nodded in agreement and I gulped. "I don't know how I feel about going into the castle without knowing what's going on."

"I'll tell you a secret," Newton scampered up onto my shoulder and whispered in my ear, "Nobody ever knows what's going on, it's part of the fun of adventures."

He leapt off my shoulder and back onto Cowie's back, shooting me a wink. There was a glimmer in his eyes that had not been there before. I crept over to the drawbridge and planted a foot on it, I froze.

"No time to waste! They'll be back before we know it," Newton held his breath and darted across the bridge at an impressive speed. I wondered what had gotten into him to help him suddenly conquer his fear of heights. His claws made frantic scratching sounds as he flew across the wooden platform. When he arrived at the other side he turned back and gaped at me, "Come *on*."

"We're loosing time, Hazel," Cowie pressed his nose into my back and prodded me forward. I took one shaky step after another. I froze three times before I found my courage and tiptoe ran the rest of the way to the other side. Safely across, I gasped for air. Just as I began to calm down, I heard the sound of hyena voices heading towards the nearest corner. They were coming back already!

Quickly we snuck through the main doorway.

"I needed my adventure book!" I announced as I ducked behind a pillar.

"What're you doing?" hissed Newton, "They're right there! They'll see you!"

"I have to find my map!" I slipped my backpack off my shoulders, undid the buckles, and unzipped the pocket. Hyena voices drew closer, they would be able to see me any second. I spotted the package of balls Marty had given me and quickly drew one out.

"Let's go to the office now, get it over with," I heard Linus call. I held my breath and carefully stepped out of hiding. Newton looked white as a ghost and tried to bolt. Cowie stepped on his tail to keep him still. When I saw the shadow of the hyena start to cross the gateway, I threw the ball as hard as I could.

"What the - BALL!" one of them shouted and began tearing down the bridge. I threw two others and watched the hyenas as they abandoned their posts, chasing the circular entertainment devices across the bridge, down the trail, and out of sight.

"Brilliant Hazel," Cowie whispered, releasing Newton's tail, "Do you have any left?"

"One more," I nodded.

"Unbelievable!" Newton blurted, glaring at Cowie, "When did everyone think it was alright to start *grabbing* dragon's tails?!"

"Shh, not so loud. Don't want to let everyone know we're here," Cowie placed a paw over Newton's mouth to silence him, "We must move quickly and quietly so we don't get caught."

Newton shoved Cowie's paw away and grumbled about how disrespectful we had all become. We crept along the hallway, through the arch furthest to the right, passed the endless stream of badger portraits, and to the staircase that went both up and down. Cowie had read in Schultz's boobytrap book that the ejection platform would not work unless a creature that weighed more than five pounds was standing on it; this was how the rat could retrieve his keys without being shot to the roof. Since Newton was the only one who was under this weight restriction, we agreed he would go down the steps alone. Cowie and I waited at the stairwell entrance as Newton fled down the steps.

"Do you think the keys are still there? What if they changed the trap? Or moved them because they knew we would come back for them?" I asked fearfully, wondering if Schultz would have noticed his book was gone and rearranged the whole castle to confuse us.

"I don't know. Even if the keys are not there, Newton will be fine, he isn't heavy enough to set off any traps."

I hoped Cowie was right. After several painfully silent minutes, there was a jangling of keys and scratching footsteps echoing through the stairs. A moment later Newton came bounding up to Cowie with the key ring clutched in his mouth.

"Splendid job Newton," commended Cowie.

Newton was sweating and breathless and did not acknowledge the praise. He climbed onto Cowie's back and collapsed in a heap. I took the keys and placed them in my dress pocket.

I followed Cowie as we crept up the other staircase. The stairs rose in twists and turns before spiralling downward. According to the map in Schultz's book, we were headed in the direction of the dungeons. Everything was going perfectly. Checking the book every so often, Cowie guided us around plants that would bite you and sound an alarm, over false stones that would drop out the moment anyone stepped on them, under trip wires that would wrap you in a cocoon of rubber bands, out of reach of falling nets, and through various doorways that led either to the dungeon or back to Schultz's office.

"We're nearly to the dungeons now," Cowie announced as we entered a narrow stone staircase with no railings and nothing but blackness underneath it. At the end of the steps we came to a long row of doors that were all labelled 11

"Is this in the book?" I asked Cowie. I hadn't seen this in any of the instructions.

"Of course it's not!" A loud dry voice called from the top of the stairs. Cowie growled deeply, Newton screamed and leapt into my backpack. A furry squirrel parachuted down and landed on the platform in front of the doors. He unbuckled his parachute and snapped his fingers. The parachute folded itself up in an instant and leapt into a pack that was fastened to his back.

"You must be . . . the breech!" the squirrel glared at us through black beady eyes. His arms were crossed over his chest and he wore a blue helmet with a emu feather sticking out of the top, "I wondered when you would arrive." He stood right in front of me and stomped his foot on the ground. "Where's my book!"

"I don't know what you mean," I said meekly.

The squirrel gasped, clenched his fists and paced before us. "Don't play innocent! I know it was you! The weasels told me that you were running around the island and sticking your nose in places you shouldn't. 'Hazel,' they had said, 'A young adventurer with the book from Bill Sploot and a great dog-' "

"And a dragon," Newton muttered from the backpack.

The squirrel continued unfazed, "They said she was coming to rescue the traveller. I sent out my spies and they saw you, they did. They saw you sneak into the forest chasing after a light," My face flushed with embarrassment and I heard Newton gasp. The squirrel continued, "Next thing you know a trap is tripped and my book disappears! *YOU* stole it! You stole my book!" he pointed a crooked finger at me.

"I didn't!"

The squirrel snatched the keys from my pocket, "Then how did you get *these?!*"

I shrugged weakly, "I forgot? I'm sorry it was an accident?" I tried.

Mocking laughter escaped the squirrel. "As if you could accidentally steal keys from the great Schultz!"

I looked at Cowie, imploring him to do something, but he just stood there and growled. Schultz continued his speech, "When I realized the information was compromised, I set to setting a trap. It's been a lot of work to move everything around; I had to recruit some beavers of course, hired some moles for the digging too, but we did it!" He laughed through crooked teeth. "And now you have fallen prey into my hands."

"Can't we fight him?" I whispered to Cowie.

"Don't be such a fool," Schultz hissed. "You don't know who you are messing with. You don't know the power we have." He snapped his fingers and yelled loudly, his voice booming through the staircase: "Linus! Schmidt! Nelson!"

No one answered. Schultz rolled his eyes, "those *useless* hyenas." He reached into his pack and pulled out a glowing blue stone. He pressed the top before yelling to the rock, "Melvin! Sharp! Kevin!"

Instantly three blue ropes raced down from the ceiling and jet black weasels rappelled down in perfect synchronization. They were very large weasels, standing taller than me on their hind legs. They had blue ties with W.S.S embroidered on the front.

"President Schultz!" they saluted.

"Take them!" Schultz glared, his eyes glinting black darkness.

"Aye sir!"

Cowie growled as an electric blue choker was tossed around his neck. The weasels tied my hands behind my back with very thick scratchy cord and Schultz took my backpack.

"You can't!" I cried.

"Can't what?" Asked Schultz, trying unsuccessfully to open the clasps.

"You - you - you *can't* take my backpack away!" I stammered through fearful gulps of air. A weasel struck me across the face with his hand. "That's enough of that," said a crude voice. "Now march!"

Feazel

The weasels marched Cowie and I through one of the doors labelled number 11. We were shoved through a dirty hallway and into a rocky elevator that clanked and clattered as it climbed up the castle. We passed a small room where mice were running along the ground to spin a large gear wheel. A tall white mouse was standing beside the gear and wearing blue coveralls that read: "Mouse Ahoy: Elevator Function & Maintenance."

Up and up, the elevator climbed until it stopped and opened to face a large light milky purple double door. The W.S.S. weasels all cleared their throats and adjusted their ties before knocking firmly on the door eleven times.

"Enter," a feeble voice called.

One of the weasels pushed the doors open and we were shoved into a throne room that was decorated in the same milky purple as the door. A fat badger was sitting in a gold throne with soft purple cushions. On his head, a silver crown with purple gems sat precariously to the left. His purple robes were gathered around him like a blanket and he was eating mint chocolate chip ice cream out of a blue bowl that was balanced on his stomach.

"What is your business?" he asked, squinting in our direction.

"We have spies, King Feazel," announced one of the weasels. "The adventurer Hazel and her dog, Cowie."

I didn't hear Newton announce his presence. My heart sunk as I realized that he had been taken with the backpack.

"Spies you say?" Feazel huffed, moved his ice cream off his stomach, and adjusted his robes. He sat up straight, retrieved a telescope from the table beside him and peered through it. "Oh yes, yes, I see," his voice changed and he suddenly became very intimidating.

"They are here to rescue the traveller," another weasel said accusingly.

The badger glared stiffly. He put down his telescope, climbed out of his chair, and strutted across the throne

292

room to stand in front of us. He had a bit of chocolate stuck between his two front teeth and his breath smelled very bad.

"Adventurers you say," he clasped his hands behind his back and began pacing back and forth. He walked with his chest up and his nose in the air. His feet landed heavily on the ground and his cloak swooshed dramatically as he turned back and forth. "I suppose you think you are brave, seeking to help the traveller that is trapped in the dungeon." He paused and shot a glare at me, "I suppose you think you are the true hero, valiant and selfless. Yet, you know not who you are rescuing. A sorcerer, a corrupt power, a trespasser into *my* kingdom! Landing without warning, without invitation or permission, in the pass that is governed by my rule. Such an offence warrants one thing and one thing only - death!" He yelled the last word before continuing in a whisper, "Ahh but haven't you done the same?" He stood in front of me, peering into my eyes. "Trespassing, entering my territory without warning, invitation, or permission? Into the castle that I rule? Into my *home?* Well, oh brave adventurer, let me assure you that you will never, *ever* leave, this castle, again. You will go down the rubbish chute."

He turned to the weasels in ties, "I will see to this. Be gone!"

"As you wish, Sir!"

The W.S.S weasels bowed low and left us in the throne room. I heard the churning of gears as the elevator lowered through the shaft.

Feazel let out a menacing laugh, "Now, let us-"

His speech was interrupted by a voice in the shadows, "Quite enough for now, Archibald."

I froze.

I recognized that voice.

Where had I heard it before?

The badger's eyes fell and his whole demeanour relaxed. Once again he hunched over and let his stomach hang forward. He shrugged his shoulder and turned around, waddling back to his throne, "I was just getting into character. You know," he held his hands out powerfully, "King Feazel!"

"Hazel, Hazel, Hazel," the voice called again. "I have given you so many chances and yet you insist on pursuing your foolish adventure."

Cowie was growling. The voice was coming from high up in a dark corner, "I like you, you know. I wanted to give you a way out. I didn't want it to come to this. Oh dear child, why do you insist on making me do this to you?"

The delicate sound of feet landing on the heavy carpet drifted to my ears. Out from the shadows stepped a fox - Francis. I gasped. Francis chuckled, "Didn't expect to see me here? Who did you expect? Honestly, who else could run this show? Surely you didn't think that a badger could manage this castle and rule over the land?"

"You're…" I stammered, pointing a shaky finger at him, "Francis."

"Yes, I am. Francis Fitzgerald Feazel." Francis sat up proudly, "the third, of course." He flicked his tail back and forth. "I have inherited this kingdom from my father, and my father from his father, and his father from his father. *We* are the Feazels, the rightful rulers!" He gestured a paw towards the clumsy badger on the throne, "Archibald here is merely an actor."

"Thespian!" Archibald corrected, "Acting is beneath me." He looked toward me pleadingly. "I mean, I was convincing, wasn't I?"

I nodded awkwardly. I had thought he was the Feazel.

"And do you like the decor?" Archibald asked hopefully. "It is new. Milky purple is my favourite colour and I've been trying to convince Francis that we need to move away from that horrid blue that he is so fond of."

Francis rolled his eyes.

"Very well, *thespian*. Now silence Archibald before I set your brother in your place."

Archibald gasped and sat back with his arms crossed.

"See the badgers are…. The face of Feazel - the insurance, if you will. Many have gone before him and many will come after."

I watched Francis walk slow circles around me, his tail brushing against me when he spoke, "Now is your last chance Hazel. Abandon this adventure and come work with me instead."

"Never!" I nearly shouted.

"Are you so sure?" he showed his teeth and his voice lowered and hissed, "Let me make your choice clear: you work with me or you will simply be another adventurer that lands in the jaws of Angus."

I shuddered. I didn't ever want to think of meeting that hideous fish again. Cowie pushed his nose under my hand and I felt myself draw courage from him. I remembered what Wordy and Mr. Sploot had said about resilience, I remembered what was true and what was right. I looked Francis dead in the eye and said as steady as I could, "I would rather meet Angus one hundred times over than work with you for one minute."

Francis smiled coldly, "Perhaps you will get your wish. Archibald! See if a night in the dungeon won't change their minds."

"Yes sir," Archibald grunted.

I watched Francis disappear back into the shadows. Archibald called the W.S.S. Agents back into the throne room and ordered them to throw us into the dungeon. "Set the spikes and give them no food or drink!"

"Aye sir!"

Chapter 38

The Dungeon

Once again we were made to march. We were pushed through the purple doors, down the elevator, through a different door which was also labelled eleven, down a twisty staircase, and into a cold damp room full of tiny cells. I was thrown into one cell and Cowie was thrown into another.

A grizzly old rat with greying fur, missing teeth, and whiskers that were singed and bent, slammed the doors behind us before turning the locks.

"Steal my *keys* will you?" a croaky voice squeezed out of the rat, "This will teach you." He pulled a lever down and long spikes shot out of the walls of both the cells. Now there was not enough room to sit on the ground without sitting on a spike. I was pressed against the cage wall that Cowie and I shared with hardly any room to breathe. Cowie was looking quite uncomfortable in the cell next to me. He had been tied to the wall by his choker, and a spike had shot out and nicked the end of his nose.

"Well this is a twist," Cowie said calmly.

The rat crackled a dry laugh. "I'll show you a twist," he said. He clamped three additional padlocks on Cowie's cell door and onto mine, "No good adventurers."

I was too tired and too scared to cry. We watched silently while the rat scribbled something in a book on the dungeon desk, taking great gulps from a metal canister, and smoking a very short but very round pipe that shot little flames out and kept igniting his whiskers. After writing, he leaned back in his chair, crossed is arms behind his head, propped his feet on the desk, and began to snore.

When I was sure the rat had fallen sound asleep I whispered to Cowie, "What are they going to do to Newton?"

"Don't think about that right now," he answered. "See if you can cut your cords on the spikes."

Cautiously I turned my head and stepped backwards so a sharp spike stuck into my bonds. Carefully I moved the spike up and down my restraints, cutting little threads each time. I was just about through them when the dungeon door swung open with a bang. The rat startled and jumped awake, knocking his chair over, and spilling his drink.

"Really, again Roy?" a weasel pointed to the spill, "Now I have to take you to Schultz."

"Nope, not going, can't make me," Roy scribbled something down in his book and pointed to an empty cell. The weasel rolled his eyes, opened the cell, set the spikes, and threw a very limp Newton inside.

"Come along now Roy, let's not do this the hard way," he said as he took the rat's arm and led him out the door, slamming it shut behind them.

"Newton!" I stared at him, making the final cuts to free my wrists. "What's wrong with you?"

He lay flat on his back with his limbs splayed on the floor, "Wrong?" he smiled sleepily, "Nothin's wrong! See? I got no hiccups!"

"Newton," scolded Cowie, "you're only supposed to take that for height induced hiccups."

"Don't get mad at me, it spilled in the backpack. I just cleaned some of it up before it could er'... do any damage." A burp escaped his throat and he covered his mouth shyly. "Don't get mad Cowie... you getting mad at me makes me nervous."

"Well maybe you should be nervous!" I snapped, "We're stuck in the dungeon. We're supposed to be the ones rescuing someone and now we will need someone to rescue us. We're going to the rubbish chute."

"Calm down Hazel," Cowie chimed. I took a deep breath.

"Well it's not all my fault!" Newton defended himself. A burp gurgling up again.

"It's no one's fault," said Cowie, "and there's no point in arguing about it. We need to put our heads together and figure out what to do next."

"Yes, Cowie!" Newton jumped, "That's the spirit. First one to have an idea wins!"

As if this was a game, Newton was being ridiculous. I rolled my eyes. Everyone sat in their cells in contemplative silence. Newton sputtered every few moments: "Oh oh oh I know!!" followed by a brief pause and, "oh dear but that would never work" and something ridiculous like "where would we find a unicorn seashell at this hour?" or "no, Angus probably wouldn't just let us leave the lake even if we asked nicely." I wondered just how much of his medicine he had taken.

Water dripped down from the roof and splashed on the floor of my cell in a chilly rhythm. We couldn't see the sun so there was no idea of knowing how much time we had spent in the castle so far, days could have passed for all we knew. I shuddered at the thought. I was starting to feel rather hungry and thirsty.

"Underground Postal Service!" a voice called from behind the cell wall. There was a creak as a gopher pushed one of the spikes out of the wall and wriggled into Newton's cell, pulling his mail bag behind him.

"From your mother," the gopher passed Newton a large package. "Sign here," he said as he held out a clipboard. Newton had already become distracted by the package. He opened it and found a large canister of blueberry juice and a box of pumpkin squares.

Newton, Fritz sent me your note. Glad to know you are safe. Let me know if you need anything. Love Mom.

"Sign here," the gopher called again.

"Really?" Newton snapped, staring at the letter, "We're in jail and the postal service can get here to deliver squares and blueberry juice but not keys?"

"We're keeping you connected wherever you go!" said the gopher proudly. "Sign here, please," he pointed to the clipboard.

Newton grumbled, "Well keep us connected with keys why don't you."

302

Newton's medicine must have been wearing off, he was finally getting irritable again.

"Please," the gopher looked confused, "it's my first day… can you just sign here?"

"Can you just get us keys?" Newton scribbled his signature on the clipboard.

The gopher took the pen and scribbled something down on the paper, "I'll see what I can do!" The gopher swung his carrier on his back and headed back out the hole, replacing the spike behind him. Newton carefully passed some squares through the gap in the cell walls to Cowie. Cowie took two then kicked the rest over to my cell. I reached through the gap and took them gratefully. My stomach growled greedily and I savoured every bite of the pumpkin goodness. Somehow Newton managed to squeeze the canister of juice through the gaps as well. It was delicious. I felt much better with a full stomach.

After another hour or so of silence Newton asked, "Any ideas yet?"

"No," I said, "Not a one."

Cowie didn't say anything, he just sat thinking silently.

"We need to get out of here," I said, looking helplessly at the padlocks on the door.

As Newton's medicine wore off he became more and more agitated. He started pacing up and down the cage, rattling doors, and getting the hiccups. By the time the gopher reappeared a second time Newton was so nervous his hiccups were twice their regular size and he singed the poor gopher's fur.

"Forget the signature!" the gopher squeaked, tossing Newton an envelope before darting back through the hole, avoiding another streak of fire that nearly scorched his tail.

Newton, sorry to hear you're in jail. I couldn't find any keys lying around but here's a hair pin. I read in one of my mystery books that you can pick any lock with this. Have fun on your adventure! Love, Mom.

Newton looked dismayed. He held up the hair pin, "Seriously?!" he screamed. Fire blasted the pin and it melted like a popsicle, landing with a splat on the ground.

"Newton!" I jumped up happily. He looked at me confused.

"The padlocks!" I pointed.

Murky River

Newton's eyes lit up all at once when he realized my plan. He climbed up his cage door and blasted the lock, which after several bursts of fire, melted away into nothing. He pushed on the door and it swung open freely.

"The keys!" I called.

Newton nodded and darted over to the desk and retrieved the rat's keys which he placed in my hands. It took a great deal of fiddling and testing different keys but I finally unlocked each padlock on my cell and the door swung open. While I had been working on my own locks, Newton had been blasting the locks on Cowie's door and had successfully opened it. I ran out of my cell and pulled the spike lever. I watched the weapons snap back into the wall with a heavy click.

With the spikes gone, I snuck into Cowie's cage and helped him take the blue choker off his neck. Soon, we were all free.

Newton declared he was lightheaded from melting all the locks and so he rode on Cowie's back as we exited the cell and crept out of the dungeon.

"Hooray for you," I patted Newton on the back, "You saved us."

He smiled groggily and closed his eyes.

When we left the dungeon we realized we had no idea where we were going. Cowie had memorized a great deal of the map from Schultz's book but it seemed that Shultz had been very successful in his efforts to change as many things as possible. There were signs we didn't recognize, labels that were foreign, and new boobytraps that had been set up around every corner. We crept along slowly and carefully for quite some time before anyone dared to speak.

"Cowie?" I whispered, "Why didn't he just throw us to Angus?"

It was a horrible question but I had thought about it a great deal while we were stuck in the dungeon. If we were really just a thorn in Feazel's side, why wouldn't he just throw us down the rubbish chute? Why give us until morning to decide? And if he was after me, why did he spare Newton and Cowie?

"He wants your power," Newton muttered, "And mine and Cowie's."

"What do you mean?" I asked.

Cowie whispered, "Adventurers and guides are not exactly like everyone around them. They are special. They travel between worlds, meet all sorts of people, collect tools of wisdom, and are given great gifts... gifts that they can use for good or for evil. You, Newton, and I have all chosen to use our gifts for good. Francis... well he has made his own choice"

A shudder went through my spine.

"Is Francis evil?" I asked.

Cowie was silent for a moment. We turned and walked down a hall to the left. "I cannot say if he himself is evil," he replied, "but he has chosen to use his gifts to do wrong and so he fights for evil. He takes the easy ways, believes in shortcuts, spreads lies, and hurts anyone who opposes him. There is not very much truth, kindness, or goodness in him if there is any at all."

"There's not any at all," Newton retorted.

Cowie clucked his tongue, "That is not for you to say Newton."

"So, why hasn't he sent us down the rubbish chute?" I asked again.

"Didn't I already explain this?" Newton sighed.

"Because you have power," Cowie answered. I didn't feel particularly powerful. He continued, "The more power he can get, the better. He thinks he can scare us into choosing his side."

I was aghast, "I will never choose his side, not in a million nights in the dungeon."

Newton smiled at me proudly.

"Not everyone is so strong," Cowie said. "Many creatures have chosen his side because they are afraid of him. It would surprise you who has."

The corridor came to a very mossy staircase that went down. We crept along silently. At the bottom of the steps ran a greenish grey river. There was a splash and a sputter as Fritz jumped out with his green bag and his book.

"I've been waiting for you. What took so long? Honestly, making old Fritz wait in the Murky River all day," he chuckled and gave a fake shudder. He reached into his bag and passed me my backpack. I squealed with delight, clutching it in my hands. "These young adventurers," he said. "Always cleaning up after them.

Didn't you know your mother isn't on this trip with you?" He winked at me.

"Thank you, Fritz!" I said.

"You're welcome," He bowed gallantly, "Lucky thing I got it when I did. I had to wrestle it away from one of the eels."

"You did?" I was shocked, Fritz certainly didn't look like he'd win in a tangle with an eel.

"Don't look so surprised. I've been fighting eels since I was knee-high to a seahorse. Once you've fought one you've fought them all. You're lucky you had the waterproof clasps closed, kept your books safe. Those fools can't ever open the clasps."

"How do you fight an eel?" I felt the need to prepare myself in case Francis ended up throwing us down the rubbish chute after all.

"Well the same way you fight anything that works for the Feazel ma'am. I must be off. Much to do, Wordy has called a circle for later today. Only a few hours from now. I will see you there I hope."

Fritz disappeared with a splash and was gone before I could ask any questions.

"What does that mean? Same way you fight anything that works for the Feazel," I asked distraught,

I didn't know how to fight anything that works for the Feazel.

Cowie chuckled, "One battle at a time Hazel. You will learn how to fight the things that work for the Feazel. Besides, Newton is a dragon, he can protect us all from the eels."

Newton's eyes bulged out of his head and he swallowed hard.

While we walked along the river I checked my bag. The thing-a-ma-jig was now bent beyond function but my adventure books were both in tact, my letters from Wordy still tucked safely away, and the rock that Fritz had given me was nestled in the bottom. An empty bottle of Height Hiccup Healing Herbs was tucked in the folds on the side.

"You drank all of it?" I asked, holding up the bottle to Newton's face.

"I was stressed!" he defended, a hiccup shooting a flame out of his mouth.

Tucked in the very bottom corner of the bag there was something I didn't recognize, a glass jar with a black cork tightly wedged in the top. Dark blue liquid splashed in the bottom. I checked my adventure book. There was an entry written in someone else's hand: *Only what is true can pass through the blue*.

I wondered who had written it and what it meant.

"Come along," Cowie called, "Got to keep moving."

I returned the item to my backpack and closed the clasps, trying to guess what the blue liquid might be. We followed the river to the end of the hall. The river turned left and travelled through a very small pipe and the corridor turned right and led into an increasingly narrow passage where the floor had gaping holes. At first I didn't think I would be able to jump far enough to cross the gaps but leap by leap I gained more confidence.

We had finally made it to a place where the hall widened and the floor was cohesive when I heard a cranking of gears turning behind the stones. I turned to Cowie, "What is that?"

Before anyone could answer, a door in the wall slid open.

Chapter 40

Teetor-Totter Corridor

We ducked behind a rotting wooden beam and crouched low, hoping the shadows would keep us from being seen by the elevator occupants.

"I told you we went too far down!" one hyena called out from the shaft.

"How was I supposed to know?" barked a second. "He's just added the dungeon to the extra enhanced inspection, I've never even been there. I swear I'm going to quit if he adds one more thing to our list!"

The elevator doors closed with a thud, the gears carrying the hyenas back up the castle. We all crept out of hiding and let out a heavy sigh.

"You know what this means don't you?" Newton asked solemnly.

"What?" I turned to face him.

"They will know we're gone."

The gravity of that statement hung in the air for a moment.

"Right, better move along then," Cowie finally said.

At the end of the hall there was a black door that led to a round narrow staircase that was weathered and crumbling. Along the way down there were entire steps missing and we had to jump across the gaps to avoid falling into the darkness below.

"How has this castle not fallen to shambles?" Newton shook his head.

Moss made the steps slippery underfoot and Cowie caught me as I began to fall down the stairs several times. I went as fast as I dared and tried very hard not to think about how Francis would soon be notified that we weren't in our cells. I didn't want to imagine what would happen if he caught us and tossed us down the rubbish chute.

Consumed by my private anxieties, I lost total track of time. The walls dripped grey water as the murky lake seeped through and made the air chilly and humid. It was very unpleasant. We came to a door with nothing written on it. The steps continued down but I felt we must have walked far enough to reach The Stinky by now.

"Is this The Stinky?" I asked.

"We haven't walked down far enough yet," Newton said, "The Stinky is very deep under the dungeons."

"We are very deep under the dungeons. Have you been there before?" I asked.

Newton shook his head but he insisted that he had enough friends who had been down to The Stinky and so he knew better than I did where it was and that we had *not* walked far enough.

Curious, I turned the door handle and pushed it open. The door swung back with an echoey squeak and collided with the adjacent wall. An eery thud drifted through the chamber. A long skinny walkway, something like a balance beam, stretched out from the doorway. It reached to another door on the opposite side of the chasm.

Tentatively I stepped one foot on the stone beam. It creaked loudly under my weight. I stepped my other foot forward and the whole beam started tipping down. Cowie picked me up by my backpack and pulled me back through the doorframe as the beam started to drop. As soon as my feet left the beam, the floor righted itself and swung back in line with the two doors.

"I should've known," said Cowie, "It looked different in the drawing."

"What is it?" I asked.

"The Teeter-Totter Corridor," Cowie replied. "It's the shortest way to The Stinky but I'm afraid that it is the most dangerous."

"It doesn't look that dangerous," I gazed across the teeter totter.

"Think again," Cowie retorted. "If you time anything wrong and slip off the beam, you will be dumped into the bottom of the chasm."

"What's at the bottom of the chasm?"

Cowie shook his head, "Best not to think about it."

"Angus," Muttered Newton.

I steadied myself, "Do you think we can we make it across?"

"We can," Cowie said. "If you listen very carefully and do exactly as I say - both of you," he looked at Newton who rolled his eyes.

"Let's do it," I nodded my head.

"Newton, you will go first since you are the lightest," instructed Cowie.

Newton muttered that by lightest Cowie actually meant the most expendable.

"Do you think that you can jump up and hold onto the handle to turn it?" Cowie asked.

Newton scoffed, "You doubt my abilities?"

"It is quite high," I reminded Newton.

Newtons face looked slightly green and I heard the beginning gurgles of hiccups. "Well," he said, "there comes a time to just do what needs to be done."

"When did you get so brave?" I asked.

"Well we get out of here today one way or another," he said, "across this thing or down the chute."

I didn't reply, that was a fair point.

"Run fast to the middle and wait for the beam to balance itself before running to the other side," Cowie instructed.

Newton nodded and fixed his gaze sternly ahead, stifling hiccups.

"You will be fine," Cowie reassured.

Newton cleared his throat and stepped towards the edge of the doorway. He leapt on the platform which groaned menacingly. In a bright orange flash, he ran to the middle of the walkway. The beam shifted up and then down and gradually righted itself. A hiccup escaped Newton's mouth and a short burst of fire flashed in the air. As soon as the beam stopped moving, he darted to the other side. He leapt so high that he nearly missed the doorknob, catching it with the corner of his tail as he started plummeting down. Bracing himself against the door frame, he turned the handle, and swung the door open. He leapt through the doorway and collapsed on the ground, sending up a stream of fire before signalling a thumbs up.

"Would you like to go now?" Cowie asked.

I shook my head furiously. I told myself that if I watched one more time I would be more prepared, really I was just scared.

"Alright," he agreed.

Cowie stepped gracefully down onto the platform which immediately started swinging down under his weight. Carefully but quickly he walked to the middle. The teeter-totter had swung so low under his weight that it was a scramble for him to reach the centre. Before the beam had righted itself, when the side closest to me was at a very low point, he raced up the other side. With a great leap he launched himself from the beam and through the doorway. The platform made several tremendous reaches upward and downward before stopping to connect the doors one again.

"It's your turn," Cowie called, "Make sure you close the door behind you."

Oh dear, I hadn't thought of that! How was I going to manage walking and closing the door? My mouth dried up and my knees knocked together.

"It's alright," Newton called. "If I can do it," hiccup, "so can you!"

I reached around the entrance and took hold of the door handle. I tiptoed onto the beam and swung the door shut behind me with a bang. The slam shook a vibration up and down the chasm with an aggressive echo. I could feel the beam dropping under my feet, reaching down the chute. I could see that Cowie was yelling instructions at me but I couldn't hear him. I could only hear my heart in my ears. Everything slowed down. I stared dumbly ahead, only waking up when I felt my feet start to slide backwards. Suddenly my legs found their strength and I ran up to the middle of the beam, barely making it to the centre. I lay on my stomach and clung to the side of the teeter totter as it rocked up and down in a wild effort to find balance. Even when the beam righted itself I stayed frozen on the ground, too terrified to move forward.

"Come on Hazel," I finally heard Cowie calling. "You have to keep going."

I turned my face to see Cowie and Newton staring at me with concerned eyes. "You can do it!" Newton called.

I stood up carefully and looked towards the door.

"Come along Hazel," Cowie barked. "Just run as fast as you can and then jump."

I closed my eyes and steadied my breathing. Wordy's voice drifted through my mind, "*When it takes all your strength, all your strength you must muster.*" I locked my eyes on the frame. Three counts went in my head and I raced along the beam, I felt the ground dropping lower underneath me and watched the doorway get a little bit higher and a little bit higher. Mustering all of my strength I leapt up as high as I could. My fingertips barely landed on the edge of the doorframe. I tried to grip the stone and pull myself up but the dirt and dust made it slippery. I felt all at once that I was about to fall backwards and be lost down the rubbish chute.

Chapter 41

The Final Bridge

Just as my fingers began to loose their last grip, the beam swung back up and pushed me through the door. I crashed into Cowie and knocked him onto the floor. Newton patted my back and cheered in my ear. Cowie stood up, licked my cheek, and helped me to my feet.

"Well done!" They said over and over.

Nervous laughter escaped from my throat. My arms and legs were still shaking with adrenalin. I looked down the hall to see what scary thing we had to meet next. At the end, there was a round room with no doors and no windows. In the middle of the room there stood something that looked like a merry go round.

"Where do we go from here?" I stood on the contraption, confused.

"Why, have you never seen a merry go round before?" Newton asked, sounding rather delighted. He scampered over to the centre and sat on the floor, "These are my favourite. They're the old school elevators."

"Old school elevators?"

Newton nodded. "Yes, they used these before they got the mice to power them by running through the wheels. These haven't been used in decades."

Cowie started moving the merry go round in circles. It creaked and protested for a moment before sputtering a dusty smoke and picking up speed. Cowie leapt on just as it started to spiral downwards. It moved terribly slow and at times I was concerned that it had stopped moving all together and we were going to be permanently stuck in a hidden elevator shaft.

Eventually we did stop.

We had arrived at the bottom of the elevator shaft and into another round room that had the nauseating stench of rotting earth. Blue light glowed in rock lanterns along the wall. Water dripped from the ceiling and splashed in puddles on the muddy floor. Everything was slimy and scummy and I tried not to gag every time I breathed in.

"Is this The Stinky?" I asked.

"Not quite, we are nearly there though," Cowie replied. "If my guess is correct, I'd say we'll be coming up on the doors soon."

"The doors?"

He nodded slowly. The corridor looped in circles and led into another round room that was lined with doors. Each door had a strange shape on it. I stared at them, turned my head one way, turned my head another, and asked Cowie and Newton if they knew what they were. Newton looked as puzzled as I was and Cowie shook his head but I had the feeling he wasn't trying very hard to help figure it out. Suspicious.

I stared at the doors and tilted my head so I saw the symbols upside down.

"They're letters!" I shouted.

Newton lay on his back and looked at them upside down before gasping and agreeing with my conclusion. Cowie nodded his approval.

I scanned around for G but it wasn't there, "There's no number G."

"Of course there's not," Newton scoffed. "G isn't a number."

"No…," I said, "it's a letter," I counted, "the 7th letter."

Quickly I scanned the the doors and looked at the figures, sure enough there was an upside down seven on one of them.

"This one," I pointed to it.

"There's no handle," Newton gestured.

Of course there wouldn't be a handle. Nothing on this adventure could be easy. This was getting so much more complicated than I had been prepared for. I pushed on the door to see if it would swing open, nothing happened. I looked around for a button or a rope or a lock, there was nothing. Then I remembered Feazel's throne room and I knocked on the door eleven times, just as I had seen the W.S.S. weasels do. The door quivered and shook before sliding to the left and revealing a shaky wooden bridge. There were so many steps missing that it would be impossible to cross it. The ropes holding it up looked feeble and unreliable. I stepped to the edge of the door frame and peered down.

Underneath the swing there was a blanket of white fluffy clouds, I couldn't see what was beneath them. I glanced up and gasped horrified.

"What is it?" Newton scampered up to my shoulder and looked up at the sky.

Above the bridge, dreadfully close to my head, was Murky Lake. The water rippled above us as eels swarmed, trying to reach through the water to get at us. I heard Newton swallowing hiccups beside me.

"Don't do that," Cowie said. "You'll get heartburn."

Newton took several steady deep breaths and poked my shoulder, "you better check the book."

I flipped through the pages and found a line from Wordy's letter. I read it aloud: *"To cross the final bridge, you must look over not under."* I snapped it shut. "Is this the final bridge?"

"I believe so," Cowie nodded.

I glanced up over the bridge at the swarming eels. "You're sure?"

Cowie squeezed beside me and looked up at Murky Lake, "I'm sure."

I looked down at the clouds. I was considering how much easier it would be to go under the bridge than over it. After all, I had walked across clouds before.

I had also learned that "easier" was a mistake more often than not. I had to find a way to look at this all the way through.

I got an idea.

I took my backpack off my shoulders, taking care not to knock Newton over, and took the remaining bouncy ball out of my pack. I stepped one foot on the bridge and it squeaked under my weight, I could feel that the ropes were about to snap. I threw the ball and watched it bounce on one of the boards, breaking it instantly. The ball plummeted down and landed on the cloud which opened to reveal red steaming lava which devoured the ball in a heap of flames.

There I had it, going down was not an option.

Looking up I turned my attention away from the eels and started looking for a way to get through the lake. There only seemed to be one entrance, a trap door with a red sign that said: BEWARE: EELS ON DUTY. I lifted my hand and reached for the latch.

"It says beware," Newton pointed out.

I turned to face him, "If you see another way to go over, I'm open to hearing about it. This is the only way I see and Wordy said we're supposed to go over."

Newton looked around desperately but ended up agreeing that this door was the only one. The eels were ramming their heads against the door, their teeth biting at the glass. I was afraid, but I had faith that this was the way Wordy told me to go and so it was good. I pulled the latch on the door.

Chapter 42

Stinky of Stinkies

When the door opened I held my breath. I expected a downpour of eels, water, and to come face to face with Angus. Instead of water, I met blackness. Darkness spilled out of the door and crowded all around us. The door faded, the bridge and the clouds beneath it faded, and I found myself floating in mid air with Newton still clinging to my shoulder and Cowie pressed against my side. I could not tell whether my eyes were opened or closed for a moment. Then just as the blackness had come, it vanished. We were standing at the top of a series of steps that led to a dingy dungeon that smelled positively putrid.

Moss covered the walls, water leaked through the roof and trickled down, and in the middle of the slanted floor, there was a black cage trap door that looked something like a vent.

"The Stinky," Cowie whispered.

As we descended the steps I looked into one of the cells and saw stacks of bones in the shadow. I shuddered and closed my eyes. At the bottom of the steps I heard something, it was coming from below the caged door. A gentle melodic hum.

"Hello?" I called, rushing over to the vent.

The humming stopped.

"Is someone down there?" I peered through the black metal.

"You don't sound like the rat," a voice answered. It was a girl who sounded no older than I.

"It's not the rat," I replied excitedly, realizing we had found the traveller. "It's Hazel. Hazel with Cowie and Newton. We've come to rescue you!"

My words were met with a heavy sigh.

"You can't get down here," the girl said. "And besides, you're probably not even real. I'm probably just imagining you like I've imagined all the others. No one can get down here."

"You're not imagining! We are real," I assured her. "And why do you say we can't get down?"

"Because you can't, there's no way down and there's no way up. I'm trapped down here forever. This is the end of my story," she started humming her dreary tune again.

I looked to Cowie and whispered so the girl couldn't hear, "What do we do? We haven't come this far to get stuck now!"

Newton was scrounging the dungeons for anything useful. He shook his head solemnly when I asked if he had found anything. I peered through the door, I couldn't see anything. The stench was so powerful that I nearly became ill when I breathed in. I wondered how the traveller below must feel.

"Don't worry we will get you out," I called.

The girl chuckled softly before she resumed her humming. A soft glow appeared under the neck of my dress as she hummed. I felt the chain that Wordy had given me when he painted the sunrise. In all the excitement I had forgotten all about it. Why was it glowing? I unfastened it from my neck and placed it in my hands to get a better look. It was a small sun pendant. In the centre there was a swirling yellow glow. I turned it over in my hand. Engraved on the gold back were the words, "in case of emergency break glass." I placed the necklace on the ground and picked up a loose stone, I raised it above my head before bringing it down heavily on the glass face.

"What are you doing?" cried Newton when he saw me violently attacking my necklace.

"This is an emergency," I said, taking a final swing at the pendant and shattering the glass. A gold shimmery liquid ray of sunshine trickled down through the cracks in the stones, dripped through the vent, and shone into The Stinky of Stinkies.

The girl under the vent shrieked, "What is that?!"

"It's liquid sunshine!" I called, "It's alright!"

There was silence down below. The light expanded into a shimmering gold staircase. "Come up!" I called to the girl.

"No," said Cowie, who had been unusually quiet this whole time, "we go down."

"Why?" I asked.

"Do you trust me?" Cowie's gaze fixed on mine.

One by one we climbed down the steps of the sun rays. Mice skittered across the floor below. At the bottom of the stairway we met a very dirty girl with wild brown hair and bright blue eyes. She was sitting huddled in a corner, looking like a stack of bones that was wrapped in skin. Her green clothes were ripped and torn and there was blood on her pants.

329

"Are you a ghost?" she asked me.

I shook my head and thought that she looked much more like a ghost than I did. Her skin was pale and had cracks running over it. Newton scampered up to sit on my shoulder very quietly. Cowie walked over to the girl slowly, keeping his head down low. The girl backed away frightened. "It's alright," he reassured her. He walked patiently to the corner she was crouched in and nudged her hand with his nose until she pet him.

"What's your name?" I asked gently, my words vibrating through the stone dungeon.

"I'm Cadence," she said. Her eyes were fixed wide open and she stared at Newton and I like she didn't fully trust that we were real.

"Cadence is a nice name," I said. "It sounds like music."

She smiled slightly. "As a true dragon healer's name should," she said.

"Where are you from?" I asked.

"I am from Theoze," she replied. "Under the Crystal Sea."

She stroked Cowie's head softly and kissed his nose.

"I am sorry I don't quite know where that is," I said.

"Far from here," her face fell and her eyes looked sorrowful. I wondered how long it had been since she had seen her home. When I asked her how long she had been in the castle she didn't know, "I lost track of time because there's no light."

"Well would you like to stay down here and figure out how to keep track of time or shall we be off?" Newton chimed in, sounding rather stressed.

"How are we going to get out?" Cadence asked.

"Same way we got in," Cowie smiled.

"Oh, I wish I hadn't lost my spiggle to those birds when I arrived," Cadence muttered.

"Spiggle?" I had never heard that word before.

"You wouldn't know it," she sighed and waved her hand. "To you it would just look like an ordinary rock."

Cowie led the way up the stairs with Cadence, Newton walked behind, and I followed last. I watched Cadence's fragile frame hold onto Cowie for support. I wasn't sure what sort of person I had expected to find in the bottom of the most desolate dungeon in the world, but I had not expected them to look quite so ghastly. I felt sorry for her and wished we had some squares and blueberry juice to give her.

What was the word she had said?

Oh yes, Spiggle. I wondered what one looked like; hadn't she said if I saw one it would seem like an ordinary rock? Fritz had given me a very ordinary looking rock. We reached the top of the sun staircase and I was just slipping my backpack off my shoulders to search for the rock when Newton interrupted."Going to leave a mess for Fritz again are we?" He joked, pointing to the shattered glass from my necklace. "Tsk tsk tsk."

I smirked at him and picked up the remnants of the gift, a solid gold ring on a delicate gold chain. I draped it around my wrist and again reached for my backpack but was stopped by an all too familiar voice that called from the top of the stairs: "Not so fast!"

Chapter 43

The Blue Tree

Francis Feazel was perched at the top of the stone steps leading out of The Stinky, blocking our only way out. He was sitting up regally with his tail twitching back and forth. His smooth voice crooned, "Hazel, my dear, you have put me in a very awkward position."

I steadied my nerves and asked as calmly as I could, "How's that?"

Slowly I crept behind Cowie and took my bag off my shoulders. As I placed it on the ground I snapped the buckles open and undid the zipper. Francis watched me carefully but evidently thought he had the upper hand and therefor was unconcerned that I was digging through a bag.

"I had wanted to give you another chance but now you have shown me such immense disrespect that you have forced my hand," he said, "I am afraid that I have to kill you."

My stomach lurched and I felt my heart skip a few beats. I was not ready to die. I had so many other worlds to see and adventures to have. Francis slowly rose to his feet and started to walk very casually in our direction.

"You see," he sighed, "now you are of no use to me. You have made your stance clear over and over again. I have given you every opportunity to escape death, truly. Alas, it seems you have chosen it. You refuse my good graces and go behind my back to free my prisoner. How could our relationship ever be repaired, Hazel? I offer you wisdom and opportunity and you just throw it away." He shook his head and I watched a dark spark flash in his eyes.

Newton started hiccuping.

I kept my eyes on the approaching fox while I dug around the inside of my backpack. My hands landed on smooth glass. I remembered the strange blue vile that had been inside when Fritz returned it and the note that was written in my adventure book: *Only what is true can pass through the blue.* There was no truth in Francis, I knew that, this could help! I closed my fingers around the bottle and took it out of my bag. Francis's eyes fixed on it suspiciously as I drew it out. "It's Newton's medicine, for his hiccups," I spoke as confidently as I could.

Francis didn't seem to believe this explanation, he glared at me and started walking towards us faster. He called several names and the door behind him opened. Weasels started pouring into The Stinky and racing down the steps, chattering madly. Newton ran in front of me and yelled hiccupy fire-filled threats at the entourage. Cowie growled and pawed the earth. As quickly as I could I uncorked the bottle, ran forward, and threw the contents onto the ground in front of Francis.

Cowie pulled me back by the collar of my dress as the liquid spread across the path between us and Francis and his weasels. A cold note hung in the air for a moment and everyone stood still. The note grew into an enchanted melody as a deep blue vine grew to cross the stairway. Growling, Francis stepped his foot over the vine. As his fur landed on the blue there was a great sizzle, smoke rose from his paw, and he leapt backwards with a yelp.

The vine thickened, twisted and reached upward, unfolding into a majestic blue tree that spanned the width of the path. Unable to stop themselves, weasels tumbled into the branches and were thrown back, over the staircase, and sucked into the waters above. Shrieks of hungry eels flew through the air. Francis yelled angry threats and made several attempts to cross the tree which was still singing its steely blue song and burning his paws.

But then it stopped.

All at once the tune of the tree held its breath and everything froze in its place. My breathing and pounding heart were the only sounds to be heard. Nothing moved. Everything was still, as if I was standing in the middle of a picture or a painting and not real life. I looked around at the posed figures: Cadence was ducking behind Cowie, Cowie was in a snarling pose with his eyes locked on the fox and teeth bared, Newton was white with terror but standing his ground with fire streaking out of his mouth, the tree was standing frozen and silent with its blue light shining but no longer moving, and the weasels were tumbling over one another, hanging in mid air, and half sucked into the water above.

Francis was sitting motionless on a step. I stared at him and he blinked. I gasped and he laughed as he leapt into the tree. I could see smoke rising from his paws and hear them being singed as he walked. His feet turned black, his eyes glowed red, the hair on his back bristled up, and he seemed to grow at least two feet taller. He walked across the tree and came to stand right in front of me. He looked like a monster. I could feel his breath on my face, hot like fire. He held up a silver pocket watch and clicked a button to open the face.

"Did you ever wonder why 11 is the Feazel's favourite number?" he asked in a patronizing voice.

I offered no reply.

"Come on now Hazel, play along," he sang.

I refused.

He walked slow steady circles around me, his red eyes felt like they were burning my skin and my clothes.

"11 is my favourite, every Feazel's favourite, number," he continued, "because at the precise moment where both of the hands on the clock point to the 11, *I* am the keeper of time."

He pushed a button on the top of his clock and everything around me flashed to life for a second:

Cadence cried out, Newton's fire shot forward, and Cowie lunged at Francis. Francis pushed the button again and everything stopped. A silver forked tongue slithered out of his mouth as he laughed in my face.

He stood up on his legs, growing even taller, and puffed out his chest.

"Oh Hazel. You obstacle in my path. You meddler in my plans. You slave to the *lies* of goodness," his eyes were glowing very bright red now and smoke was coming out his mouth. He crouched down and twitched his tail back and forth, ready to pounce. "Any last words?"

I steadied my breathing and mustered all of my strength. I squeezed the blue vile tight in my hand and said as calmly as I could, "There is no truth in you, you only tell lies. These won't be my last words."

Francis laughed and pounced, his jaws open wide. I fell to the ground and raised my hand up, thrusting the blue vile over my head. I felt his jaw close over my hand and his teeth meet my arm but I didn't feel any pain. There was a loud pop and Francis screamed before he flew backwards, his watch clattering to the floor. He crashed into the blue tree and began rolling over, yelping as blue light shot through his mouth and nose. He pawed clumsily at his face as vines grew

338

around his mouth and bound it shut. I grabbed the watch and opened it. I took hold of the bigger hand as blood dripped down my arm and onto the ground. I pulled at the watch hand with all my might. For a moment nothing happened, I pulled harder, clenching my eyes and gritting my teeth Finally I felt the gears click and the hand give way. Everything leapt back into motion. Newton fainted, Cadence covered her eyes, and Cowie lunged for Francis. I fell onto my back and closed my eyes. I heard an eery foxy cry echo down the chamber and a splash of water followed by an eel shriek.

Then I could hear nothing but the ringing in my own ears. I let go of the watch and let it clatter to the floor. Time slowed down and the world became fuzzy. I saw the gold light of several Grynns fluttering towards me and then felt my body go limp.

Chapter 44

Council Circle

I shook my head and tried to will my eyes to focus.

"Hazel, come on wake up now," Cowie licked my face.

I saw the roof of The Stinky take shape and then Cowie's face staring at me full of concern. I sat up in a daze. My arm was wrapped in white cloth.

"What happened?" I asked.

"You beat Francis," Cowie explained calmly, "but we still need to get out of here."

He nudged the ring that was dangling off my wrist. I slipped it off my hand and passed it to him. He balanced it on his nose and threw it up into the air. Just like the emerald, I watched the ring spin up above me and carry us upward.

The ring swallowed the room in a fire of gold, carried us through a windy tunnel, up across the sky, and into the middle of a large group of people. Animals were sitting on a gold painted bench in a large circle. Edith was there, knitting furiously, pausing only to stuff small pieces of yarn into her project. Mr. Marty and Mrs. Marty leapt up and cheered when they saw us with Cadence. There was a llama wearing pink pyjamas and a night cap, an otter with a water wings and a party hat, a sheep with several birds nests in the wool of its back, and countless other creatures I hadn't met. Everyone was sitting very still and looking at us. This must be the meeting Fritz had been talking about; I looked around and didn't see him.

"Where's Fritz?" I asked Cowie who just shrugged a reply.

Jack the moose was standing behind a tall table at the head of the circle. When he saw us arrive, he proceeded to bang his antler on the tabletop.

"Attention attention Council Circle," he said in his lazy tune. "I am Jack, the Mister Speaker of the House."

"You're just the Speaker of the House, Jack," Edith rolled her eyes. "We only call you the *Mis*-Speaker of the House to tease you because you say words wrong."

"Yes, I realize that, but *I* am a *Mister*," he cleared his throat before continuing. "As I was saying, I am Jack, the *Mister* Speaker of the House," he shot Edith a look, "And we need to dress the elephant in the room."

An elephant was standing behind Jack. He had thick spectacles, baggy wrinkly skin, and wore a black judge's robe.

"It's *address*," the elephant correct patiently.

Jack banged his antler on the tabletop again, "Honestly if you are going to give me a job to be the speaker then you better let me speak!" He cleared his throat and began again, "A dress, for the elephant when he enters the room. Though I think he looks much better in a nice suit if I do say so myself."

Edith rolled her eyes again and her knitting needles moved even faster. Jack was made to sit down and the elephant took his place at the table. "Thank you for the address Jack," he elephant said. "Now, let us get to business."

Before he could say more, a gopher shot up out of the ground and called, "An announcement from Wordy!"

"Please, go ahead," the elephant helped the gopher to stand on top of the table. The gopher cleared his throat and read from a letter:

"Addressing the Council Circle:"

Jack shook his head indignantly, apparently annoyed that Wordy didn't know how to properly use the term 'dress.' The gopher continued,

"I am truly sorry that I cannot attend,
There's a mix in the time that I have to mend.
The Feazel has been vanquished! His reign is no more,
This is your chance to make life better than before.
But you must not be lazy, you must act fast,
This new beginning is sure not to last.
I warn you new trouble is already at hand,
Darkness worse than the fox to try and rule the land.
Hazel and Cowie, and Cadence must go home,
But new Senior Guide Newton will ensure you're not alone.
Sincerely,
Wordy."

The gopher rolled up the scroll and disappeared down the hole.

"Sounds like they're leaving us with all the work!" a beaver piped up, pointing at Cowie, Cadence, and I, "I say we make 'em stay, make 'em work."

"Now, now," the elephant spoke softly, "really I think they have done quite enough work for us for a lifetime."

The beaver crossed his arms and sat back grumbling.

343

A large polar bear and a dog came walking into the circle. "So sorry I'm late," he interrupted, looking positively miserable.

"Welcome Mitch," the elephant greeted. "We are glad you could make it. Is everything alright?"

"It would be if we could get the donkeys to obey the signs!" he scowled. "I pulled two out just this morning, both with broken legs. Wandering in the bear scout territory without a senior guide. Walked right past a sign and over the ridge."

"Oh dear," the elephant clicked his tongue. "We will have to do something about that. But first, we have to say goodbye to our dear friends Hazel, Cowie, and Cadence. It is too late to get started across the stars tonight, isn't it? Let us have a feast to honour their work!"

Everyone cheered and the circle was dismissed so everyone could begin preparing the festivities. Mitch came over quickly after the dismissal to say goodbye and good luck. He was not going to attend the feast since he didn't enjoy crowds and had to work late; but he said he was very grateful that I had obeyed the rules and it was a pleasure to meet me. I hugged him and patted his dog goodbye.

The rest of the evening passed in a blur. Tables were brought out to the beach, a bonfire was lit, hot dogs roasted, s'mores cooked, music played, and everyone danced into the night. Edith gave me the project she had been knitting, a stuffed owl. "So you don't forget us," she said.

I hugged her with a tear in my eye and reassured her that I could never forget them. I was placing the gift in my backpack when I found the rock that I had forgotten about.

"Cadence," I called.

The girl was laughing and dancing with Mrs. Marty who had given her a new dress and brushed out her hair. The Grynns had healed the cracks in her skin and fixed the light in her eyes. Eating, drinking, and dancing had brought the colour back to her face and a special music back into her laugh. She looked and sounded much more alive than she had in the castle.

"Is this your spiggle?" I asked when she ran over.

"Yes!" Cadence leapt up with excitement. She cradled the rock in her hands, grinning ear to ear.

"What is it?" I asked.

"I'll show you," she whispered. She took my hand and led me into the bushes where it was quiet and dark. I thought about how lovely it was to be able to walk into the forest at night without fear of Francis. She held the rock flat in her palms and began singing a tune. It was a beautiful tune, as soulful and blue as the ocean itself. As she sang, the rock began to glow and twitch and jump. Cracks began to form and purple light shone through. The pieces peeled back and revealed a small creature curled inside. It was a delicate figure in a purple dress with long purple hair. It's skin was also purple but her eyes glowed a crystal white. It stretched and little sparks flew off of the trails of the dress and out of her fingertips. Elated to be awake, the spiggle floated through the air and zoomed around before settling on Cadence's shoulder. Cadence whispered something into the spiggle's ear. I wasn't close enough to hear exactly what it was, but I thought it sounded more like music than words. The spiggle nodded several times and then darted up into the darkness.

"What *was* that?" I asked, open mouthed with surprise.

"I told you," Cadence giggled. "A spiggle! They're messengers for the healers. She's going to find my dragon."

I was awestruck, "She's beautiful."

"I missed her. She would have come and found me but she was asleep when I got captured and only healers can wake a spiggle so she's been cramped in her rock this whole time."

After watching the little light disappear into the night, we crept back to the festivities and danced until our feet felt like they were going to fall off. Exhausted and silly with excitement, we all collapsed in a sleepy heap on the beach. I fought to stay awake. This was the best night of my life and I never wanted this adventure to end. Newton curled up on my shoulder and reminded me that we still had to get Cadence home. "The adventure isn't quite over yet," he promised.

Chapter 45

Goodbye at the Beach

The next morning was full of too many goodbyes. It seemed everyone from the island had turned up to wish us well. I even met Newton's mother who was a very old dragon with a walker. She wore bright red lipstick and followed him around reminding him to have good manners. When she came to say goodbye, I hugged her and told her how wonderful her squares and notes had been on our adventures.

"Any time dear, any time," she had replied, beaming at the praise.

Mrs. Marty passed me a package full of scones and gave me a teary hug. "Such a pleasure to meet you, you are such a brave young thing," she said over and over. Mr. Marty shook my hand and congratulated me on a job well done.

"Look at all the things you thought you couldn't do, all behind you and done." He looked as proud as if he had orchestrated it all himself.

Edith checked us all over for mites and made sure we were safe to leave the island. Even Jack was sorry to see us go.

Once everyone had gone and we were ready to leave, Cadence's spiggle came rushing through the air in a frenzy. She dashed over to Cadence's ear and sang a song that sounded rather like wind chimes. Cadence beamed and ran ahead on the beach. A great shadow swept overhead. Newton froze and turned white. I looked up to see a great green dragon, not a bearded dragon, but a *dragon*. Its head was the size of a motorcar, its neck stretched out like a tower, its wings looked nearly as large as the beach itself, and a great winding tail was lined with bright yellow spikes. It flew along the beach and snatched Cadence up by her arms. She squealed with glee as it carried her through the air in several large loops before coming down to rest on the beach.

I ran over to catch up to her. When I approached, the dragon wrapped itself around her protectively but she stroked his side and convinced him to let her say goodbye to us. "They're my friends," I heard her telling him, "they rescued me from the dungeons." He huffed and uncoiled to release her but I didn't go anywhere near him as he looked quite unapproachable.

Cadence stepped away from her dragon and hugged Cowie around the neck, whispering something in his ear. Newton extended his hand and she shook it gratefully.

"Thank you for everything," she said when she stood in front of me.

I didn't know what to say so I gave her a hug and one of Mrs. Marty's scones from my bag. I wished that Cadence and I had gotten to spend more time together. I felt that we would be good friends, that she might have become like a sister.

"If you are ever in Theoze do come and find me," she smiled.

"How would I find you?" I asked.

"Under the Sorpes, knock on the knothole."

Cadence's dragon started stomping on the ground, an action that shook Newton into the air. "I have to go," she patted the beasts neck and climbed on its back. "I do hope I see you again my friend. I owe you my life."

"It was my pleasure," I said.

We sat on the beach and watched Cadence's dragon flap its wings and leap into the air. It glided into the sun. The sky opened like curtains and soon they were on the other side of the sky, no longer visible. Newton looked exposed on the beach and was trembling like a leaf.

"Don't worry," Cowie said sympathetically. "You're still a dragon."

Newton shot a glare at him but smiled.

"Shall we be off?" Cowie asked.

"I haven't said goodbye to Wordy!" I insisted.

"Don't worry, he will be around," he assured me.

I climbed on Cowie's back and Newton scrambled up onto my shoulder.

"Hold on," Cowie barked as he ran across the beach, across the water, and into the sky.

Chapter 46

The Adventure Hut

It was different crossing the sky this time. I could see what was going on in the clouds since it was daytime and the sun was shining. There were many travellers going from island to island in the sky. Boats taking creatures to and fro were piloted by pelicans, sword fish, sea lions, and things that I didn't recognize.

We left one sun behind us and started running towards another. In between the suns there was a great blinding flash of light and clouds that swirled all around us. We ran across the white misty blanket for quite some time before the clouds dissolved into a vast ocean. I peered down through the crystal water and watched a crab skirt across the bottom of the ocean floor, pulling a cart full of fruit behind him.

In the middle of the infinite water there was a little red rock island with a crooked wooden shed resting on it. The inconspicuous little shed had a colourful sign hanging above the door: "Adventure Hut."

When we landed on the rock, I climbed off Cowie's back and followed him into the hut. It was an extraordinary place. Along the walls were gears. Some had pebbles of all shapes and sizes that rattled down through a great maze when they were turned, others created bubbles in liquid chambers, and some let out great gasps of colourful steam. Wooden floorboards creaked under our feet as we stepped inside.

There was a neat little desk which sat in front of a row of cubbies that were all piled with stacks of interesting looking things: books, crystal balls, mirrors, backpacks, picture frames, pocket watches, and contraptions completely foreign to me. On the neat little desk there sat a small silver bell with a red handle. Beside the silver bell there was an ink bottle and pen. The ink bottle was green glass and twisted into something that resembled a mermaid.

Newton crept over to the bell and reached out for the handle.

"This is Hazel's adventure," Cowie nudged Newton away with his paw.

Newton grumbled that ringing the bell was his favourite part of the whole adventure.

"Am I to ring it?" I asked rather foolishly.

Newton crossed his arms in a distinct pout. "What else are you to do with a bell?"

I took the red handle and closed my fingers around it. A tingle shot through my arms and I got the feeling that this was indeed the most magical thing I had done so far. The most delicate chime that sounded like angels laughing escaped the bell when I shook it. Newton had been watching me so intently that he didn't notice the baby beach crab sneak up onto the desk and take an interest in his tail. At the sound of the bell, the whole room lit up and floated in a frozen moment.

A strange contraption leapt out of one of the cubbies. It was camera lens on saxophone body. It had a jet pack attached to the back that sported spinning gauges and flashed orange and white. A great flash came from an umbrella that jumped out of a nearby cubby as the camera took a picture.

At the exact moment the umbrella flashed, the baby crab closed its pincher on Newton's tail. Newton leapt into the air and screamed, fire streaming out of his mouth and singeing a whisker or two on Cowie's nose. Cowie yelped. Newton upset the ink bottle which

354

spilled shimmery green liquid all over the neat desk and down onto a clean stack of paper.

"Oh dear, oh dear, oh dear," Fritz clucked as he leapt out from behind one of the gears, which was actually a door. He rushed over to the desk and placed his very large procurement book on the ground safely away from the ink spill. Reaching into one of the wall cubbies he pulled out several rags and sponges which he placed on the desk and which began instantly mopping up the mess. I wondered if I could take one of those rags home to help me do the dishes.

Behind Fritz, items were leaping from one cubby to another in a frenzy. A picture frame bolted up three cubbies and across one, a flash of glitter escaped from an upper cubby and landed two down, colours, textures, smoke, and light collected in a mad cloud of flurry and frenzy.

"Now that is going to take a moment I am afraid," Fritz propped his hands on his hips and shook his head at the desk.

"I'm awfully sorry," I said as I placed the bell down on the counter. I wasn't quite sure why I was apologizing, but I felt an obligation to. Someone had made a mess and someone ought to apologize.

Fritz shook his head back and forth in a fast blur, "Not to worry my dear, not to worry. Let me see your backpack."

Confused as I was, I took my backpack off my shoulders and placed it in his outstretched arms. He looked through all the pockets, took a small tool out from the desk drawer, and adjusted the buckles. He removed the thing-a-ma-jig and passed it to a hand that reached out of one of the cubbies before he inspected all around the edges for rips and tears. He muttered to himself as he worked "Oh yes what a mess we have here.... I will have to fix that with a whimsadriver I think... perhaps a tiltywilty... and yes a new top as well, yes that would do quite nice." He was in his own private world of fixing, jotting down notes as he worked.

When the backpack had been emptied and examined, and everything fixed, he carefully returned my adventure books and my goodbye gifts to the pocket and passed it back to me. Humming quietly to himself, he reached up into one of the cubbies and pulled out a small yellow snake skin case.

"Follow me," he said as he turned and skittered back through the gear door on all fours. I walked through the door after him, trailed closely by a chuckling Cowie and a rather cross Newton. Behind the door there lay a whole other world. The walls were made of gears and cubbies and ribbon roads connected each door to another.

We walked along a green ribbon which rippled under my feet and waved out in all directions. It was an interesting walk. We passed many oddly shaped gears, seahorses, though they looked much more like regular horses than the seahorses we see in our stories, and storage closets which were labelled "things," "nothings," "stuffs," "odds and ends," "priceless treasures," and the like. Fritz talked as we walked, "Now Hazel I must impress upon you this very important truth. The more you have seen in other worlds, the more you will see in your world."

"I'm sorry I don't quite understand," I said.

"I mean that before you came here, you didn't know anything about the keeper of time, or the office of procurement, or magic, or dragons, or anything of the sort. You probably would not have even considered those things to be a possibility."

I paused for a moment to consider his proposition.

"You see Hazel," he continued, "now you have seen that there is more to life than what you knew and you know that there is still more to learn. Yes?"

I nodded.

"Well, what you know alters what you see. When you go back to your world, you won't find it just the way you left it. You will notice things you would have missed before and you will see what others are blind too."

"I will?"

"Yes," he said solemnly. "People cannot see what they do not know is real. You couldn't see the magic in your world before, though it was around you all along."

"How come I couldn't see it?" I asked.

"Because you did not *know* dear," he put a great deal of emphasis on the word know. "And no one could have told you the magic was there, you would not have believed them."

"How do you know?" I challenged. I did not appreciate Fritz telling me that I would not have been receptive to magic being in my world.

"What would you say if someone had come up to you when you arrived at your new home and told you that a letter had arrived for you from a gopher and it was written by an owl who was going to open the sky so you could ride a talking dog to another world?"

I fidgeted my toes and scrunched up my face. I couldn't honestly say that I would have believed them.

Fritz belly laughed, "I'll tell you what you would have said. You would have said that person was mad. And quite rightly so! For I find that humans cannot believe what they cannot first see."

"I believed Mr. Sploot didn't I?"

"Yes you did. But Mr. Sploot did not tell you anything that he did not first show you. Isn't that right?"

Fritz was better at this game than I was.

"Believe me," he said, "there was much you couldn't see that Bill could, and he chose not to tell you about it."

My jaw dropped. "How do you know that?"

A twinkle glimmered in his round platypus eyes. "You think the office of procurement doesn't keep in touch with Bill Sploot?"

I hadn't thought of that.

"Bill Sploot has travelled to many worlds and seen many things. In his time he has become very wise. I would in fact say that there is no one in your world who has collected as much wisdom as dear Mr. Sploot."

"There's not?" I gasped.

Fritz removed his glasses and looked at me very intently, "No there is not. That is why it is such a great honour."

I didn't know what to say. I didn't know what was such a great honour.

"It took Bill over fifty years to pass on his first adventure book," Fritz explained.

"Why?" I whispered.

"Because he wanted to be wise with it of course. The adventurer's books are, after all, the adventurer's legacy and Bill Sploot has one of the grandest legacies of them all. He wanted to give his book to someone he believed would perpetuate that legacy.

"Perpetuate?"

"Live out, learn from his stories and keep learning from theirs."

The gravity of the gift rested on me, in a little nook between the top of my neck and the tips of my shoulders.

"He always said that when he met a person with the correct light in their eyes, he would pass on the book. And after fifty two years and seventeen days from the first day of his very first adventure, he met that person," he looked at me intently, "he met *you* Hazel."

I wouldn't realize for many years just how big of a legacy had been passed down to me. I was only beginning to see the tip of a very large iceberg.

"But I digress," Fritz placed his glasses back on his bill and his eyes resumed their abnormally large appearance. "As I was saying, you must be mindful and patient. People will not understand the things you see and the way that you think. That can get lonesome sometimes. You will be misunderstood and taken as a fool more often than not I am afraid. Whatever happens you must remember what you know."

I nodded though I didn't completely understand what he meant.

We came to the end of the green ribbon road to a giant clock. The clock was an unusual one since it had many numbers and many hands. I didn't know how anyone would ever be able to make heads or tails out of such a contraption. I watched a shooting star fall from a number 74 and land near a number 3, one of the hands stepped up over another, apologizing as it went, and a door in the top half of the number 8 opened. Wordy peered his head out of the door and waved a wing in greeting.

Chapter 47

Goodbye Newton

"Hello Wordy!" Waved Fritz.

"*Helloooo*!" Wordy's billowy voice replied.

"I'm afraid this is where I leave you," Fritz said sadly. He took the snake skin case from under his arm and passed it to me, "Do you remember?"

I took the snake skin in my hands and shook it, it grew to the size of a sheet of paper. Again I shook it and watched as the snake skin slithered away and revealed a beautiful gold frame with waves lapping up against the edges. I looked to Cowie for direction but he just smiled at me. Fritz tapped his fingers together expectantly and Newton rolled his eyes in exasperation of my ignorance. I tilted the frame and watched the waves shift and begin to splash out of the picture. Carefully I poured the water out, it trickled down from the frame in a steady stream and landed in a puddle on the ribbon beneath our feet. I watched as the puddle began to flit and flap and the clear blue water turned into a soft blue butterfly. The butterfly glided into the air and through the maze of gears. I pointed and yelled in amazement, "Did you see that?" Everyone smiled and laughed, even Newton gave into the joy of the moment.

I turned my attention back to the frame; inside was a picture of a girl at a desk. I stared at it for a moment before gasping, "It's me!"

"Yes!" Fritz clasped his hands together.

He whistled a little tune that went up and then down and up again. All at once the picture jumped to life. The me in the picture picked up the bell and rang it, Newton bolted up and knocked over the ink bottle, and Cowie yelped. A flame shot out of Newton's mouth and left a black burn mark on the side of the gold frame.

"No, no, no! This is just all wrong!" Newton was staring at the burn mark distraught. "It was the crab's fault! He pinched my tail! He is to blame for the spilled ink!"

"Calm-" Cowie was interrupted before he could finish telling Newton to calm down.

"Don't you understand?!" Newton cried in distress, "I've been framed!"

Fritz chuckled and he took the frame from my hands. "Oh grow up and own your actions Newton," he winked.

Newton hiccuped and stomped his way back to Cowie's shoulders, muttering the whole time how it really was the crab who caused the spill and complaining that picture painted him in entirely the wrong light. Fritz returned the frame to normal size, tucked it safely away inside the snake skin case, turned me around so he could lock it away in my backpack, and turned me around again to hug me goodbye.

"I have to get back to the main office," he said with a tear glimmering in his eye. "Well done Hazel, well done. You have set yourself in a good direction. Maintain it."

Suddenly it hit me. All the goodbyes on the beach were really goodbyes. I hugged Fritz furiously and promised him that I would maintain my good direction. In an effort to keep the tears from blubbering out of my eyes, I shifted attention to Newton's complaining about being incorrectly immortalized in an incriminating act that was really not his doing.

Wordy told Newton to hush and act like a proper grown up dragon, he also told Newton that it was time for him to say goodbye too. Newton suddenly stopped grumbling. He looked at me quite solemnly and I swear that I saw a glimmer of emotion in the very bottom right corner of his left eye.

"No," I whispered. "Why?"

"Because we are going home," Cowiesaid as he nudged my hand gently. "And Newton belongs here, he has important work to do"

I was not ready to say goodbye to Newton; not so suddenly, not like this. A tear rolled down my cheek.

Newton cleared his throat, "None of that nonsense Hazel, that's too much drama for an adventurer like yourself." He reached out his hand. "This is goodbye then."

He sounded very serious but he wouldn't look at me in the eyes. I shook his hand and said, "Thank you for everything, Newton."

He sniffed and his voice quavered, "Well, you weren't quite as awful as I thought you would be, for such a young adventurer." He smiled softly, his lips quivering as he sniffed again, "You better go."

Fritz passed Newton a soft handkerchief. I bent over to kiss the top of Newton's scaly dragon head. "Goodbye Newton," I said softly.

Cowie led me along the ribbon to the door in the top of the number 8. I wasn't sure how I was going to fit through such a small door but I found that when we arrived at it, it had grown a good deal and I could walk through it without crouching or ducking. I turned to give one final wave to Fritz and Newton, who was now bawling uncontrollably into the handkerchief, and then I walked through the door.

Chapter 48

Goodbye Wordy

There was a soft click as number 8's door closed behind me. It was very black behind the clock, I kept my hand on Cowie's neck to make sure I didn't somehow get left alone. I couldn't feel the ribbon under my feet anymore, I couldn't feel anything.

"Where are we?" I asked, my voice sounding very eery as it echoed through the nothingness.

"Behind the stars," whispered Cowie. "Waiting for the sky to open."

I had never realized there was a 'behind the stars.' I heard a series of clicks as the hands on the clock behind us moved. A turn of gears sounded followed by a pop and a swoosh.

"One more minute until you cross through the door,
Back home and safe in your own world once more."

Wordy's voice was quiet and billowy. Everything about the land behind the stars was very still. I didn't like it very much. Sitting in silence, waiting to be sent back home, knowing that a wonderful world of adventure was already behind me. How had it gone so fast? I felt like I had only just arrived.

"That's it? Adventure is over?" a tear rolled down my cheek, I didn't want to leave.

A pop sounded and a single star appeared in the distance. I could see the reflection of it in Wordy's eyes as he looked at me.

"Maybe your time in this place is done,

But your days of adventure have only begun."

I stroked Cowie's neck with my right hand and brushed a tear away with my left, "They have?"

"Yes, just you wait. You will have many more,

That teach you more truths that you didn't know before.

Many places to be,

Many people to meet ,

A collection so full, you could never believe."

I remembered Mr. Sploot's briefcase and how he said he collected worlds. "Will I ever come back to this world?"

"Alas, dear one, that is not for me to say.

For you would never leave, if I had it my way.

This chapter is done and the pages must turn.
Though it is time to move on,
You keep the lessons you've learned."

Another star appeared in the distance and then another beyond that one.

"Climb on," Cowie nudged me.

I swung myself onto his back. Wordy placed a wing on my shoulder.

"Worry not, young Hazel, adventure calls when it does,
Be grateful for what is and not lost in what was.
Be patient while you wait for excitement to begin,
There is extraordinary joy in the stage that you're in."

A great whooshing and popping zoomed through the air as millions of stars flooded the space all around us. I heard the final turn of the gears and the click of the hands. All at once I knew with absolute certainty that the door in the sky had closed behind us; Wordy was on one side of the door and we were on the other. Tears spilled down my face and I hugged Cowie's neck as he carried me home.

Chapter 49

Cinnamon Buns

When I opened my eyes I was sitting on the back step at Uncle Art and Auntie Gladys's house. It took my eyes a second to adjust to the light. I was leaning on Cowie's side. Had I fallen asleep? I could smell cinnamon buns, hear Auntie Gladys singing, and hear the phone ring.

"Hello?" I heard Uncle Art's strong voice, "John how good to hear from you! Yes, she's just outside, let me call her in." He placed the receiver on the kitchen counter and leaned his head out the door. "Hazel, your father is on the phone."

I scampered inside and picked up the receiver, "Hello?"

"Hazel!" Father's voice was crackly through the phone, but it was his. I felt like I hadn't heard it in so long and my smile grew to stretch from one ear to the other.

"How are you?" he asked.

"I miss you! But I am doing very well. How are you? And Mother? And Richard?" I asked quickly without pausing to allow a response.

He chuckled, "We are fine. I have good news, Richard is done his medicine and we are coming home tomorrow."

"Really?" I jumped up and twirled, almost knocking the telephone off the stand.

"Careful now," Aunt Gladys patted me on the shoulder affectionately, laughing as she stabilized my near disaster.

"Yes really. We will be there before the sun goes down. You be good and hang tight one more day. We can't wait to see you," his voice sounded tired but I could tell that he meant it. I told him I loved them and then passed the receiver back to Uncle Art. I trailed after Auntie Gladys into the kitchen with Cowie close behind.

"Did you hear that?" I whispered to him. "They're coming home!"

Cowie wagged is tail and stuck his tongue out like a regular dog. Auntie Gladys situated me at the table in front of a fresh cinnamon bun.

"Did Lori-Anne give you that backpack?" she asked.

I had hardly noticed it was still hanging on my shoulders. I was speechless. She winked and walked into the kitchen, humming a pretty song.

"I can't believe it!" I said to Cowie as quietly as I could. "It was all real."

He cocked his head to the side and acted like he didn't know what I was saying.

"Come on Cowie," I whispered, "I know you're not an ordinary dog."

He whined and pawed at my plate. I sighed and passed him a healthy slice of my cinnamon bun. He deserved it - he had saved my life after all.

Dedication & Thanks

Thank you God for giving me this story to tell. In loving memory of Gramma Hazel who was the first adventurer I knew, Betty Wiebe who gave me the gift of creative writing, Uncle Art who was a pillar of strength, and Auntie Gladys who modelled courage, faith, and unrelenting joy through struggle. To Auntie Kathy and Uncle Scott who gave me a home in the city and loved me like their child, to my family who have held my hands while I walked through fire, and to my angels who have lit my life up with magical kindness; I love you all beyond measure and this story is for you.

Auntie Lori, you read Hazel's story first and encouraged me to see it through. Thank you for nurturing me as a writer since elementary, for building into me as a person, and for loving me as a friend. I could not have written this story without you.

Kait - thank you for all the phone calls, letters, and messages that keep me sane; you are an anchor in my life and I am grateful for your sisterhood. Hailey - thank you for your friendship and for proof reading the original draft. You are the little sister that I never had and I am overjoyed to have shared this writing experience with you.

Thank you Jennifer, Kirsten, & Micaela, you have all kept me going in the darkest of times. You are my angels and I would not be writing without you. Thank you Coach Aimee Everett for giving me your Garage Mind journal and for being an example of courage, resilience, strength, and grit.

I could write an entire book acknowledging everyone who brought this story into existence but I will save that for my autobiography. For now, I hope you all love Hazel as much I do.

Love,

Jo

Manufactured by Amazon.ca
Bolton, ON